Undead and Done

Anthologies

CRAVINGS
(with Laurell K. Hamilton, Rebecca York, Eileen Wilks)

BITE
*(with Laurell K. Hamilton, Charlaine Harris,
Angela Knight, Vickie Taylor)*

KICK ASS
(with Maggie Shayne, Angela Knight, Jacey Ford)

MEN AT WORK
(with Janelle Denison, Nina Bangs)

DEAD AND LOVING IT

SURF'S UP
(with Janelle Denison, Nina Bangs)

MYSTERIA
(with P. C. Cast, Gena Showalter, Susan Grant)

OVER THE MOON
(with Angela Knight, Virginia Kantra, Sunny)

DEMON'S DELIGHT
(with Emma Holly, Vickie Taylor, Catherine Spangler)

DEAD OVER HEELS

MYSTERIA LANE
(with P. C. Cast, Gena Showalter, Susan Grant)

MYSTERIA NIGHTS
(includes Mysteria *and* Mysteria Lane, *with P. C. Cast, Susan Grant,
Gena Showalter)*

UNDERWATER LOVE
(includes Sleeping with the Fishes, Swimming Without a Net,
and Fish out of Water*)*

DYING FOR YOU

UNDEAD AND UNDERWATER

UNDEAD AND DONE

MaryJanice Davidson

BERKLEY
NEW YORK

BERKLEY
An imprint of Penguin Random House LLC
375 Hudson Street, New York, New York 10014

Copyright © 2016 by MaryJanice Davidson
Penguin Random House supports copyright. Copyright fuels creativity,
encourages diverse voices, promotes free speech, and creates a vibrant culture.
Thank you for buying an authorized edition of this book and for complying with
copyright laws by not reproducing, scanning, or distributing any part of it in any
form without permission. You are supporting writers and allowing Penguin
Random House to continue to publish books for every reader.

BERKLEY is a registered trademark and the B colophon is a trademark of
Penguin Random House LLC.

Library of Congress Cataloging-in-Publication Data

Names: Davidson, MaryJanice, author.
Title: Undead and done / MaryJanice Davidson.
Description: First edition. | New York : Berkley, 2016. | Series: Undead/
Queen Betsy ; 15
Identifiers: LCCN 2016025586 (print) | LCCN 2016025763 (ebook) | ISBN
9780425282946 (hardback) | ISBN 9780698407251 (ebook)
Subjects: LCSH: Taylor, Betsy (Fictitious character)—Fiction. | Vampires—
Fiction. | Hell—Fiction. | BISAC: FICTION / Romance / Paranormal. |
FICTION / Fantasy / Paranormal.
Classification: LCC PS3604.A949 U44 2016 (print) | LCC PS3604.A949 (ebook) |
DDC 813/.6—dc23
LC record available at https://lccn.loc.gov/2016025586

First Edition: October 2016

Printed in the United States of America
1   3   5   7   9   10   8   6   4   2

Cover design by Lesley Worrell and Katie Anderson
Cover illustration by Craig White
Book design by Kristin del Rosario

For Ethan and Cindy,
who helped me go from the trailer park to the bestseller list.
I know I've said this before, but hey—it bears repeating:
you're the greatest!

Author's Note

Well, here we are! The final book in the Undead series. When I started *Undead and Unwed*, I was neck-deep in an SDJ (stupid day job), working fifty hours a week while trying to write after the kids were in bed. Or during my lunch break. Or when I was supposed to be transcribing my boss's notes. (I wasn't a very good employee.)

Fast-forward: writing is my SDJ, which is really a WDJ (wonderful day job), and I've written a whole bunch of books and, even better, sold a bunch, too. *And*, since I work for myself, these days I'm a slightly less terrible employee. (My boss is the worst, though.)

I have no idea how this happened.

I'm not kidding. No clue. I've always written because I've always wanted to. I never gave it much thought beyond that. It's been my great good fortune to stumble across talented people who are great at their jobs, who love books as much if not more than I do, who thought I had a voice worth hearing and wanted to help me ~~punish~~ share it with the world.

Although I'm most known for the Undead series, after fifteen books it's time to take a break from that universe and explore new ones. I never wanted to be the writer who kept churning out books to pay for the pool house and, in the process, lost all regard for her characters.

That's not to say I'll never, ever write about Betsy and the gang. I foresee characters from the Undead universe showing up now and again in various novellas. I couldn't keep that bitch away even if I wanted to.

A few things worth noting . . .

The Mall of America is actually pretty great. (As I'm writing this, I'm about to leave to sign stock at the Barnes and Noble store, suck down a bowl of ramen at Masu Sushi & Robata, and maybe grab a Cinnabon, because my self-control is in shreds.) I don't think it's Hell on earth, except on Black Friday. And Blue Tuesday. It was just the best way for me to grasp an infinite space and make it relatable. If anything, Hell's more like Coachella or Comic Con . . . it's not as terrible as you feared, but you still can't leave until they let you go.

Everything Betsy says about *InStyle* magazine is true. Everything.

There really is a KARE 11 news channel, and as of this writing, Diana Pierce really anchors there. Wait, that doesn't sound right. Diana Pierce *is* an anchor there? That's probably better. Anyway, I've been on KARE 11 a few times, and they always invite me back regardless of their instincts. I always thought if Betsy had to do an interview, she'd go with a local she liked. So for the final book in the series, I couldn't resist pairing a real person with a fictional character.

For those of you whose Greek mythology is rusty (and I put myself on that list), the Augean stables were one of the twelve labors of Hercules. Once upon a time, the strongest alpha male on the planet went crazy and killed his kids and his wife (the Disney movie left that part out, though casting James Woods as Hades was inspired). So to make up for it (as if anything could), King Eurystheus set Hercules twelve unbelievably difficult tasks. Like, *Wait, you're auditing my audit?* difficult.

One of these was mucking out the Augean stables, a job that wasn't just supposed to be almost impossible, but also humiliating—Hercules was the son of Zeus, king of the gods. Herc probably thought "stable boy" was never going to show up on his résumé. The horses weren't just healthy; they were immortal and never got sick. They sure did shit a lot, though, in the manner of healthy mammals everywhere.

Well, "dung scooper" *did* end up on his résumé. Along with lion tamer, hydra decapitator, hind stealer, boar grabber, snake wrangler, man-eating-bird catcher, bull rustler, mare catcher,[1] belt stealer, cattle herder, apple grabber, and three-headed-dog catcher.

Long story short, Hercules forced a river to flow through the Augean stables, doing all the dirty work for him, which was ruled as cheating, but that part isn't relevant to this book.

Oh, and the reason he went insane and killed his family in the first place? His stepmother *made* him insane. As in, it wasn't his fault at all. As in, Hera was an asshat! Why is the moral of most Greek myths "Family is the worst"?

The Saint Paul Hotel really exists and so does the fabulous Ordway Suite. For the purpose of this book, I gave it three bedrooms instead of two. If you get the chance, and can handle a second mortgage, it's well worth checking out. Parlor that seats eight, a kitchen, two bathrooms, amazing king-sized beds, a stocked wet bar, robes that feel like warm, fuzzy clouds, dark glossy wood all over the place . . . it's like

---

[1] The Mares of Diomedes were huge flesh-eating horses! Ack! Can you imagine? Gives me the creeps just thinking about it.

a penthouse suite decorated by George Washington's mom. The whole place just stinks of class. If you get the chance, check out the magnificence: www.saintpaulhotel.com /accommodations/ordway_suite/.

Bacon cookies exist! You can get the recipe here: www .myrecipes.com/recipe/bacon-cookies.

The Little Bighorn Battlefield National Monument is worth seeing. I'm an amateur Civil War buff so I'm into it, but the place is fascinating if you're into what happened in the years after the war, or learning what too much pride can cost you, or how indigenous people shouldn't be fucked with, or if you just like to look at amazing countryside: www.nps.gov/libi/index.htm.

Port-a-cribs are wonderful. That is all.

There is some discussion of suicide in chapter twenty-three, when a character in Hell recalls how she killed herself. If you think this might be a trigger, please avoid. Also if you think vampires, zombies, grumpy mermaids, reminiscing about decapitation, betrayal, explosions, incontinent puppies, and far, *far* too much profanity might be a trigger, avoid chapters one, two, th— You know what? Just put the book back on the shelf.

Lutefisk is a traditional Nordic dish, and we got screwed. You know what other countries' traditional dishes are? Lasagna. Baklava. Fish and chips. Crêpes. Astonishing and delicious things designed solely to nourish and make you happy. Meanwhile, lutefisk is dried fish soaked in cold water, then lye (which, yes, is a poison), after which it's soaked in water again to make it edible. Because, a reminder: it was soaked in *poison*.

You know what isn't soaked in poison as a preparatory step to consumption? Lasagna. Fish and chips. Baklava.

I have eaten lutefisk.

Once.

If you're ever in Boston, put the Faneuil Hall Marketplace on your "Must See and Drool Over" list. It's the best food court ever, where you can buy a bagel and half a dozen raw oysters and sushi and pizza and a frappe and cookies and a salad, all to go, in the same place. This place is a miracle.

Smoothie Nation is not a thing. But it damned well should be. Fortunately, blackberry Creamsicle smoothies *are* a thing. Pinterest, is there anything you can't do?

And that was the October week when they grew up overnight, and were never so young anymore.

SOMETHING WICKED THIS WAY COMES,
RAY BRADBURY

Who is the liar but he who denies that Jesus is the Christ? This is the antichrist, he who denies the Father and the Son.

1 JOHN 2:22 ESV

One Betsy . . . to rule them all.

NO ONE EVER

Let no one deceive you in any way. For that day will not come, unless the rebellion comes first, and the man of lawlessness is revealed, the son of destruction, who opposes and exalts himself against every so-called god or object worship, so that he takes his seat in the temple of God, proclaiming himself to be God.

2 THESSALONIANS 2:3-4 ESV

I just want to focus on my salad.

MARTHA STEWART

He shall speak words against the Most High, and shall wear out the saints of the Most High, and shall think to change the times and the law; and they shall be given into his hand for a time, times, and half a time.

DANIEL 7:25 ESV

Undead and Done

The guards finally took a break, and by lunchtime most of the skin on his torso had grown back. He sat down in the food court and contemplated his burger, cooked just the way he liked it (well-done, with a pucklike texture), with most of the bread scooped from the bun (not that he had to worry about hatefuldelicious carbs anymore), sweet potato fries with a sprinkle of sea salt, a dish of flan for dessert, and to wash it down, a tall glass of sweet iced tea, no lemon, with a shot of cream.

It was perfect.

He hated it.

He ate it anyway. While he chewed and sipped, he looked around the food court, still amazed at all the changes that had happened in such a short time. The place hadn't always looked like the Mall of America, and the devil hadn't always been a vampire. He was pretty sure. Time was funny here.

In fact, the devil was dead, killed in combat by the vampire queen, who then took over Hell and started running it by—he still couldn't believe it; no one could believe it—committee.

Hell had always been gigantic, so its transformation into a mall made weirdnormal sense. Some poor idiots had thought—and worse, said, and that was always a bad idea; someone was always listening—how bad could a mall be? They soon learned. An enormous mall where the stores never had things in your size and the food court only served things you hated or screwed up the food you loved and all the best rides in the amusement park were closed and it was always Black Friday was Hell indeed. The new devil, the vampireangel devil, was reluctantly, instantly admired for the depth of her cunning. Suddenly it didn't seem so impossibly strange that Betsy

(*betsy????? what????*)

had killed the Morningstar.

Except the devil wasn't dead; she'd only been hiding, had taken another form and had hidden in plain sight.[2] But the vampire queen had somehow known, and hurt her, and yelled at her, and banished her in front of everyone. He hadn't been in the food court at the time—Thursday the guards drowned him in sweet tea—but he saw it all like he'd been sitting ten feet away. The guards, too. Everyone saw. Hell had trembled, teetered . . . and was slowly settling back. Or at least settling down.

So! The terriblewonderful vampire queen was in charge. Meet the new boss, perhaps not the same as the old boss. Maybe he had a chance. At last, one chance. Because she was letting some of them off. And she was letting some of them leave. At least, that was the rumor. And in Hell, rumors had more power than they ever had in life.

---

[2] It's complicated. The weirdness can be found in *Undead and Unforgiven*.

So! Why wait? People could get a second chance; there were people in Hell who simply . . . weren't there anymore. It wasn't like there were going-away parties, but still: people who had been here a long, long time suddenly weren't. And there didn't seem to be any pattern. Men, women, and children had left. Catholics and Muslims and agnostics had left. Killers and thieves, blasphemers and telemarketers—they could leave. Anyone could leave. You just had to meet with the new devil, talk to her. Explain things. She didn't tell everyone yes . . . but she didn't tell everyone no. She was terriblewonderful that way.

And . . . hadn't he paid and paid? From birth to death and now beyond, he'd suffered. Where was his fresh start?

But speculating was one thing. Making it happen was tricky. He was leery of approaching the new one on his own—everyone was. HeavenHell knew the old devil didn't encourage fraternizing. But the word was if you got the ear of a committee member

(not really you can't really get their ears it's just a saying if you tried to hurt a committee member she got sooooooo maddddddddd did they ever find that guy's face?)

that committee member would take you to see her. Or at least put in a good word for you. Several good words, sometimes. He glanced around the food court but saw no one he could trust . . . no one he even dared approach. They were all filthycrazy. He couldn't even look at them; he'd never be able to approach one. And *speak* to them? No, no.

He chewed and pondered and drank, and like an answer to a dreamprayer

(!!!!!!!!!!!!!!!!!!!!)

there she was, gliding past the Dairy Queen like a bright-eyed goddess. Perfect hair, perfect skin, perfect body. She was real and clean and sane. And there, right there, and he was so stupid, he should have thought of her earlier. She'd help him; of course she would. She couldn't refuse him a thing, no more than he could refuse her.

"It's you!" he cried, abandoning his perfecthorrible lunch without a second thought and running to her, ignoring the chewing and slurping and drinking and bitching and moaning that made up virtually everyone's conversation during meals.

He saw her shoulders stiffen, and then she swung around. He noted with pleased pride that she recognized him at once; her eyes widened, then narrowed. She looked clean and perfect, her dark blond hair in an intricate French braid, her feet sockless in battered oxblood loafers, her faded jeans rolled at the cuffs, and wearing a blue T-shirt with white lettering (*Jesus is Santa Claus for adults*).

She sucked in a breath (unnecessary; they were both dead, but old habits) and he had a moment of pure joy at being the focus of her attention, a moment where he didn't feel

(*filthy filthy filthy*)

dirty. He'd been unclean in life and soiled in death; dirty up top, dirty down below, but now she was here, and she would help him be free; they could both be free and clean, clean forever and—

Oh.

God.

Ow.

"There!" she cried as he clutched himself and flopped to the floor.

Fun fact: getting kneed in the balls hurts just as much in the afterlife as it does in life. And the vicious beating that followed was impressive. *This could be her job*, he thought when she broke his nose with a small fist. *Men and women hurt me all day every day, and she's making them look like amateurs. What a marvel she is!*

"You son of a bitch!" Stomp. Smash.

He coughed out three teeth. "I love you."

"Shut up!"

"I really, really love you." He'd curled up, protecting his tender bits, but that gave her a clear shot at the rest of him, and she took full advantage and wasn't that something? He'd never had his elbow broken in Hell before now.

"Get a grip, fucknut!"

"Whoa, whoa, *whoa*." And *she* was there, the new devil, the one who wore a red-and-white name tag that read, *Hello, My Name Is Satan 2.0*, because her friends thought it was funny. "Cathie, what the hell? Sir, are you—oh yuck," she said as he knuckled blood out of his eyes and blinked up at her from the floor. "You are all kinds of gross and bleeding right now."

"This—this—" She was sputtering and rubbing her hands on her pants as if frantic to get his blood off her fingers, then took a breath and forced calm. "This repellant fucknut is the guy who murdered me."

"Ha! Repellant fucknut, that's— Whoa." The other devil's blond brows arched. "You're the Driveway Killer?" She bent to take another look, her shoulder-length hair swinging forward and obscuring her face and brightbright eyes for a second, and then she nodded. "You're the Driveway Killer. I couldn't tell right away, on account of how your nose is spouting blood and has been moved over an inch. Yikes, Cath, you really did a number on him." This in a tone of mild admiration.

"I'm not done, either." This in a tone of whatever the opposite of mild admiration was.

"Yeah, you are, though." The new devil extended a hand. He expected a slap, or a trick, but she just waited and he eventually took her hand and climbed to his feet. "What's on your crazy fractured mind, Driveway Killer?"

"Ben." That name, that terriblecorrect name the newspapers

stuck him with; he'd hoped it hadn't followed him down here. "Ben Sporco."

"Yeah, I don't care. Why'd you pick a fight with my friend?"

"I didn't pick a fight with her." Shocked. The idea. Oh, he would never. "I needed her help."

Cathie made an inarticulate sound that sounded quite a lot like rage. "I'll help you," she managed through gritted teeth. "Right into a fractured skull and multiple amputations, I'll help you. Someone get me a blowtorch."

But the new devil was looking at him thoughtfully. "Huh. You've heard about the changes. You're looking to get paroled, I'll bet."

Yesyes! He nodded so hard blood and mucus flew in strings from his nose. The new devil dodged, saving her sweater.

"It's a brand-new program," the new devil explained, which was nice of her, because the people in charge didn't have to explain anything, anywhere, unless they wanted to—something else that was the same wherever you were trapped. "And we don't even know if it'll work. Baby steps, y'know?"

He didn't, but he nodded anyway. She reached into her pocket, pulled out her hand, scowled, reached into her pocket again, pulled out a large clean handkerchief, and handed it to him. "Ta-da! Uh, I don't want that back, by the way."

"Thank you," he managed. What was happening, exactly? Was he in trouble? Was he getting out? Was this a new version of torture? "You're much nicer than the old devil."

"That's a low bar." Still, she seemed more amused than anything else. "And maybe I'm not. If I was really nice, I'd have cured your injuries."

"You don't have to cure me," he said, then took a break to blow snot and blood into the handkerchief. Both women grimaced, which was fair. "Just let me out. I want to get out."

The (last) love of his life made a disgustedhappy sound. "And you thought I'd help you? Jesus, you really *are* crazy."

"I'm not crazy," he said. "I just want to leave."

"Actually, those two things aren't mutually exclusive. Well, c'mon," the new devil said. "Let's go to my office and talk about it."

"Really?" This in unison with the (last) love of his life—ah, even in Hell, they were one.

"Oh, Betsy." She sounded equal parts appalled and interested. "You're not serious. Are you? No. Can't be. Wait. Are you?"

"Never hurts to talk, Cathie. Listen, are you okay? D'you want to get out of here for a while?" That was another thing about the new devil's friends/committee members. They didn't have to stay in Hell. She helped them pop in and out all the time. He had the sneaking suspicion one or two of them weren't even dead. Disgusting.

"No, I'll stay." A glare that could shatter glass. "He's not driving me out. This is my turf. *Everyone knows the food court is my turf.*"

"Well, if not before, they sure do now. Let me know if you change your mind." The new devil put a solicitous arm around his love, which all the people pretending not to watch couldn't miss. "You want to take the day off? Do something that isn't . . ." She glanced around the food court. "This?"

So, this one was clever like the last one. *My friends can kick the shit out of someone here, and I'll be worried about* them. *I'll show concern for* them. *Not any of you. See?*

"No, like I said, I'll stay. I'll want to talk to you." He met Cathie's gaze as best he could; his left eye was swelling shut. The other eye had no trouble picking up on her baleful glower. "After."

"Oh, I'll bet." The new devil grinned, then looked at him. "Come on, then, Driveway Guy."

"Ben."

"Still don't care."

He fell into step behind her, wondering why she didn't just whisk him away to her office in the security wing. Then he realized she wanted everyone to see him follow her out.

, New, but learning quickly. Oh yes.

He had just finished explaining. It hadn't taken long. Which was just as well, as he'd never taken a meeting with the devil before. Or a vampire. And certainly not in a room that looked like the dispatch office of a busy Midwestern mall. A row of screens showed what was happening in several corners of Hell, though she thankfully had the volume off. No clocks, of course, and no calendars. No family pics anywhere, or posters. Bare walls and banks of screens showing eternal suffering; Hell was always efficient.

They had come in and she had plopped down in the big chair behind the desk dominating the room, and he'd gingerly taken a seat opposite her as he was wondering where to start, how to start, when he got his first good look at her.

For the first time he noticed what she was wearing—he'd been too distracted earlier by Cathie. And pain. And by how *normal* a devilvampire looked: pale skin, blond hair, light eyes, light eyebrows. Minimal makeup—just that shiny lip stuff women put on when they wanted something fancier than ChapStick but not a full-on date-night mouth. And she was too tall, and her eyes were all wrong. He'd never have chosen her to be his love if he'd seen her in life. Cathie had that honor, not this new devil.

(Putting that aside, if he had seen her in life and tried to make them as one, would he be a vampire now? Or just in Hell? Or both?)

Never mind any of that; on the outside, at least, there were millions just like her in Minnesota alone; she was nothing special. Her clothes were just as unexceptional: khakis in that style that made it look like they were too short (capris?), a light blue sweater, high heels of some kind.

She was suddenly sucking on a straw and he realized she'd gotten a large cup of something, though he hadn't seen her order anything in the food court, and she'd left with only him, not him and a drink or

(so much better!)

Cathie and him and a drink.

"Is that . . . uh." Was he really? Was he going to chat with the vampiredevil like this was an ordinary office and he was an ordinary man? Ask her about her diet, for God's sake? "Are you . . . um." *There is no polite way to ask Satan 2.0 if she's slurping blood out of an Orange Julius cup. None. None at all.*

She figured out what he was (not) asking and shook her head. "Strawberry smoothie."

"Oh."

"It's less gross than blood," she explained, "though there are more seeds to contend with."

"Okay."

"I *love* blood. But I don't like it. Y'know?"

"Yes."

"So then. Let's have it."

"What?" The slurping. The slurping was working on his nerves like a small string of firecrackers tossed into a dirty street, just *pop pop pop poppoppop and smoke and more unbearable loud sharp sounds and dust everywhere, filth all over this was a bad idea this was a VERY BAD IDEA.*

"Hey! Stay away from the light, pal. Keep your focus. Your life story," she prompted.

So he told her, and she nodded here and there and grimaced a few times, but mostly she let him talktalktalk, and when he was done he felt a little better, not clean, exactly—only Cathie could make him clean—but a bit less wretched.

"Wow," was all she said after a long moment. She sucked in more smoothie and then

(thank you thank you)

put the cup on the desk, leaned back in her chair, and stretched out her long, long legs. "Your entire life."

"Yes?"

"Was severely fucked up."

"Yes."

"Which you decided to take out on several innocent women who had never harmed you in any way."

He said nothing. It seemed safest. And they weren't *several women*, they were his loves, his terriblewonderfuls.

They sat in silence for a moment, until she broke it. "So . . . dying didn't get rid of the crazy."

He blinked. "The crazy what?"

"I mean, this is exactly how you thought when you were killing short, dark-eyed blondes in their driveways, right? D'you know, my friends were worried you'd come after me?"

"I would never," he protested, trying not to stare at her legs, ugh, the gangly things took up half the office it was so off-putting women were supposed to be short so men could

(help them have them save them use them and GET HOLD RIGHT NOW)

"You're not my type," he managed, and oh thank God she seemed more amused by that than anything else that had happened in the last half hour.

"No? You'd never have tried to bag me for your collection?"

She grinned at him and he noticed how white her teeth were. And . . . sharp. Of course. "That's too bad. My friends were worried, but I'd kind of hoped you'd try something."

He shook his head. "Never." He felt like retching; her legs alone were problematic; he would have needed an extra suitcase at the least. And her eyes were wrong, wrong, all wrong.

"A discerning serial killer!"

"I— What?"

"Picky. Is that better?"

He had no idea. And now came the strangest thing in a very strange day; he could feel himself warming to her. Liking her, even, and it was so strong it almost

(almost)

buried the fear. "I . . ." *Almost don't loathe and fear you*, but even he wasn't such a glutton for a beat-down that he'd say such a thing. "You're very patient."

"Sure." She shrugged and shifted in her chair, looked down and smiled, and he thought her self-deprecation and modestly lowered gaze were charming until he realized she was smiling at her shoes. They were purple high heels with a purple cuff around each ankle, which made it look like she was wearing two festive electronic tracking devices. "I'm still learning myself. As you maybe noticed, I'm new in town."

Well, yes. He'd noticed that.

"So," he began, but she cut that right off.

"You're not getting out." Her tone was hateful because there was no malice, no glee; she took no pleasure out of it, out of any of this, and that was worse than malice. You can't fight calm indifference. "No way. Not for a long, *long* time. Even I couldn't tell you how long."

Of course you could! he wanted to shout. *You're the only one who could! You could snap your fingers—like that!—and I'd be free.* He kept it behind his teeth, thank God, and what came out next was purest truth, if not sanity. "Please. I've been here too long. Your horriblewonderful mall is—is—"

"Horrible and wonderful?"

"—but I should go."

"It hasn't even been three years."

No, that wasn't—no. Impossible. No. Decades, centuries. Not three years. No. "I need to go. I have to, it's so—" He made a vague gesture, hoping it encompassed the room, Hell, the universe in general. "Out there. They need me. They're filthy until I find them. There are so many. They're lost without me."

"No, they're doing fine without you."

"Lie!" he shouted, then shoved his fingers in his mouth and bit down, hard. "Y'don' 'aveta 'orry," he managed around his fingers.

She winced. "All right, no need to devour yourself right in front of me. And it's literally my job to worry, especially about whatever it is you'd get up to if I let you out. You're staying. For a long time."

He saw the truth of it in her words and posture and her calm-yet-firm polite regret. But that just raised more questions. "But—why? Why meet with me? You knew. You knew in the food court. So . . . why?"

She looked at him for a long, unblinking moment. (No one had to blink, but everyone did. An impossible habit to shake.) He wanted to cringe away from her stare. He managed to hold his body still as his gaze skittered everywhere: her eyes her chin her nose her shoulder the wall behind her her eyes her eyes her—

"Well, I suppose I wanted to meet with someone with *no* chance of parole. See how different that meeting is from the other kind—the kid who ended up in here at age ten because he stole a pound from the collection plate in London in 1886. If you can call someone who's lived over a century a kid."

"So I was right. You weren't—you never—you wouldn't—" She shook her head.

He *stared* at her. "You're . . . worse," he finally choked out. "Worse than the other. She never—she'd never dangle getting free and then yank it away."

He waited for the flash of temper, the pain. What next? More scourging? Boiled alive every day for a few decades? Not even boiling would get him clean. It would be pointless agony—the very worst kind.

"Me being worse than Satan would be a good thing to mention to the other residents down here," she said.

"Residents?" He'd never heard the term—at least, not in regard to Hell. It sounded vile.

"Sorry. The damned? The screwed? The thoroughly, thoroughly fucked? Whatever you want to call yourselves." She said this in a tone of perfect courtesy, then smirked. "Anything else?"

"I might have to love you," he choked, and it was true, and he hated that it was true. The beautiful blondes he had made his, he loved them, too, but it was always the gift he gave them; the reward was his deep affection. *This* one, though. He felt like she was taking his love. Robbing him of it. "I hate it, but . . . yes, I might have to really, really love you."

"Annnnnd we're done," she replied, the smirk long gone (which was a relief). "Run along," she said, and between one unnecessary blink and the next he was back in the food court.

"Oh, hey." It was Jennifer Palmer, the girl who ran Orange Julius. She was the devil's friend, kind of. Not as untouchable as a committee member, but the new devil was frequently seen chatting with her. "You forgot your lunch, so we got you a fresh one." She held out the new tray, completely unmoved by the way he'd blinked into existence between the Dairy Queen, whose soft serve was too soft and slightly sour, and the ladies' room, which was always out of toilet paper. "Here you go."

"No!" he wailed, warding it off with an elbow. Serving food in Hell had given Jennifer quick reflexes, though, and though she had to juggle the tray for a second, everything righted. "No," he said again, and ran away from her. He found a seat as far away from the food as he could and sat and tried to be still and tried to quiet his brain and definitely didn't think about anything that had happened in the last hour.

It took him a half hour to stop shaking.

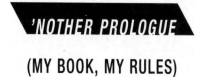

'NOTHER PROLOGUE

(MY BOOK, MY RULES)

You know the cliché about your life flashing before your eyes just before you die? It's true, and it's terrible. In those moments before death, you don't see loved ones or birthday parties or graduation or falling in love or your wedding day or your best vacation or anything, anything good.

No, you see your mistakes. All of them. Every missed chance, every bungled opportunity, every wrong choice, every consequence, every error in judgment, every left when you should have taken a right. In an endless parade, right before your eyes, right at the end, and it should take years, but it doesn't; it takes only a few seconds. And it pretty much guarantees that when you die, you'll go out regretful and deeply depressed.

That's what happened to me, anyway: my well-deserved, miserable death.

CHAPTER
ONE

I hung up on the bitchy mermaid and waited for the gate to slide back. That was new. The reporters huddled on the sidewalk, though? They'd been there for three weeks. Long enough for me to remember their names, if I were the type to remember names. There was Needs Highlights, and Enough with the Aftershave, and This Isn't My Real Job, and It's Not Like I Stepped on You on Purpose, and Seriously with That Hair? Oh, and my personal favorite: Those Shoes Aren't Terrible. I referred to all the camera personnel by the same name: Get That Thing Out of My Face.[3]

I parked in the garage, which was also new. Before the deluge

("Onslaught," my assistant/friend/devoted vodka guzzler, Tina, corrected. "Deluge means flood."

"Have you been out there? I'm sticking with deluge.")

---

[3] Whoa! Am I the only one having a prom flashback? Ha!

we'd had an outside, unconnected garage that was really long and weirdly deep (it used to be a stable that held the carriages and the horses). It was too vulnerable to Enough with the Aftershave and his ilk, though, so Tina had pulled a zillion strings and gotten a modern, safe, connected, impenetrable garage put up in less than a week. Luckily, the mansion sat on a corner lot and almost took up the block by itself; our yard was still big enough for Fur and Burr and smoothie picnics. Ah, the carefree days of smoothie picnics, before vampires went viral.

I made my way into the mansion, waking up Fur and Burr when I passed through the mudroom. I had to amuse them for only a minute; given the yawns and round bellies and bad breath, they'd just eaten, and I'd interrupted nap time. (Fur and Burr were not reporters. They were black Lab puppies.)

What was waiting for me inside the mansion was almost as scary as what was lurking on the sidewalk, though: a jittery zombie, a pissed-off Southern belle, the guy who saw dead guys (Bill? Sam? Something short, anyway), and a vampire king, all under siege.

I'd gotten no farther than a single step into the kitchen when I was seized, backed into a wall, and kissed so hard my feet left the tile. I wiggled my toes so my left shoe didn't fall off and clop to the floor. That sound was so distracting. "Finally," Sinclair murmured against my lips. "I loathe your interminable shopping trips."

"I filled up the tank and got ice, jackass; I was gone maybe twenty minutes mmmpphhh."

Should have said a vampire *queen* under siege.

I managed to fight off my husband (not without regret, but time and place, man, time and place) and put away the ice. This took, subjectively speaking, about five years, since the freezer was crammed with flavored vodkas

(Sriracha-flavored vodka, Tina? PB&J vodka? WHAT IS WRONG WITH YOU?)[4]

and dead mice stuffed into neatly labeled Ziplocs. Only in this place would the mouse population go down *after* the cat died.

"Yes, but I missed you this morning as well. I dislike rising alone." Don't worry—the king of the vampires definitely wasn't pouting. *I'm not pouting,* he'd correct while I tried not to giggle at his protruding lower lip. *I'm concentrating.* Not even a little tiny bit. Borderline pout at most.

"Yeah, well, I haven't seen Jess and her weird babies in over a week. Unacceptable! I'm still getting used to not living with her." And it *sucked.* It sucked rocks. It sucked like Trump's hair.[5]

Jessica had been my best friend since our training-bra days. We'd lived together since college. But since I'd accidentally changed the timeline, she was ~~stuck with~~ blessed with a boyfriend and baby twins.[6] It was a measure of her loyalty that she was willing to put up with her friend rising as a vampire queen and eventually taking over Hell, willing to put up with vampire roommates and werewolves who loved the pop-in, willing to put up with a zombie doctor and a perpetual shortage of ice . . . it was all fine, until the Antichrist outed vampires.

No one—least of all me—knew what would happen now. There was constant news coverage. The block was infested with reporters and had been for weeks. We were also hearing

---

[4] Sriracha and PB&J vodka exist! Run away!

[5] The great thing about that reference is, his hair has been awful for decades, and will continue to be awful, so whenever you're reading this, it's accurate.

[6] Betsy accidentally changed the timeline in *Undead and Unfinished.* Jessica hadn't been pregnant in the old timeline. Now she was a mother, and devoted to her boyfriend, Detective Dick Berry.

from a *lot* of vampires who were super pissed to rise one night and discover that, while they were sleeping, their queen had confirmed to the world that they exist.

So: exit Jessica, Dick, and their twins, Elizabeth and Eric. Also, I totally didn't cry like a wimp when I realized she'd named her babies after my husband and me.

It was for their own good. That's what I kept telling myself. When I weakened and started to call to beg her to move back in, Sinclair and Tina reminded me.

("Darling, must I confiscate your phone?"

"Try it. You ever gotten a fang in the testicle?")

Laura Goodman, the Antichrist—dumbest name for the Omen ever, by the way—motivated by a combo of spite and bitchiness, had used YouTube and social media and her legions of pathetic devil worshippers to expose vampires. And the vampires, under my direction, hadn't denied it. In fact, we'd done the opposite of denying it. Specifically, I had gone on live television and admitted that, yep, vampires were a thing and, yep, we weren't going anywhere.

Cue the deluge. Or the onslaught, if you like that word better. The interview went viral. Everything vampire-ish went viral. We were the goddamned swine flu of the Internet. That was a virus, right? Anyway, people were pretty evenly divided between two schools of thought: "That bimbo is lying!" and "That bimbo is a vampire!" The worst part? Nobody called the Antichrist a bimbo. Must have been the angel pin she wore on the lapel of the hideous blazer (corduroy!) she liked to wear on air.

"Stop that." Eric Sinclair, king of the ~~pouters~~ vampires, was once again trying to corner me for some more five-star smoochin'. "I can hear all your exposition."

"I can't help it," I protested. "Also, Fred called again."

"As I told you she would."

"Yeah, yeah, you're freakin' Nostradamus. Is it any wonder I can't help thinking about all this junk? It's what's on my mind."

"Easily fixed." Eric Sinclair's smile, slow and dark like a stream of chocolate ganache, lit me from the inside out. Better than sunshine, even. And that was saying something. He made a grab for me and I let him, and he pulled me straight to him, up against his broad chest, and oh my God the *shoulders* on the man! He'd been a farmer's son in life, a hard worker who had loved his family. His family was long dead, and so was the farm boy he'd once been. Only the muscular frame and the keen, deadly mind remained. I sometimes wondered how much more terrifying a vampire Sinclair would have been if he *hadn't* been raised by loving parents.

"Darling, I meant it—stop narrating."

"*You* stop narrating," I retorted, because he was now pressing soft kisses to the slope of my throat and it was really, really hard to think. "I'm doing just flehhh burble menh mmmm." The man's mouth was the textbook definition of sinful, and the sexy baritone was the cherry on the *oofta* sundae. (Hmm. Maybe he was right; maybe there was such a thing as too much exposition.)

But never mind! It was time—past time—to slip upstairs and try to break our fourth bed in two years. The Slumberland rep *loved* our asses.

Sinclair was now nibbling—very, very gently—on my lower lip, and I lightly bit him back and mumbled hopefully, "Upstairs?"

Oh yes! The upside to a telepathic link with your husband: you couldn't fake anything in or out of bed. The downside: you couldn't fake anything in or out of bed. But this time it was all good.

Then he did that corny thing I loved: bent and scooped me

into his arms and literally swept me off my feet. He was an undead Rhett, and I was his bitchy Scarlett, with better shoes! Oh, it was glorious, and I—

"Hey!" A familiar skidding sound followed by a thud. When he had news, Marc liked to sprint for the kitchen, nearly always misjudged the distance, and bounced off the swinging kitchen door like a Super Ball. I'd blame this on his zombie-ness, but he'd been exactly like that in life.

Sinclair closed his eyes, likely mustering patience, or reminding himself that zombies taste terrible and thus must never be chowed upon. We could hear Marc righting himself before shoving the door open and darting into the kitchen. It was really, *really* hard not to snicker. "Betsy, it's almost time for your— Again? God, you two are like rabbits."

"We are not!" Rabbits did it at least a dozen times a week, right? Sinclair and I were both so busy that we'd only managed half of that, and it was Friday already.

"It's odd that you frequently feel compelled to comment on our sex life," Sinclair pointed out with admirable calm.

"Because it's always in my face! Everyone's faces! All the time!"

Er. Not really, I was pretty sure. I think this had more to do with Bill Lesser, or whatever the guy's name was. When the "Vampires are, like, real! Whoa!" story broke, Marc ended up hanging out with one of the bloggers covering the story. Sparks flew, apparently? But Marc had this nutty idea that live people didn't want to date zombies. His old-fashioned prejudices were so quaint.

"Now you're just exaggerating and being shrill," I said, keeping the reproach out of my tone. "Besides, I already told you guys about the stuff I said in the interview."

"This isn't a lame YouTube video like your useless sister came up with; it's an actual interview on an actual news channel."

"Aw. You're so cute when you're disparaging the Antichrist to stick up for me."

"I've seen Hell and I've been audited. The Antichrist doesn't scare me."

Even Sinclair had to laugh at that.

"Though why you settled for Diana Pierce when you prob'ly could have gone on *Larry King*—"

"King creeps me out. It'd be like talking to a giant grumpy cigarette. Besides, I like Pierce." She looked great, her hair was always nice, pleasant voice, and she didn't make the sign of the cross at me when I came to the studio. Sadly, the same couldn't be said of her sound guy.

"So let's go watch it!"

"More exposition," Sinclair muttered, and got an elbow to the ribs for his pains, which was tricky since he still hadn't put me down.

Still, an excited zombie was hard to deny, and anything that got his mind off pining for the blogger was good. So Sinclair set me back on my feet and we followed Marc to the TV room, formerly one of the mansion's many parlors. No one needed five parlors—honestly, no one needed one—so Marc had taken this one over and modernized it with a vengeance: wide-screen TV, stereo sound, a bar *with* a blender (the entire household was a bit smoothie obsessed), easy chairs, a sectional sofa that five of us could slump on at a time, new plush carpeting, soundproofing, et cetera.

("It's definitely not a man cave," Marc had insisted as we stared at it a month ago, startled into silence, "so don't ever call it that. God, I hate that word. Hate it.")

Tina was already there, curled up at the end of the sectional, her short legs tucked beneath her, but she immediately unfolded and stood when she saw us. She'd known Sinclair all his long, long life—she'd been an honorary aunt to the entire Sinclair family for generations, had turned him at his request, then stuck by his side like a blond barnacle with exquisite manners.[7]

"Majesties."

Years. Years of my life wasted, asking the woman to just call me Betsy already. "Seriously, Tina?"

She was too deep into her tablet to respond. "Ah, this is excellent; we're all here . . . once we're finished watching, I would like to discuss hiring a PR firm to handle more things like this."

Yawn. Which wasn't out loud, but apparently my poker face sucked, because she followed up with, "I know it sounds unnecessarily dull, Majesty, but the vampire nation has never needed public relations before. We were rather more invested in the reverse."

"What, you think I'll have to do more of those?" Well, going on TV wasn't *so* bad. I'd gotten to debut my new navy pumps, at least.

"Nothing to sweat," Marc assured me. "You said yourself you thought it went fine."

"Oh, you bet. At first I was worried the Casadei slingbacks would be too much for daytime, but then I realized they were appropriate, but now it's occurring to me that's not what you meant." I shrugged. "It was, what? Two days ago, maybe? It was fine."

Sinclair sat on the far end of the sofa, pulling me into his lap as he got comfy. In retrospect, I'm glad I didn't kick up a fuss like calling him Handsy McGrabass and maybe dumping ice down his back, because that was the last bit of fun we had for a long, long time.

---

[7] We got the backstory in *Undead and Unfinished*.

CHAPTER
TWO

TWO DAYS AGO, MAYBE?

Green rooms aren't really green, proving once again that much of life was a lie. But it was a decent enough room to cool your high heels in, with comfortable chairs, a sofa, a full-length mirror, a fridge full of snacks and pop,[8] and a TV.

So I sat there and guzzled my third Coke in five minutes and tried not to fidget and politely returned the stare of the cookbook author who had the segment before mine. She was a pretty, curvy woman who looked to be in her early forties, with short, fluffy brown hair, pale blue eyes, and big glasses with brown rims that made her look like a cute owl. She was clutching her book so hard her knuckles were white.

Someone (producer? guy who lost the coin toss?) opened the door, stuck his head in, saw we were both in the room, nodded approvingly, left. The woman's gaze had shifted to him and she seemed a little devastated when he shut the door.

---

[8] Pop = soda, like Coke. It's a Midwestern thing. I make no apologies for it, or anything Midwestern.

As for me, I was too antsy to play with my phone and, like an idiot, hadn't brought anything to read. So, what the hell. "You're thinking, if it's true, I'm alone in a room with a vampire. And if it's not true, I'm alone in a room with a crazy lady who thinks she's a vampire."

There was a reason I hid behind humor, and it wasn't just because I was Minnesota Nice, which was code for passive-aggressive. It's because humor *worked*. Sometimes.

"Well . . . yeah," she admitted, and her mouth curved into a bashful smile. "That's pretty much the whole thing right there."

"Don't worry. I only drink . . . Coke," I said, because what's more cheering than my terrible Bela Lugosi impression? I leaned forward—she was sitting opposite me—and held out my hand. "My name's Betsy."

"Yeah, I know. I'm Carol." She moved the book to her other hand to shake mine and I let out a yelp of delight.

"*Smoothie Nation*," I breathed, delighted by the title and content. "Oh my God, everyone in my family loves smoothies! We make them every single day! We have so many blenders!"

"Your family? You mean . . . other . . . um . . . vampires?"

"Vampires, humans, maybe a zombie or two. The family I made." As opposed to my blood relatives, who, with the exception of my mother, were all degrees of terrible. "We're nuts about them. Are you going to make smoothies during your segment? Please, please tell me you're making smoothies during your segment!"

"Well, yeah." Another giggle. "Course I am. Look." She opened the book to a glorious concoction: Strawberry Colada Smoothie. Ooh, and on the facing page: Cinnamon Roll Smoothie!

I started groping for my purse. Pen, pen, *where was my pen*? "May I please have your autograph? And where can I get your book? The gang will love your book. I have to get your book!"

She giggled, which was *so* charming. "Sure. Here, I've got an extra copy." She picked up her tote bag, rooted around, produced another book and a pen. "It's, uh, Betsy, right?"

"Yeah. You don't have to say it. I'm well aware it's an absurd name for a vampire queen."

"Yeah," she agreed, and started to write.

"Would you mind terribly making it out to my husband, too?" At her nod, I added, "It's Sink Lair, two words, just like it sounds." Heh.

"Oh, is he foreign?"

"No, but he was super insufferable when we met. I just like sticking it to him sometimes." All times. But who was counting? "Thanks," I added, smiling down at my new (free!) book. "I can't wait to try these. I'm so lucky I ran into you."

"Yeah, I was just thinking the same thing. You don't seem . . . um—" She cut herself off and the color rose in her face.

"Like a drooling psychotic with an unholy thirst for human blood?" An uneasy giggle was my answer. "Yeah, don't believe everything you see on YouTube."

"I won't," she promised at once. "Y'know, my husband's on the St. Paul City Council, and I could tell him . . ."

"You'll put in a good word for me?"

"Sure." She started to say something else, then cut herself off again.

"What?"

"Nothing."

"C'mon, we're bonding over smoothies and I'm going to brag to everyone that I met a smoothie chef and you're gonna tell your husband that I'm not a knuckle-dragging psychotic, so it's all good. What is it?"

"Are you really?" She laughed again—I figured it might be a nervous tic—then added, "You're, um. It's daylight."

"Yeah, I noticed." I started flipping through *Smoothie*

Nation. Glorious, lots of color pictures and the recipes looked simple. "That happens during the day a lot."

"But you're a vampire."

"Or crazy," I reminded her. Then I got it. "Yeah, I'm out in sunlight. Or I would be, if I went outside. But I didn't teleport here, so, yeah. I can be out in the daytime." I shrugged. "Maybe don't believe everything you read, either?"

"Or see on random YouTube vids," she agreed. "That'll be what gives you the most trouble."

"Hmmm?" What's this? Blackberry Creamsicle Smoothies? What a time to be alive!

"That you guys break the rules. That what people thought they knew about vampires was wrong."

I looked up. Carol's expression was troubled, but the good news was, she didn't seem scared. Just worried. Possibly for me, even.

"Just my opinion," she added.

"Yeah, well, it's a good point." It was, and I wondered that I hadn't thought of it before. Scary news: vampires are real and always have been. Scarier: they have a hierarchy most people never noticed. Scariest: they're a lot harder to kill than legend indicated. "I'll keep it in mind."

A quick knock, and the guy who lost the coin toss was back. *"Smoothie Nation?"*

Carol popped to her feet. "That's me!" She turned back to me. "Well, it was nice meeting you."

"Oh, likewise. Good luck with your segment."

"You, too. 'Bye, Betsy."

"Good-bye, Carol."

And then there was one. One with a wonderful new cookbook! And I figured as far as omens went, Carol was a good one. Which showed, once again, how much I suck at predicting the future.

I followed him down a hall lined with poster-sized pictures of the KARE 11 on-camera gang, wondering if I should tease him about the cross around his neck. I'd never been here before; it's possible that was his everyday jewelry. Yeah, better not assume everything always had something to do with me, and here came a couple of interns and *they* had crosses, too. I rolled my eyes and said nothing. (This might have something to do with me.)

Remember how nice Carol was, I reminded myself. I also realized that one way or the other, I'd be leaving the building in twenty minutes, so all I had to do was . . . eee-yikes! Why was it so cold in here?

Coin Toss Guy—wait—was he a sound guy? Probably should have paid more attention . . . Anyway, he was wiry and efficient and fast, had opened the big double doors, and we stepped into a room so large it was like a warehouse. Tall ceiling, lights everywhere, a kitchen set, a living room set, cords snaking all over the place, gigantic cameras everywhere, and, argh, so friggin' cold! I instantly regretted my wardrobe choice of a knee-length skirt and short-sleeved sweater. I regretted not bringing a parka. Not the shoes, though. I never regretted the shoes.

A pretty young woman with short dark hair, dressed in business-casual dark pants, a red sweater, and black flats, hurried over to me. She shifted her tablet to her left hand, stuck out her right, and introduced herself as Deb, the producer.

"Pleased to meet you," I managed, shaking her small, warm hand and trying not to let my fangs chatter. (Yeah, that was all I needed . . . please, *please* don't let someone cut themselves in here. I had zero control over when my fangs came out; one snootful of blood and the game was over.)

She watched me trying not to tremble and looked worried. "Are you sensitive to cold because you're a vampire?"

"No, I'm sensitive to cold because I understand the difference between hot and cold and it's really, really cold in here."

"Sorry," she replied, trying (and failing) not to smile. "It's for the equipment."

"Your equipment's made of ice?"

"No"—she sighed, steering me toward the middle of the floor, sidestepping cables without looking—"but it might as well be. Diana? Here's Betsy Taylor."

And oooh, there she was! It was so strange to see someone I'd been watching on TV for more than a decade walking up to me like a real person and everything. *Smoothie Nation* and now Diana Pierce! What a time to be undead!

"Hi, I'm Diana Pierce," she said with a warm smile. Like a real person and everything. Like I didn't know who she was! Oh my God. Was I a fangirl?

"I might be a fangirl," was how I answered, because I'm a moron. But she laughed, thank God. *Marc must never know of this*, I vowed to myself.

"Well, we're real glad you agreed to come on the show." Unspoken: as opposed to something national, or international—CNN, maybe. "No matter your, ah, agenda." Translation: whether you're a vampire or just a crazy lady with terrific shoes—either way, ratings!

"I'm a local," I replied, scampering behind her as we walked into the nearest set: low dark-wood table, love seat, easy chairs. Like someone's living room, if their living room was in a freezing warehouse and had nothing out of place anywhere and unbelievably high ceilings. "I wanted to do a local interview." And hopefully that'd be it. I'd admit my grotesque vampire nature, foiling Laura's plan, there wouldn't be any Antichrist drama, case closed. To be honest, I was amazed this hadn't blown over yet. Americans weren't known for our long attention spans. And why couldn't we make smoothies during the interview? That would put me at ease and, also, fill my gullet with smoothies. Well, maybe I'd hit Orange Julius on the way home. I was entitled to a Julius, the week I'd— Nuts. Diana Pierce was talking to me.

"Well, this is pretaped, as you know." She sat and made it look easy: not a gorgeous reddish brown beautifully cut hair out of place, not a wrinkle in her red suit, not a smudge on her eyeliner or her lipstick. Me, I was trying to keep the easy chair from gobbling my behind, I'd chewed off all my lipstick in the parking lot, and my sports bra was cutting into the skin under my boobs. One size fits all, my ass! "Anything you don't like, or don't want to answer, we can edit that out. As we told your assistant—"

Huh? Oh, right. Tina. She'd offered to come with, but unlike me, she couldn't walk around in the daytime. The whole point was to put people at ease, which meant creeping around in the dark of night to get to an interview because otherwise my assistant would burst into flames was a bad plan. Besides, I

wanted Diana Pierce to myself. I could always use a new bestie!
(Note to self: never discuss this line of thinking with Jessica.)

"—it'll air the day after tomorrow."

"Great." I was still trying to extricate myself from the maw
of the chair without messing up my hair or dislodging my
microphone. This could be the entire interview: Vampire
Queen Devoured by Chair, Needs More Lipstick, Film at 11.
"That's fine."

Finally, I was—well, not comfortable, exactly; I was too
conscious of all the cameras and the lights, *so* many lights. And
I could feel the stares from behind the lights. Was it just me,
or were there people in the studio who had nothing to do with
producing this segment? What, they needed *all* their recep-
tionists and office personnel to be in here with Diana Pierce
and me? And the custodians? And—hey! That guy didn't even
work here! He was the UPS guy! Why were they all in here
with Diana Pierce and me?

*(Diana Pierce and me! If there was a reality show about Diana
Pierce and me roaming the countryside solving mysteries, I would
totally watch it.)*

Not everyone was wearing crosses, at least, and I think the
fact that I hadn't hissed and clawed at the ones who were
helped put people at ease. No one in here but us regular people; nothing special going on at all except for this chair, which
was the furniture equivalent of a Venus flytrap.

Because that's what I wanted. Not the chair—the attitude.
The mind-set that I was a person, like all of them. I had dumb
problems and good times, like them.

"Thirty seconds," someone said, which didn't bother Diana
Pierce one bit, but made me wriggle. Who knew navigating
chairs with a microphone cord snaking out of my sweater was
so difficult? What if the cord got tangled around my neck and
choked me? I wouldn't die, but eyes bulging while clawing at

my throat wasn't a good look for TV. How do people on those talk shows make it seem like they're just hanging out? I felt like the polar opposite of hanging out; I felt on display, like a zoo exhibit. *See the bitchy vampire queen! Notice how she is uncomfortable away from her native kitchen and on the watch for apex predators!*

". . . three . . . two . . ."

What? Already?

". . . one . . ."

Ack!

"And we're back, talking this morning with St. Paul resident Betsy Taylor, who was outed a few weeks ago as an honest-to-God vampire. Yes, you heard that right." She looked away from the camera, straight at me. "We can say *God*, right?"

"It's your show," I replied, and got a smile for that one. "Yes, of course. Vampires aren't at all what people assume." Except when they were.

"Given that most people assumed they weren't real, I think you're right." Her dark eyes twinkled at me—or maybe that was just the lights. Did that mean my eyes were twinkling in a friendly way? Ooh, please make the lights look like I was twinkling in a friendly way. "How did this happen?"

"My half sister, Laura, knows I'm a vampire. She's never approved. We're . . ." In a power struggle, except she had no power. Not since I'd taken her spot in Hell away from her and, with that, her paranormal abilities.[9] So she was reduced, in the most pathetic way, to stirring up shit.

"Yes?"

I decided to be nice. "Well, families fight. She thought by

---

[9] It's true! The coup that wasn't took place in *Undead and Unwary*. Betsy looked fabulous throughout.

telling the world I was a vampire, that'd cause trouble for me. I don't think she gives society much credit."

"So you never considered denying it."

Sure I did. Then I thought better of it. It had taken Tina and Sinclair some time to come around, though. I hated playing the "STFU—I'm the boss of you" card so kept it at a minimum. Which meant when I did play the queen card, it made an impression. "No, I decided it was time people knew the truth. Vampires are real. We're your moms and your sisters and your friends. And that's it—there's no sinister secret conspiracy. We're real, we've always been around, nothing to see here."

Diana Pierce snorted and it was glorious because even her snorts were elegant and professional. "I don't know that I agree there's nothing to see here. But you're saying that historically speaking . . ."

"We've been around going back to the beginning," I interrupted. "Yes. We've been living alongside humans for thousands of years. Nothing has changed from a month ago . . . except now people know we're real." I'd hoped that by pointing that out—hey, look! Nothing to be scared of!—we could get on with our lives. Vampires weren't running the world. Well, not overtly. Not in a way anyone would notice.

"And you're how old?"

"What a rude question, Diana Pierce!" She laughed. "I'm in my early thirties. Not every vampire is a thousand years old and rich and has a European accent and skulks in alleys."

"So the queen of the vampires is young, for a vampire?"

Don't preen. "Yes."

"And why are you the queen?" Ah, a question for the ages. "Do you have elections?"

"No . . . vampire politics are tricky, and I'd rather not discuss that right now." Translation: *My rule was foretold, I'm*

Elizabeth the One, nothing to see here. I just didn't want to get into all of that.

"Okay, no problem." She instantly shifted ground. "Some people say that this is a hoax, the way people maintain the Undersea Folk—mermaids—aren't real, either."

"Well, some people think we didn't really walk on the moon. Some people are asshats." I paused. "Can I say *asshat* on TV?"

"On this station, yes. So what do you say about Undersea Folk? Are they real?"

"I'm not a mermaid," I replied. "How would I know that?" They were real. Bitchy and horrible and in dire need of a good hair conditioner—at least the one I had met—and yes, very real. But I wasn't here to talk about them.

"Well, can you prove you're a vampire?"

"This isn't an audition. I'm not here to prove anything. I'm just going on the record as not denying my sister's claims."

"You drink blood?"

"Yes."

"How often? From whom?"

"Mostly donations, and every vampire's appetite is different." Hoo boy, that was the truth. Younger vamps could drain someone in twenty minutes. Naturally we frowned on that behavior. Older ones didn't need it nearly so often. But we all craved it. Constantly.

I wasn't about to mention that Sinclair and I preferred "donations" from asshats usually involved in assault or rape or attempted murder. When we went hunting, we always looked for the scumbags. People minding their own business? We weren't into it. Though, ironically, we could have had our pick. Other than reporters, most of the people haunting our block were people who wanted to be turned. Or just snacked on. Included in any way, however small.

"How are vampires made?"

"Well, my"—*zombie*; um, rephrase—"doctor says it's like a virus, something passed on in our blood, and symptoms include a really slow heart rate, a metabolism that's mostly stopped but causes light sensitivity, aural sensitivity . . . things like that. But it's against our rules to just run around randomly biting people to try to"—*turn them* sounds sinister; rephrase—"reproduce." Ugh. Nice mental image for the audience. *Just think of our fangs as sharp, virile, pointy penises!*

"And how long have you been around?"

"I don't know," I admitted. "There are records going back thousands of years, but I don't think we can nail down the first vampire with any accuracy. There's not a plaque anywhere that reads 'On this day was chomped the first person who succumbed to a particular virus.'" *I'm pretty sure . . .*

"Why come forward now?"

"I think we're as ready as we'll ever be now. When my sister exposed us, the first instinct was to deny, sure. But after some thought I realized that would be a mistake. Some of us are tired of hiding, and it's not the Middle Ages anymore."

"Meaning . . . ?"

"People used to think all sorts of biological conditions were a result of witchcraft or whatever, like that disease that made people look super hairy, so people decided they were werewolves."

"Hypertrichosis."

What am I, a scientist? "Yeah, sounds right."

"Are there?"

"Are there what?"

"Werewolves?"

"Oh." Well, shit. I hadn't anticipated this one. Which I should have, especially after Diana Pierce's mermaid question. This was tricky ground, because while I was leaving out some parts, I'd promised myself I wouldn't overtly lie during the interview. But the Wyndham werewolves weren't mine to reveal. "I'm just here to focus on vampires." *Shades of Martha Stewart!*

"Because some would say we now live in a world with mermaids and vampires . . . so doesn't it follow that there are other paranormal creatures of legend we just don't know about?"

What, like unicorns? They're definitely not real. I was pretty sure. "I can't talk about werewolves; I'm here about vampires."

Pierce deftly shifted ground, *finally.* "Would you compare your group coming forward to the battles the LGBT community has had to fight for decades?"

"I didn't say that," I said quickly. "It's not a contest for 'most repressed.' Look, bottom line, my sister wanted to expose us and she did. We're not denying it. The end."

"Some people have gone on record—

(Who were "some people"? And would beating them unconscious be a bad thing?)

"saying you aren't just the vampire queen—that you also rule Hell."

"Yeah, well, 'some people' just looooove to talk smack."

"So you deny it?"

Definitely not being sarcastic enough here. Or she's as tenacious as she is stylish. Damn you, stylish Diana Pierce! "Hell isn't really relevant to the topic at hand."

"Because some would argue that if it's true, that if you chose, you could prove there is a Hell and, conversely, a Heaven."

Which was exactly what Laura's end game had been: she'd wanted to prove to the world that Heaven and Hell were quantifiably real. In her mind, that would lead to everyone on the planet converting to Christianity, en masse, followed by peace on earth forever.

Which was deeply nuts.

"I don't know about that, I'm afraid."

"What would you say *your* long-term plan is?"

"Oh, I don't know—live my life?"

"But *are* you alive?"

"Of course I'm alive, same as you. Like I said, the virus slows us down; it doesn't kill us in the way most people understand death. Viruses don't work on dead people." Learned that from Brad Pitt in *World War Z*.

"Would you consider allowing medical testing? Or providing samples of the virus for scientific study?"

"Uh . . . hadn't crossed my mind, actually. You think I should spit in a test tube and FedEx it to the CDC?"

"That's one way to do it," she replied, still twinkling away. "What if a vampire breaks the law?"

"Then vampires deal with it."

"So you have a legal system, courts . . . like that?"

"Kind of." Well, no. Not really. It was a good idea, though.

"So if a vampire broke the law and was arrested, you would allow them to go through the human justice system?"

"We're all human," I said quietly, "and vampires have been through our justice system. Look, most of us lie low." Shit! Sounded shifty. Recover, recover! "They work hard to stay out of trouble. When they can't, or won't, then we take care of it."

"So you don't consider yourself a sovereign nation, entirely separate from the rest of the world?"

"No, of course not."

"Do you have anything else to tell people about vampires?"

The end, finally in sight. "Just that in most ways, we're like you. Nothing to be scared of—I mean, we're all capable of savagery. You don't have to be a vampire to be a jackass. I guess I would want people watching to know that their lives aren't any different today than they were last month, before you knew vampires were a thing. Let's just—y'know, everyone can get back to business now."

"Not that we would, but . . ." She leaned down and picked up her coffee cup. "Say this was filled with holy water—"

"Are you on a cleanse diet or something?"

"Ah, no."

"Because you look great."

"Thank you."

"You don't have to cleanse with holy water."

"If this was holy water," Pierce continued doggedly, "and I tossed it at you—"

"Rude."

"—would it hurt you?"

"No."

"Can you show us?

"No. As I said, this isn't a circus act. I'm not here to convince you, or your audience. Just to let my sister know that I'm not contesting her latest crap." Nor was I about to mention that my gorgeous blond jackass of a sister was the Antichrist. It would just lead to more questions I didn't want to answer, as well as stooping to her level of jealous tattletale.

"Thank you very much for coming to talk to us today."

"Thanks for letting me come."

"Did we have a choice?" she joked.

"Um, yeah, of course—"

Cut. "And we're out!"

So that was that.

CHAPTER
FOUR

THE PRESENT

Tina cleared her throat. "So. About that PR firm . . . ?"

"What? It was fine." They were all staring at me. "What? It was! I mean, I felt a little on the spot with the werewolf question—"

"You looked like a deer about to be mowed by a semi," Marc pointed out. "*Two* semis. The first would've creamed you; the second would have made sure you stayed down."

"Oh, please, exaggerate a little more." I scoffed and, when that seemed to have no effect, scoffed harder. "Besides, I couldn't out werewolves without their permission. Like I need the Wyndham pack breathing down my neck—literally breathing down my neck and probably drooling on me—along with everything else going on this month?"

Sinclair actually shuddered. "No, you do not. But I'm afraid this interview has done nothing but raise more questions." Infinitesimal pause. "As I warned you it might."

"And here we go with the 'I Told You So' dance. Well, too

bad. You guys are the ones who said I shouldn't guzzle holy water on camera. You're the ones who said I wasn't a circus performer."

"No," Marc agreed, "your outfit was all wrong for that."

I shot him an exasperated look. "Look, Laura made her little video, I went on TV to refute, end of story."

"No one is saying that you did a bad job," Tina began in that "treat the idiot with kid gloves" tone I hated. "But—"

"By denying we're a nation, you just opened up the chance for any vampire to be arrested, charged, and tried in a court of law . . . *not* by our laws," Sinclair said.

"Which is . . . bad?"

Vigorous nods.

Sinclair went on. "Every vampire who sees this will now wonder if you have not simply exposed them, but they will wonder if you made a deliberate decision to leave them without protection, either."

"Which is super-*duper* bad."

"Yes. Further, by mentioning vampire politics, you have raised the question among our people: Why *aren't* we more political? Why do you and I rule? Perhaps we should embrace politics and hold elections."

"Oh." Huh. Okay. Hadn't thought of it like that. What surprised me most was that my first impulse wasn't: *You want the job? You can have it. Best of luck.* No, it was: *I'm not the queen by popular demand. I'm the queen because I'm the queen.* "Okay, well, this is how we figure out what else we have to do." I refused to see this as a fuckup. "The whole point is that it's time, right? Well, nobody ever promised it'd be drama-free. Or that it'd be easy." Though I'd been hoping. "I still think you guys are making something out of nothing. I'm telling you, it'll be fine."

Suddenly everyone's phones shorted out at the same time.

No, wait, they all started ringing and trembling at the same time. A cacophony of ringtones filled the air, startling everyone in the room. For the first time I wasn't amused by Marc's Darth Vader ringtone, or the *Pink Panther* theme, which sounded so *weird* coming from Tina's phone. Sinclair used the old-fashioned bell ring—no, wait, that was the kitchen phone ringing, the one hooked into the landline. (Yeah, we still had one of those.) Sinclair had his set so only dogs and vampires could hear it.

I cut off my own ringtone

("Piiiiiiigs . . . iiiiiiin . . . spaaaaaaaace!")

when I answered and was greeted with, "Oh, you silly bitch. What have you done now?"

"Antonia," I groaned. There were two women named Antonia in my life and they were both pains in my ass. One was my dead stepmother, who helped me run Hell. The other was the bitch (literally—Antonia was a werewolf) on the other end of the line. She'd lived with us in the mansion for a few months until she fell in love with a feral vampire and they both moved west. (I know how it sounds. These are the days of our lives.)[10]

"Did no one prep you, you shoe-obsessed moron?"

This was Antonia-ese for *I'm a little worried about you.*

"It was a ten-minute local interview," I whined. "It went fine."

"I didn't know it was possible for someone to have their head *that* far up their ass." *As your friend, I'm concerned you haven't thought through all the ramifications.*

"You don't call me for six months and when you do pick up the phone, it's to yell at me?"

---

[10] Antonia's backstory can be found in *Dead and Loving It.*

"God knows the cringing sycophants you live with won't do it." *With respect, the others lack my objectivity.*

"Always so nice to hear from you, Antonia."

A rude noise, like she farted into her cell phone. I wouldn't put anything past that bitch. "Look, when the gang gets to town, call me. I might be able to save your dumb ass from the well-deserved smackdown coming your way." *I'd like to help you but it's not in my nature to just show up—I'd like an invitation so I don't feel I'm imposing on our friendship.*

"The others? What others? Wait, are you telling me the— Dammit!" Antonia hanging up was like anybody hanging up: conversation over.

My phone promptly rang again

("Piiiiiiiigs . . . iiiiiiiiin . . . spaaaaaaaace!")

and I glared at it hard enough to shatter the case. This time, luckily, it was my mother. "That was, um . . . you looked very nice."

I sighed. "Apparently it was the worst television interview in the history of the medium and I was a fool to contemplate it much less go through with it."

"Oh no, it wasn't *that* bad."

"Thanks, but you're biased."

"That doesn't mean I'm lying, honey. Nixon looked much worse than you did when he debated Kennedy."

Sigh. "Thanks, Mom."

"The reason I called . . . was . . . ah . . ." Hmm. Hesitancy was not a trait she was known for. This was a woman who all but kidnapped Tina so she could pump her about the Civil War. She practically chained her up in the basement. This was a woman who, if she thought my new $450 Manolos were ugly, *would say so*. Fearless! So whatever she was about to say was nothing I wanted to hear. "I know we talked about bringing BabyJon back to the mansion tomorrow . . ."

I closed my eyes, because I immediately saw the problem. My brother/son, BabyJon,[11] ostensibly lived in the mansion with the rest of us. And we adored the incontinent drool machine. Except he was spending more and more time with my mother these days. What started out as a temporary arrangement in times of emergency

("I'm going to Hell. Not sure when I'll return; it depends on whether or not the devil kills me. I'll try to bring you back something nice, though!")

was becoming permanent. And my mom had gone from resenting her ex-husband's late-in-life baby to absolute adoration. Which was wonderful, except it meant that these days, BabyJon was more a visitor than a resident of the mansion. But it had to be done, for the same reason Jessica and her weird babies had to move out. You couldn't dick around with the safety of innocents. You just couldn't. It was decidedly uncool.

He was starting to walk, and he'd already cut his first few teeth. And I was missing all of it . . . the first tooth, first solid foods, first talking back, first scribbling on the wall, first stealing my car, first time getting drunk and throwing up in the kitchen sink . . . all the stuff I'd looked forward to as a mom/big sister hybrid.

"Betsy? You there, hon?"

I pinched the bridge of my nose. "I'm here, Mom. You'd better keep him for a few more days. I think the deluge is going to get worse before it gets better. I'll come see you both tomorrow."

"All right, hon." Her relief was unmistakable. "I think that's the best option for now."

"I'm really sorry."

---

[11] BabyJon is Betsy's half brother, the child of her father and her late stepmother, Antonia. Betsy is his legal guardian.

"It's not your fault." A generous lie. "Take it easy, sweetie—this too shall et cetera."

Sure it would.

("Piiiiiiiigs . . . iiiiiiiiin . . . spaaaaaaaace!")

Nope. I angrily stuffed my phone down between couch cushions. My phone was dead to me. And so was Diana Pierce. Well, no. Just my phone. How could I stay mad at Diana Pierce when she knew how to sit down without strangling on her microphone cord?

"I'll be hiding in my bedroom if anyone needs me," I announced.

"Aw, c'mon. Don't do that. Let's adieu to the kitchen. This is nothing a blender of smoothies can't fix," Marc cajoled. "Or at least distract us from."

I shook my head. "I'm not thirsty." And perhaps would never be again. Who knew when I'd get my appetite back? *Smoothie Nation*, I have failed you.

"Perhaps our feedback was unduly constructive," Sinclair
said, closing our bedroom door and moving to sit on the bed,
where I was sulking, facedown, into my pillow.

"Y'think?" I mumbled into memory foam.

"But as you said, this is a learning experience for all of us."

"Ugh." I could feel him stroking my back the way he knew
turned me into a puddle of grumpy goo. But it would take a
lot more than a back rub to oh yeah right there. "Mmmmm.
Umph, gggnnn nnmmph."

"Your endearments always make me melt." He eased me
over on my back and bent for a kiss. "Now complain about the
dearth of ice in our home. The shriller you get, the more
arousing you are and the more irresistible you become."

I *barely* stopped the smirk in time. Whew! Close call. "You
can't seduce your way out of this one," I warned, "so just—
Hey, get back here. I want another one."

He laughed and swooped back in, planting one right on my
mouth, then moving lower to nibble at my neck. I brought my

arms up around his neck and pulled him closer. "I still think it was a good idea to do the interview."

"As you like."

"I do, though."

"Of course."

"I think it'll work out fine."

"Time will tell."

"Man, you're just begging to be cock blocked, aren't you?"

"Now, there's a bluff I may call," was the smug reply. So naturally my only option was to tickle the bejeezus out of him, which wasn't unlike trying to tickle a tree trunk. When we called a temporary truce, he was on the floor and I was on my back on our bed with my head hanging over the edge.

"Plenty more where that came fr— Yeek! Argh, get off. If you stretch out my sweater, I'll set your suits on fire!"

"Well worth it."

"It'll be an inferno in there! Kids will come over and roast marshmallows!"

"A small price to pay for the pleasure of your company."

"You know how deeply nuts you are, right? You're the only man I've ever known who finds shrill to be 'maddeningly arousing.'"

"Soon all vampires will love you as I do."

"First off, that's a truly alarming thought. Second, you know they won't." The playful mood had vanished, because when it came to predicting vampire behavior, Sinclair was nearly always right. Something was coming and it was going to get worse before it got better. If it got better. "You know what we're going to have to let them do. And then what I'm going to have to do."

"We," he said softly. "What we will have to do."

"Yeah. We. I just wish—"

"No point to it, beloved. Wishing is a time waster. Focus

on doing. Focus on *we*. You see? That makes all the difference. And in the meantime . . ."

"Yeek! God, your hands are freezing!"

Soon enough the room filled with threats, giggles, more threats, and flying clothes. Sinclair's dark eyes basically became my whole world, and that was fine, because my much less dramatic eyes were his world, too.

After, he leaned over and picked up the book off my night-stand. *"Book of Shadows?"* he read aloud, then started flipping through the book. "Banishing spells, cutting cords, banishing negativity? This is a book for Wiccans."

"Duh, I'm the one who checked it out of the library. Hey, be careful! Don't bend the pages; you do not want to mess with the Dakota County librarians." They were super pleasant and helpful . . . right up until you damaged a book. Then it was a bit like "I am become death, destroyer of worlds." I mean, they didn't do that work because the pay was so great. There wasn't a librarian on the planet who was in it for the money. It was strictly out of love for books. So when you hurt the books . . . I shivered. It was one time, I'd been fifteen and had dog-eared a dozen pages (all the sex scenes in *The Flame and the Flower*), and the resulting lecture haunted my nightmares for years.

"Darling, you're not a Wiccan."

"Again: duh. Why are you telling me things I already know? I just liked the looks of the book and wanted to do some research. You remember when I banished the devil from Hell?"

"Exquisitely." The dark throb of his voice hit me nice and low; if we hadn't just finished, we'd be going again. After I'd given Satan the boot, Sinclair and I had come back to the mansion and he'd taken me on all fours in front of the full-length mirror. It had been . . . memorable.

"Well, I get the feeling that kind of thing might come in handy. So I wanted to study up. And don't give me that look. You know I can do research when I have to."

"I know you *enjoy* research. It's one of your more charming secrets. You are the only woman I've ever known who takes offense when people assume she's intelligent."

"I don't like raising expectations," I muttered. And I didn't like this conversation, either. I took the book away from him and put it back on the nightstand.

"You like taking people by surprise," he added. His hands skimmed over my buttocks, and then he rolled on his back and pulled me on top of him. I braced my palms on his chest so I could look down at him. "God knows that's all you've done to me since the moment we met."

"You love it," I accused.

"I *adore* it. And you."

Well. When you put it that way . . .

"Round two?" I ran my palms over his nipples, feeling them harden.

"And then three. And four."

"Oh, that's a bluff I'll call," I teased.

(It wasn't a bluff.)

CHAPTER
SIX

"Wow, it's great to be back in Hell." **Then I heard myself. This** was what my life had become—the media was so obnoxious, the fallout from the interview was so chaotic, the vampires were getting so demanding, that running Hell was more a respite than anything else.

"That bad, huh?" For a wonder, Cathie seemed genuinely sympathetic.

"What the hell were you thinking?" my dead stepmother exclaimed. "How could you not see the potential fallout here?"

Of course, not everyone was sympathetic. Several thought I was in a mess of my own making. Which was true. However, if I may indulge in a bit of childish behavior, stupid Laura *started* it, so *nyah-nyah-nyah*.

"Apparently I've not only exposed every vampire on earth but they're all now vulnerable to the human legal system, which is so weird since that wasn't my intent at all." Or was it? Could I get away with the "I totally meant to do that" argument? "And there might be a vampire election."

"Just tell the vampires to STFU since you're not just their queen; you're also the devil. That ought to fix them. *And* the election."

"Yeah, I've been trying to get away from that whole absolute-dictator off-with-your-head-if-you-don't-like-it thing since the day I woke up dead."

"Why?" Cathie asked and, ye gods, she was serious.

I had to laugh a little. "What, why? Why d'you think? My entire platform—not that I ran for office, and not that I *will* run for office—is that vampires are no different from any-one else, and definitely not above the law. They don't get to get away with bad shit because once upon a time they got chomped to death."

"Well, too bad, because if you *had* run for office, I'd have voted for you. That's a platform any murder victim can get behind."

"Yes, it's right up there with 'a chicken in every pot,'" An-tonia teased. She was as she always was, though she didn't have to be. In life she'd worn lots of loud polyester

(ladybugs on a lime green background? why?)

and went through a can of hairspray a week. Her pineapple blond hair (color *and* texture) was pulled back and piled high in a sort of Kardashian meets Bride of Frankenstein effect, but not as classy as what you're picturing. In life she'd also been shallow and bitchy. In Hell she was shallow, bitchy, and help-ful. When she felt like it.

Meanwhile, Cathie had been murdered on laundry day and refused to go through the rest of her afterlife in granny pant-ies. So she didn't. Everything in Hell was mind over matter, including how we looked on the outside.

"Let's move on," I suggested. We were just outside the long, narrow conference room that, in the real Mall of America, was the Lego store. Cathie liked to build conference rooms out of the gigantic pieces (each Lego was the size of a brick), then dismantle them, then build them again. She found it soothing. I found it aggravating. Also, I kept tripping over the bricks she didn't use. "Marc's on his way; he stopped off to say hi to George Washington's mom." Have I mentioned Hell-bound old ladies loved Marc? They absolutely did.

"I thought he had a date." My stepmother and my zombie had grudging, reluctant respect for each other. Thus her tone was polite, while her expression was that of someone who smells poop on a skunk. "At least, that's what he was babbling about the last time. Some reporter? Ooh, is Marc going to be your mole amongst the media?" The Ant actually made this sound like a cool plan.

"First, never say 'amongst'; I hate that. Or towards. I hate that, too." *So much!* "Second, I might be a cynical bitch—"

"Yes, I know."

"—but that doesn't mean I think Marc should prostitute himself so I can one-up the Antichrist."

"Hell is no place for your tiresome morality."

"Wrong! It's exactly the place for my tiresome— Okay, first, my morality isn't tiresome." I pushed past them into the conference room. "It's a breath of fresh air here. That's my story and you won't shake it."

"So he must have missed it," the Ant finished, shrugging off my tiresome morality in favor of her one-track mind. "Or rescheduled."

Cathie frowned. "But he was really looking forward to it— why'd he skip?"

By now I'd collapsed into a chair made of Legos, which was exactly as uncomfortable as it sounded. "What, like *I* know? I can barely keep track of my own social life." Pathetic thing that it was these days. But even I knew that bitching about the dearth of date nights would be in really, *really* bad taste here.

"He's hiding," Cathie announced. "He finally met someone and he can't handle it so he's just avoiding the whole thing."

"He's not; it's just a coincidence," Antonia countered. "He lives to come down here, the goofy bastard. One of a few pathetic saps who were dumb enough to volunteer to help my stepdaughter."

"You're on that list," I muttered. They both ignored me, because my life sucked.

"He's hiding from his date," Cathie insisted.

"Nope."

"You wanna make it interesting?"

"Terms?"

My eyes, which had been slowly closing

(Do I have to be here for this? Sounds like I don't have to be here for this. I wonder if that candy cock ring came from Amazon yet? Sinclair's not a fan of sticky stuff on his nethers, so this will take some fast talking on my part. Which I am totally up for. Because— Wait, what?)

flew open. Bets were a *very big deal* in Hell. It was a deadly serious business with enormous stakes. Beyond life and death, even. Unlimited opportunities to crow about it if you won. Endless piles of scorn heaped on you if you didn't.

"I've got terms. If I'm right and we find out he's hiding because he doesn't want to get back out there," Cathie said, brow furrowed as she thought of something the Ant would find sufficiently disgusting and/or unpleasant, "you have to . . ." What? Eat live snakes for every meal every day for fifty years? Sleep with Henry VIII and let him cut your head off when you break up? Shovel out the Augean stables with a salad fork? (We had those down here—the stables, I mean—and they stank like you wouldn't believe.) ". . . say at least five nice things to Betsy every time you see her for the next hundred years."

"No!" we both blurted, then stared at each other, appalled. Probably for different reasons. The Ant likely found the thought of being nice to me, her nemesis since I was a teenager, to be revolting and impossible. I found the idea of working with her for the next century equally revolting and impossible.

I knew I'd formed the committee to help me run Hell, but I wasn't thinking of it in terms of, y'know, eternity. Though maybe I should have. Yeah, I definitely should have. Anyway, I figured one or two decades in, we'd have the kinks worked out. Hell pretty much ran itself anyway. It was difficult and confusing now only because I was making so many changes.

"Three nice things," the Ant countered, and who could blame her? Even I couldn't say three nice things about myself every time I saw myself. Two, maybe. If having great taste in footgear counted as one nice thing. "And I don't have to say the three nice things the second I meet her. It's per visit." She shivered. "I'd need a minimum of several hours to come up with something. Anything. Anything at all."

Cathie's triumphant grin lit up her face. "Done! And if you win . . ."

"If *you lose*," the Ant said, eyes narrowing (pale blue eye shadow? Was it 1976 in Hell?[12]), "if we find out he's not hiding from dating, you have to give me a massage every time I ask for the next hundred years." Hmm. Interesting! Cathie had just gotten her massage license when she was murdered, so she presumably knew what she was getting into. "Whatever you're doing, you have to drop everything and work out my kinks."

To steal an *Archer*-ism, "Um . . . phrasing?" Since they both died before *Archer* was a thing, it went over both their

---

[12] Trick question! It's all times in Hell.

heads. In fact, I was pretty sure they'd forgotten all about me. "Guys? Did you hear me? Because she said kinks? Guys? See what I did there?"

"Done," Cathie said, and they shook hands so firmly, their knuckles went white.

I sneaked a glance at my watch. The watch was incredibly important, because it was the only timepiece in Hell that told me how long I'd been away from the real world. When I first started trying (and failing) to get a handle on this job, I'd go to Hell for a couple of hours and come back and find I'd been gone three days. The havoc this wreaked on my love life was insane. I'm embarrassed to tell you how long it took me to think up (ta-da!) the newfangled invention known as a wristwatch.

Nothing to fear—even though it felt like I'd been here a day and a half

("You're gonna lose, and it'll be terrible for you."

"*You're* going to lose, and I'm going to laugh my ass off whenever you have to pound my glutes.")

it had been only five minutes.

"If you two are done gambling the next century of your afterlives away, maybe we can get to business?" Times like this, I *almost* missed Satan. She'd been the one who'd been a stickler for meetings starting on time. For meetings at all. Sure, she'd been trying to obstruct me at every turn, but by God, we stuck to an agenda and meetings ended on time. Not that I knew she was the devil then. Because nothing's ever simple, y'know?

"Yes, yes, we can start," the Ant replied, waving away my whining. "We just have to— Marc! Hoo-hoo! *Marc!*"

"Hey!" Cathie let out an eardrum-shredding whistle. "Over here, Marc! Get your butt over here!"

Marc, who'd been hurrying through the food court, looked momentarily surprised to be greeted so enthusiastically. He shot a cautious glance at me and I shrugged. It wouldn't be fair to tip him off. Also, it would be huge fun to see my stepmother and favorite ghost falling all over him to figure out the state of his love life so they could decide which one would be the other's slave for the next hundred years. Why would I ever stand in the way of that?

With each step, Marc looked more and more bewildered. It was a good look for him, though, because Marc was criminally cute. Black hair he kept chopped in a Caesar cut (which he insisted on calling a George Clooney cut), bright green eyes, pale skin—like most of us, because (a) dead and (b) Minnesota—long legs, quick and clever hands. He usually wore scrubs so often washed they were almost velvety (as well as going from green to a washed-out gray). An ER doc in life, he didn't trust his zombie reflexes to do much more than skilled first aid in death.

I thought he was being overcautious—it's not like the flesh was rotting off his bones or anything. He'd delivered Jessica's weird babies with no trouble. (For him. Jessica was pissed that he was unable to rig an epidural in her bedroom. I can still hear her: "I *get* to push? What, like it's something I won? How is that an incentive? *What the fuck is wrong with you?*") In fact, as long as we hung out together, Marc would only ever appear to be seconds dead. Maybe just *one* second dead; that's how (ugh) fresh he was. He could also heal with ridiculous speed, which made *no* sense.

The trouble would start if I abandoned him. Or took my power away from him . . . not that I had any idea how to do that. I still had no idea how I'd turned him into a zombie in the first place.[13] Argh, hindsight! That's how I should have

---

[13] Ancient Betsy, an older Betsy from an alternate timeline, did it. Then she vanished forever without explaining herself, because she's an asshat.

answered all of Diana Pierce's questions: "I have no idea how I did that."

Moot, anyway; I'd never leave him. He became my friend the day I woke up dead and has stuck by me ever since. Not to belittle my mom or Jessica, but they'd loved me before I died. Marc only knew me as a bitchy vampire and he still thought I was worth getting to know. So there wasn't much I wouldn't do for him.

Except warn him where this was going, of course. I got so few kicks from running Hell, I wasn't keen on derailing this train until we knew who won.

"—just tell us why you were late already!" I could see the Ant had gotten tired of her version of subtlety and was just nagging the shit out of him so they could settle the bet.

"But why do you even care?"

"Of course I care!" the Ant yelped. Boy, talk about a half-truth. She cared, but only because she didn't want to be my compliment slave. Also, *I* didn't want her to be my compliment slave.

"What difference does it make if I had plans?" He was looking from one to the other with a dazed expression on his face, like he was trying to focus on a tennis match after several beers. "I'm here now."

"Did you have plans?"

"Why?"

"Just answer the question."

"Did Will put you up to— No, wait. That's idiotic. Right?" He looked at me. "Will doesn't have any influence down here. You haven't even seen him since your mom beat him up."

"She did not beat him up!" By now I'd gotten up off my chair and was standing in the doorway. "She gave his ear a twist, which under the circumstances was excellent. She *did* catch him sneaking into our home, remember?"

"On a scoop! That's what journalists do!"

"Not to be mean, but I'm not sure a weirdo with a ghost blog qualifies as a journalist."

"He is *not* a weir— Um, he is too a journalist!" He rounded on the Ant and Cathie. "And why are you two so interested? I don't think I've ever seen you work together for a *good* cause. Why's my famously arid love life so interesting all of a sudden?"

"It's a bet," I explained.

"So? Why does—whoa." I could see he got it right away; like I said, bets in Hell were major.

"So there you go. Serious business is afoot. Anyway, Cathie thinks you're hiding from what's-his-toes—"

"Will Mason."

"Right. She thinks you're too chicken to date him, which is why you're in Hell instead of trying to get some among the living. But Antonia is betting it's just a coincidence, that it was just a scheduling conflict and of *course* you're not hiding from dating. Or sex."

"That brings up a new one," Cathie said. "Can you even have sex? Do you . . ." She made a vague gesture toward Marc's crotch, horrifying every single one of us. "I mean, can you get an erec—"

"Marc, if you answer that question I am going to *freak out*," I warned, and the Ant nodded so hard her hair almost wiggled. "And I've got no time for a freak-out today. The earliest I can lose my shit is Friday. And even Friday's pretty crowded."

"That's what this is about?" Marc had an odd look on his face, as if anger and amusement and horror and glee all got together and his expression was the result. "My emotional state is something to bet on?"

"Damned straight."

"Sorry, Marc, but everything here is something to bet on.

You know why." We all did. The worst thing about Hell wasn't the unrelenting torture some had to tolerate. It wasn't separation from life or loved ones. It wasn't knowing your life was over. It wasn't knowing you were trapped in the worst place humanity could think up.

It was the boredom. Even waterboarding got dull after a few decades when you couldn't really drown.

"So which is it?"

"It's neither. We were supposed to . . . but Will had something come up fast so he texted to reschedule."

"And there it is," I commented as Cathie and Ant looked crushed. "The definition of an anticlimax, right before your eyes."

Marc snorted. "Sorry one of you couldn't profit off my social life. Or the lack of one."

From Cathie: "Boo."

The Ant: "Oh, fine."

Me: "Guys? So, work time? We can work now? Guys?"

Marc gallantly presented his elbow, and I let him lead me back to the worst chair ever. Behind me, almost too low to hear (and definitely too low for Marc), I heard Cathie mutter, "Still on, right? Might take a couple of days to figure."

"Damned right we're still on," my stepmother hissed back. "I'm not tolerating the next century with knots in my neck."

Oh, goody. This could only end perfectly for all involved. Nothing to worry about. Also, whoever won would be gracious in victory and whoever lost would accept the consequences like an adult and oh my God, I couldn't even finish that thought without snickering.

Was I too late to get in on this?

"Okay, so, Jennifer Palmer. First candidate for parole. She's been here . . ." I tried to remember. Failed. There were a lot of people to keep track of. I figured I knew a hundred souls by name at this point. A hundred out of billions.

"Thirty-one years," Cathie said. "On food court duty where she slings Orange Juliuses. Juliuses? That doesn't sound right. Julius-ii?"

"It sure doesn't, the poor dope," the Ant murmured, because she thought Orange Juliuses tasted like ass, and a job serving them appropriately hellish.

"I need a . . ." And poof! Except without any noise, and now I was holding my Helltablet™, patent pending. I used to walk around with a magical clipboard, until I remembered it was the twenty-first century. So I converted my clipboard. Like everything here, it was a symbol to help me grasp the abstract. I mean, Hell didn't really look like the Mall of America. And I wasn't really holding a tablet. It was just the best way I could wrap my brain around the whole thing.

My Helltablet™ held any info I needed on anyone here. It was also waterproof. And fireproof. Nobody could read it but me. And I never had to charge it. Or maybe I was constantly charging it—I might be its battery. It always worked, was my point. Plus it perpetuated the illusion that I knew what I was doing. That was always valuable.

"Okay, yeah. We assigned what's-her-face as her buddy." Yes! One of the first things we'd implemented: the buddy system. No more did the damned have to suffer an afterlife filled with torture *and* not have any idea what was going on or where they were or where the bathrooms were or if you even needed bathrooms anymore. Now you had a buddy who would show you the ropes during your years of torment. "You know, the girl Lawrence the Vampire helped bring up."

"Cindy—"

"Tinsman!" I shouted after sneaking a peek at my Helltablet™. "The cheerleader turned vampire turned resident of Hell." And her father was one of the reasons life up top was so chaotic right now. (Argh, it wasn't "up top." We weren't below anything! Was I gonna have to put the MoA on top of a cloud so we all stopped referring to Hell as down below? And why did it bug me so much?)

"Okay, so . . . why her?" When Marc and I both looked at the Ant, she put her hands out in a "whoa, hear me out" gesture. "Whoa, hear me out." (See?) "I think your parole plan is incredibly innovative."

"Oh." Um. A compliment from the Ant. I had no idea what to do. Where to look. What to do with my hands. Everything: blank and frozen. Was she mentally preparing herself to lose the bet? Getting in practice? I didn't think I could handle three of those a day from her. "Thanks."

"Insane, and bound to cause problems, but it's a new idea, and in Hell, that's rare." Whew! Now we were back on familiar passive-aggressive territory. "I mean . . . this place has always been in the business of punishing people and keeping them. You're talking about doing the opposite—no punishment, and letting some of them go. So why Jennifer Palmer? Because if I know why you picked her, we'll—your committee—we'll have a better chance of recommending people you think should get out. Time-saver, get it?"

"Yep."

"So why this one?"

Because we had to start somewhere. And she was one of the first people I got to know here. Her story made me feel bad, which, in *this* place? Was a good trick.

"If you didn't have to be here, where would you go?"[14]

"I . . . I don't know."

"Well, think about it." I sucked up Julius and waited. I was as patient as a mannequin: unmoving, blank faced, and dressed in trendy clothes. Finally . . .

"I guess I'd go home. Tell them I'm sorry. Tell them the whole story. My folks are still alive, my sister, and he *is, too."*

"Oh yeah?"

"The fire was an accident, but they thought it was on purpose." Definitely warming to her subject, no pun intended. The side pony-tail bounced as she gestured. "I couldn't tell anybody . . . I mean . . . Tammy died." *Bounce. "All because I wasn't paying attention, y'know?" I didn't, but nodded anyway. "They thought it was on purpose and I couldn't— Someone went to prison for it. I could've said something. I didn't. I was," she summed up, shaking her head so the bouncing turned to swaying, "chickenshit."*

---

[14] From *Undead and Unforgiven*.

"And not surprised to find yourself in Hell."

"Suicides go to Hell," was the flat response. As if catching her mood, the ponytail went still. "So no. I wasn't surprised."

"Okay."

"Can I ask you something?"

"Sure."

"Why didn't you know that?"

"I could've gotten the info. I wanted to hear what you have to say."

"Oh." She paused. Swallowed. Then, in a small voice, and with a smaller smile: "Thanks."

"Sure." Aww. She was sweet, for an accidental murderous arsonist who watched an innocent man go to prison while never saying a word for fear of incriminating herself. And it wasn't her fault she died on a terrible hair day. Oh. Wait. It was. Well, no one was perfect.

"She did something awful—and she's paid for it, every day, for three decades. She's exactly the type of person I want to try parole out on. What purpose is served by keeping her here? What is she going to learn, or unlearn, or think about, that hasn't happened in thirty-one years?"

Nods all around—which didn't happen as often as you might think. *Maybe* in our kitchen at home, if I talked everyone into more strawberries in the smoothies, and less blackberries (they were *all seed*!).

But we were all on board with the parole plan, and not just because the original Satan fucking hated it. Although that alone would have been a good reason to go for it. She'd hated my plans for a newer, gentler Hell so much that she took another form and undermined me all over the place. She wasn't even clever about it, at the end. The really sad part? That wasn't the first time I got the drop on her. And when a shoe-obsessed former administrative assistant who flunked out of college can fool the devil? Time for new management.

I just hadn't thought it'd be *me*.

"I think it's great," Marc said. "Man, the first time I saw a kid getting dismembered and fed to bears— Y'know that's the first time I've thrown up since med school? Fucking *bears*."

We all had nightmare stories to share that none of us were going to share. But it's why I started thinking about the people I wanted out of Hell. The kids, obviously, and the sooner the better. The children who'd gone to Hell because they thought they deserved it—they were the first ones I wanted out. Of course, most of them weren't children anymore. There had been a pair of twins—brother and sister—who yelled at their mother and then went off and fell through the ice and drowned and woke up in Hell because they'd broken the fifth—fourth?—commandment.

And they never questioned it. Never once. In two hundred years. They've been drowning over and over again, reliving their last day as first graders for centuries, and for what?

So in my first few weeks I rounded up the ones who wanted to leave, the ones I agreed could leave, and we had the Talk: "I don't know how this is going to go. This is all new to me. I don't know what'll happen when you leave here. I'm just saying you can go, if you want."

"Where?" one of them finally asked, one small question out of the sea of bewildered faces.

"Wherever. You ended up here for whatever reason because you willed yourself here. Now you can will yourself somewhere else. Back to earth? Up to Heaven? Argh, not up. Or maybe you just want to fade away . . . I don't know. I don't." I threw up my hands. "My point is, it's up to you now."

Now, I wasn't expecting a parade. But a few thank-yous, maybe? Sure. Alas: I'd set that bar unreasonably high.

A few left, gone who knew where. Most stayed. It took me the better part of the week to figure out why: They thought it was a trick. Or a trap. Nothing had changed here in forever, and all of a sudden there was a new devil and she was telling some of the people they could leave anytime they liked, no strings attached, nothing to worry about, certainly not a hidden agenda, so just go already, what's stopping you?

Yeah, when you put it like that, I guess I'd have trouble believing it, too.

I also explained that those who didn't want to leave were welcome to stay as long as they liked, and they didn't have to be punished anymore. It was all minor shit, absolutely nothing worth an eternity of torture. There were kids who'd stolen candy bars; there were women who'd cheated on their husbands; there were men who'd coveted their neighbor's homesteads: Fly, be free! Or at least stop putting up with torture.

Don't get me wrong: the baddies weren't going anywhere. Dahmer needed to stay right where he was. So did Elizabeth Báthory and Walter Disney.

(You want to hear something that makes no sense? Hitler wasn't here. *Why the hell was Hitler not in Hell?*)

But the ones who wanted to stay? Some of them partnered up, and even formed little groups, and went off into Hell and set up their own living situations that weren't eternal torture. There were whole apartment complexes starting where the parking lot would have been in the real MoA. The duplexes of the damned, Marc called them.

Cathie pulled me back to the meeting with a gentle kick to my ankle. "But you don't want Jennifer Palmer to just gallop gaily off into the sunset, right?"

"Right. No gay galloping. I mean, she really did do something bad; she's not like the little kids. So she can leave, but she has to do what she can to make amends back in the real world. And for that we need Lawrence and Cindy." I paused. "Well, just Cindy, but I have to talk to Lawrence about vampire stuff anyway."

"Getting ready for a new TV interview?" the Ant asked with a smirk. "Figured you'd get the opinion of a vamp who doesn't adore you this time?"

I shuddered. "Noooooo. To both of those things." Then, louder, "I want Lawrence. Right now."

And there he was. It was just that easy. I read somewhere that Hell is other people. The writer got it wrong . . . Hell is me, mostly.

CHAPTER
EIGHT

Lawrence cut himself off—he'd been talking to someone when I summoned him—looked around, flinched at all the Lego bricks, saw me. He instantly went to one knee. "Dread queen," he said in that wonderful courtly manner of his. This guy would be killer on the radio. If anyone still listened to the radio. His manner went well with his black suit, shiny black dress shoes, deep blue dress shirt, blue-and-black tie, and blue silk handkerchief. He was like a suave escapee from *GQ* circa 1890. An issue on sexy undertakers, maybe. Or sultry haberdashers. "How may I serve?"

"Stop that; get up." As he eased to his feet I continued. "We wanted to talk to you and Cindy about Jennifer Palmer. And there's vampire stuff going on that I wanted to ask you about."

"As you will. Cathie. Mrs. Taylor. Dr. Spangler." They all got a courteous nod. Cathie didn't let anyone call her "Miss" anything, which Lawrence had found out the first time he tried it.

"I want Cindy Tinsman, too," I said, and so there she was. Her face lit up when she saw Lawrence, like always, and she found polite smiles for everyone else. Even me, which was an improvement. She was a little skittish around me since I'd cut her head off a few weeks ago.[15]

I cleared my throat. "We wanted to talk to you about Jennifer."

The smile dropped off her face. "Listen, whatever it was, I'm sure she didn't mean it."

"If you don't know what it was, how d'you know she didn't mean it?" Cathie asked.

"Because everybody's walking soft these days. No one knows what'll happen next. So, whatever it is, I promise, *promise* she didn't mean it. What?" This in response to Lawrence's "argh, don't talk to the queen like that; you're embarrassing me and might get us killed again or worse" expression. "We're supposed to watch out for our buddies. That's one of the new rules. Well, Jenn's my buddy. So this is me, watching out for her."

I smiled. Good answer. "It's okay, she's not in trouble. Nobody's in trouble. Well, in this room anyway. At this exact moment." Who knew *what* shenanigans the Ant would get up to later in the week? "In fact, we— Listen, will you two unclench and sit down, please? You're looming *and* cringing, which is amazing if you think about it."

Cindy instantly plopped into a Lego chair, closed her eyes in pain, wiggled in a vain attempt to get comfortable, gave up, opened her eyes. Meanwhile Lawrence had done something elegant and classy like *float* into his. Was it the years and years

---

[15] *Undead and Unforgiven.* So gross.

of being a vampire that taught innate grace? Or did people born more than a century ago just naturally have better posture?

"Thanks, that's better. Listen, Jennifer might have told you she's on the short list for parole."

The sentence was barely out of my mouth when Cindy shook her head. "Nope. She sure didn't. Because if she talked about it she might get her hopes up. And that's the worst thing that can happen down here." Her level brown gaze nearly pushed me back, it was so unwavering. "So no. She definitely hasn't said anything about parole."

And that was it right there. The devil was in the business of making people suffer. So how about raising hopes impossibly high, then smashing them in their faces? Wouldn't that be the most diabolical mind-fuck ever? Worthy of a new devil out to make a name for herself? A real attention getter?

"Dammit, I'm not diabolical!" Then I remembered I hadn't said the other stuff out loud. I coughed. "What?"

"Nothing. No one here wants to argue. Well, we do, but not about that." Cathie turned to Cindy. "No strings. No tricks. Betsy wants you to talk Jennifer into going back to the real world. But it's not a free ride. While she's there, she's got to make amends for the people she hurt, for the thing that landed her here in the first place. And if she can do that, she doesn't have to come back. If she can't, or won't, she's got to come back here, maybe forever." She looked at me. "Did I miss anything, chief?" When I shook my head, Cathie sat back. "That's it. That's the deal on the table."

"I'll talk to her," Cindy said at once. "She *wants* to, even though she's scared. If she knew it wasn't a trick she'd be on board. Well, probably. Hell's awful, but it's, like, a *known* awful."

I studied her for a few seconds. She'd ditched the cheerleading outfit within days of arriving and now went around in standard teenage chic: boyfriend jeans, a butter-soft black T-shirt, blue ballet flats, no socks. Her black hair was pulled tightly back, which made her dark brows arch, and an occasional dark curl tried to escape its scrunchie. Her gaze, once she'd realized no one was going to shout at her, or decapitate her, was disconcerting.

"You've changed," I said after a long moment. "It's only been a few weeks, but you're different now." Not that I knew her that well before I killed her. But still, the difference in a few weeks was remarkable.

"Time to grow up," she replied, her tone all sorts of no bullshit. "School's out. This is real. I threw my life away; I'm not gonna make that mistake with my afterlife. Besides, I—" She glanced at Lawrence, who was watching her with a face carefully blank so she wouldn't see the depth of his pity. "I don't have to do it alone. I've got Lawrence; I've got Jenn. She's introduced me to some others; most of them are nice. And—and—" She pulled in a breath and the rest of it just rushed out, *blah*, all at once: "MaybeifitworksforJennyoucouldletLawrencegotoo?"

"Uh—"

"Cynthia Rose Tinsman!" Whoa. I'd had no idea Lawrence's killer radio pipes could get that high. Like, opera-soprano high. Nor did I know Cindy's middle name until just now. He really nailed the tone, too. Everybody knows they're in deep trouble when an authority figure uses all your names at once. I was the queen of Hell and I *still* ran for cover when my mom did that. "Do not trouble the queen with trivialities! And do not *ever* presume to ask the sovereign a favor on my behalf!" He rounded on me and made a visible effort to control himself. "Please forgive her impertinence; she's young. I'll remove her immediately from your sight."

Hmm, I could get used to that. Why wasn't everyone here like Lawrence? *Your bitching offends me; someone remove the Ant from my sight! And anyone else who looks at me funny this morning! Wait, is it morning? It might be lunchtime . . . remove lunch from my sight, too! Just—everybody remove everything from my sight, all the time!*

"It's fine." I turned to Cindy, who looked gloriously unrepentant. "One thing at a time, okay? Right now you need to be focused on getting Jennifer to agree to try parole. Got it?"

"Yes, ma'am."

"Ugh, no. How many times? Betsy." Cathie's "chief" was the least annoying moniker, which is why I'd let it go. "I'm the queen—or the new devil—no matter what you call me. So just—Betsy. Betsy. Betsy." Argh, I was doing that thing where after a while, your own name starts to sound like gibberish. "Betsy. Betsy. Betsy."

"Stop that at once," the Ant insisted.

"I might be—Betsy, Betsy—stuck."

Lawrence was the only one in the room with sufficient self-control to *not* roll his eyes. A good man, that Lawrence. He and Sinclair had been buddies back in the day. Man, he must have stories.

"That's it for now," I said, but the others were already getting up, possibly realizing that when I kept saying my name over and over and over, that meant the meet was over and over and over, too. "Except you, Lawrence. I wanted to talk to you about the vampires going public."

"Ah," was the reply.

"I could use some advice from a silver-tongued dude like yourself. That's what the Native Americans called you back then, right? The Sugar Guy?"

"No-Sugar-in-Your-Mouth.[16] Yes, the Indians were kind enough to give me such a name."

"A good trick," I commented as the others filed out, Cathie and Ant already plotting literally behind Marc's back. "Getting one group of people to work with another group of people. Both of them not at all sure of the other—scared of the other, maybe even hating them a little."

"I may have deduced why you wished for my company this day, great qu—Betsy."

"Well, no one ever said you were a dumbass, Lawrence. Not that I know of, anyway."

"As ever, you are generosity personified."

I laughed and he fell into step beside me as we started heading east, where Sears would be in the real MoA. As usual, people ebbed and flowed around us, all trying their best to look like they weren't paying attention while watching everything we did. "So you probably heard, the Antichrist outed vampires."

"Yes. And you exercised your royal prerogative."

"I sure did. I exercised my prerogative right in her *face*. By which I mean I didn't deny any of it."

"Bold."

"More lazy than anything else. And it's causing problems."

"To be expected. I have all confidence you and my lord will overcome any difficulties this may cause you."

"Thanks for the vote of confidence, and this is a great chat we're having, but I've got no time for yes-men." This was the dichotomy of my life: none of the people around me were yes-men, so naturally I kind of wanted yes-men, except when I had one. Then I remembered they were useless. Super pleasant

---

[16] Lawrence was a real guy! He helped the settlers work with the natives and vice versa, and yep, that's the nickname he got for it.

to be around because they made you feel great about yourself, but useless.

He blinked at that. "Forgive me, I only ever had dealings with your predecessor.[17] He, ah, encouraged positive feedback."

"Oh, I'll bet. All positive all the time or he'd kill you and drain you. Or drain you and kill you. Or just chuck you into a pit o' Fiends. Or bury you in a cross-wrapped coffin for a few decades."

"Yes, those were some of the ways he expressed his displeasure."

"But he's extremely dead now and very gone, and Sinclair and I are running the show these days, which you probably noticed. So . . . advice?"

He talked. And *talked*. But some of it was interesting. Maybe even helpful. Basically, *I'm not sure how but your blundering seems to be working, so maybe keep blundering?*

"And there have been some hints that the vampires might push for an election."

Lawrence just looked at me. Too startled to speak, maybe? So I kept going. "Which just seems dumb. But who knows? Maybe they'll feel better if we let them— What?"

He was laughing. The kind of laughter that you can't hold back; it just explodes out of you. I could tell he was trying to stop and couldn't.

"As a rebuttal," I said when he'd calmed down, "that sucked."

"My apologies. And I agree, most definitely. You and my lord should absolutely hold an election. Walk right to the front of the room wearing a cross and holding a Bible. Then take them on a tour of Hell. Then challenge anyone to do the same."

---

[17] Nostro, frequently referred to by Betsy as Nostril, *Undead and Unwed*. He was a humongous dick.

I got it. "Landslide."

"Oh yes." He grinned at me and I saw the predator for the first time.

"That's pretty good. I'll have to— Nuts." My phone was buzzing. I pulled it out and saw I had a text from Sinclair.

Young master Mason has burst in upon us insisting he speak to you immediately. He is most distressed. Perhaps you would consider cutting your visit short?

"Yep, you bet." And not just because I was done with Lawrence. Well, mostly because I was done with Lawrence. I looked up. "To be continued."

A half bow. "I am always at your service."

"Good to know."

"If I may ask a question?"

"Hit me."

"Never in life or death. How is it your cell phone works in Hell?"

"I don't know. Nobody knows. It's nothing I'm doing. For whatever reason, AT&T works in Hell. I can't think about it very long or I'll get really, really scared of AT&T." By now our walk had brought us past one of the food courts, which was usually where Marc could be—yep. "Marc! Your sweetie's freaking out back home."

"Will? Why?" Marc instantly lost interest in whomever he was talking to and whatever they'd been talking about. He actually hopped over a couple of tables to get to me quicker. Zombies: spryer than you'd think! "Is he hurt? What happened? Oh my God, did a vampire get him? Or—oh shit—a member of the press?"

"Let's find out. Oh, and also, I think you're in lurrrrrrvvv."

"Shut up," he snapped back. "Get me back there now."

"Shut up, *please*. Get me back there, *please*." That's right,

Lawrence, soak up how a real leader operates. You didn't have to be an unrelenting douche canoe to command respect.

"I know the combination to your safe and I know exactly how flammable your shoe closet is."

"Right, well, not a moment to waste." Marc was probably kidding, but I was taking no chances.

Some things you just don't joke about.

CHAPTER
NINE

To my joy, Jessica, her weird babies, my mom, and BabyJon were all at the mansion when I popped in. I hugged Jess so hard her feet left the ground, which I've been doing since we were in junior high and which she's pretended to hate almost as long. "Yay! Hi!"

"Ooof, jeez, take it easy on my bones." She shook loose— she was like a bundle of sticks, all pointy edges and gorgeous sharp elbows and bony knees—and thrust a baby at me. "Here. Make yourself useful."

"No way, I've been useful enough for one day." But I took it, cradling the baby like it was a soft little football that smelled like milk. Her twins were still too little for me to tell them apart, though they were fraternal, not identical. This one—I had it narrowed down—was either Elizabeth or Eric. "Hi, Mom."

"Hi, honey." My mother was holding my brother/son (bron? srother?) comfortably, his diapered bottom snuggled against her arm. She was the way she'd always been; my first memory was of being held the exact same way, snuggling into her shoulder and twining my teeny fingers into her white curls. (I'd found out later she'd brought me, age three at the time, to the Little Bighorn Battlefield National Monument. She was a Custer fangirl.)

Mom had gone prematurely white-haired in high school and had had a head of natural white curls as long as I'd known her. She was the type of woman I'd like to be when I got older, the kind who are told "you look good" as opposed to "you look good for your age." She was a little plump, but only enough to make her huggable—she still traveled the country visiting Civil War sites and climbing all over everything. Her picture (*"Do not admit!"*) was up at Fort Sumter *and* Shiloh.

She was in her usual gear—dark slacks, tennis shoes (oh the *years* I wasted trying to teach the woman about quality footwear), a red turtleneck, a cardigan. The clothing of a woman of a certain age, you might call it, except she's wearing the same thing in all her class photos. The woman was a nut about comfortable shoes and cardigans even as a teenager.

BabyJon was resting his head on her shoulder, either ready for a nap or just getting up from one; he blinked those big beautiful blue eyes at me and smiled. I leaned in to nuzzle his teeny nose and got a sleepy giggle for it.

Mom patted him and turned so she was looking at me. "You're really getting the hang of popping back and forth, aren't you? It wasn't so long ago that you couldn't do it without Laura."

"Stop! She's dead to me, Mom. Never say her name; it's the verbal equivalent of a hate crime."

"And after you kicked *Laura* out of Hell," my cruel, cruel mother went on with relentless cheer, "you needed those shoes to figure out how to teleport back and forth."

"Yes, you had to click your heels together." From Jessica, who was also cruel. Because this was the life I had chosen: free of yes-men. "There's no place like Macy's; there's no place like Macy's—"

"I hate you both," I announced. "So much." Why were these terrible women entrusted with infants? Was this why society was screwed?

"But now you don't even need the shoes."

No, I didn't need the shoes anymore. But for the longest time, no matter how often I practiced, I'd go from Hell and end up in the garden shed. Every damned time. Took weeks of practice just to 'port into the house. These days, my control was better, but I don't think it was because I was improving. I think I just worried less, because we had bigger problems. And when I worried less, things just fell into place.

"No, I don't need the shoes anymore."

"So you just . . . what?"

"I focus. I concentrate." I waited for the scorn and guffaws. "And then I'm there."

"I'm not sure what's stranger . . . how you're changing or how quickly we're getting used to the changes."

I shrugged as she popped BabyJon into the portable crib she'd set up in the corner. She had a point—five years ago, I was still alive; I had a day job; I was dateless and not a little aimless. My biggest worries were avoiding the Ant and not strangling the executives I worked with, the ones who thought dumping a box of paper clips into a copy machine meant the copies would come out clipped.[18] If this was a TV show, the "previously on the Betsy show" part would take hours.

---

[18] This actually happened to me at one of my day jobs. He was bewildered that Plan Paper Clip didn't work. I was bewildered that someone had given him a master's degree.

"How come you're here? Not that I mind, but I thought we agreed the babies were safer elsewhere until the ruckus died down."

"They are," Mom agreed, "but that doesn't mean we can't visit."

"Actually, I thought that was exactly what it—"

"Dick had to quit the Cop Shop," Jessica said abruptly, putting a twin down beside BabyJon. Port-a-cribs, I was coming to learn, were one of the greatest inventions ever to spring from the mind of (wo)man. They were right up there with the telephone in terms of convenience. Thirty seconds to set up! Ten to take down! Goddamned miraculous is what it was, and oh hell, that was bad.

"Well, shit," I said, dismayed. Detective Richard Berry, also known as Jessica's boyfriend and sire of weird babies, had been in our lives before I'd died (the first time). I'd been attacked outside Khan's Mongolian BBQ by a pack of feral, yowling, howling vampires, fended them off with well-placed kicks from the toes of my pointy shoes (thank goodness I'd avoided round-toed shoes that day) and my purse, like it was 1955 instead of the twenty-first century. I didn't know it then, but that had been step one of my evolution from out-of-work administrative assistant to reigning queen of vampires/Hell.[19]

Anyway, Detective Dick had been the cop assigned to my case. We'd flirted with the idea of flirting, but to be frank, wealthy blonds with swimmers' builds didn't do it for me. I didn't know it at the time, but I liked them tall, dark, and vampiric. (And also wealthy. But in fairness to *moi*, I had no idea Eric Sinclair was rich when we met. Mostly I was focused

---

[19] *Undead and Unwed.* All the madness starts here!

on how much I loathed the very sight of him. We did not meet cute.)

"But Richard loves being a cop," my mother said. She'd gone right over to Jess and patted her, and Jessica sort of leaned—casually, like she wasn't consciously doing it—until she was basically slumped onto my mom like a gorgeous gangly leech. "He never needed that job."

Truth. Richard Berry was rich, rich, rich. Almost as rich as Jessica, who was probably the wealthiest person in the state. Wealthiest *live* person, anyway. Not sure how I started out as a middle-class suburban kid and ended up surrounded by millionaires, but it happened. I am the poor white trash of our set. (Note to self: stop bragging about being the poorest, dumbest person in the room.)

"He does love the job," Jessica agreed, still slumping. "But the news about vampires and all the media attention—it put him in a tough spot. They even caught him on camera a couple of times, and you can bet his bosses had questions."

"I'll bet." *So, how long have you been living with vampires? Or crazy people who think they're vampires? You understand if they faked their deaths, that's against the law, right? Let's talk.* Ugh.

"So he resigned before they could suggest a permanent unpaid leave of absence."

"I'm really sorry." That was it. That was all I had.

Jessica shrugged, almost dislodging herself from Mom's shoulder. "There are worse problems than having the means to be a stay-at-home dad with someone you love. He might go into private investigation in a while—we want to see how everything shakes out first."

"Okay." My brain was already churning. Maybe he could be a cop-to-vampire liaison? He had a unique perspective unmatched by that of any other cop anywhere. Which, it was now occurring to me, was probably why he felt he had to leave. But couldn't it be turned into a positive? Knowing vampires shouldn't be a liability.

And not going along with the Antichrist's plan to force the world to convert to Christianity shouldn't be causing all the trouble, but it was. Because as much as I liked to bitch about my father and my sister, I was also responsible for the mess we were in up to our necks.

CHAPTER
TEN

LAST MONTH, ON THE BETSY SHOW . . .

"I'll definitely prove there is a God!"

"—pires to the— What?"

Laura nodded at me with a big smile that wasn't scary at all. "I'm going to prove there's a God. Prove it to the world."

I just sat there and tried to let that seep into my brain. It was so far from what Sinclair and I assumed she was up to, but I couldn't tell if that was good or bad.

There she sat, my half sister, Laura Goodman (subtle, fates or God or whomever), dressed in her Sunday best (she had a horror of people who wore jeans to church): a high-necked pink blouse, a rose-colored knee-length skirt, cream-colored tights, chunky black loafers. Chunky loafers is what women wore in the winter when the weather wasn't bad enough for boots or good enough for pumps. Laura's were especially hideous, like lumps of tires fashioned into a vague shoe shape. We had a few things in common; our fashion sense wasn't one of them.

Besides, she was so irritatingly, thoroughly gorgeous, she

could have been wearing newspapers. Light blond hair halfway down her back, perfect fair complexion with a natural rosy blush, big blue eyes that went poison green when she was angry, or murderous, or murderously angry.

Nobody ever looked at Laura Goodman and thought, *Spawn of Satan? Oh, sure. Knew it the minute I laid eyes on her.*

I stopped pondering her annoying good looks and managed, "Could you say that again, please?"

"You cheated me of my birthright."

"No, no, the other thing." So not in the mood for the "Satan and I tricked you into running Hell but now I want to bitch about the consequences" chat. I'd warned her at the time that getting your own way was often as much a curse as it was a blessing. See: Sinclair's life, death, and afterlife, also mine, the Ant finally landing my father, and anyone who voted for Hitler back in the day.

"This *is* the other thing," she corrected. "You want the background, don't you?"

Not really.

"I can't do what I was born to do—"

"Be effortlessly gorgeous while sitting in judgment on pretty much everybody as you ignore your own sins?"

Her lips thinned but she continued. "But I can do this. I can bring faith to the world."

"How?"

"Any way I can." She leaned forward, warming to her subject. Leaning away from her would probably be interpreted as unfriendly. Maybe I could pretend I didn't want to catch her cold? If she had one. And if I could still catch colds. "Lectures, videos, websites. I already started a few while I was waiting for you to get back." Was there a tiny hint of reproach in her tone? No. I decided there wasn't, because if there was, I'd have to slap the shit out of her with a hymnal. "So I've been preparing the ground, so to speak, talking about our adventures and Hell and such while waiting for you."

"That's why Sinclair thinks the plan is to show the world vampires exist," I said, thinking out loud.

She shrugged. "Yes, I imagine his undead spies keep him well informed." When I raised my eyebrows she added, "Yes, he called me a couple of times, but I'm not obligated to explain myself to him." Adding in a mutter, "I don't know how he keeps getting my number . . ."

"So he was tipped off after he heard about the *Betsy and Laura: Time-Travelin' Cuties* show." God, Marc would have a field day with this . . .

"What, every other sinner can have a YouTube channel but I can't?"

"Um . . ." *Stay focused.* I was already envisioning the conversation my husband and I would have: *Good news! She's not outing vamps. There's a teeny bit of bad news, though. Why don't you lie down while I tell you about her Great Idea . . .*

Meanwhile she was obliviously babbling. "I'd be different from the regular preachers . . . They're talking about faith, which is all well and good for someone who isn't *us.* I can offer proof. Look what just you and I have seen in . . . what? Less than four years? I always believed in Him, and I think you did, too—your mother failed you in your teenage years but she did make sure you went to Sunday school long enough to—"

"Do not say one
(church you're in church)
dang word against my mother."

Laura cut herself off and even flushed a little. "You're right. That was inappropriate. I like your mom."

"I know you do." I had to shake my head at my little sister's many dichotomies. Skirts in church and brownies in the basement when not plotting to dump Hell on the vampire queen and murdering random serial killers. Genuinely fond of my mom—she called her Dr. Taylor and occasionally stopped in just to chat, or to play with our half brother, BabyJon—but wouldn't shed a tear at my funeral. Blithely ready to shove God onto the world whether the world wants it or not, but gets embarrassed when called out for being rude.

"You were telling me," I prompted without grimacing or clutching my temples, "about your Great Idea." God, now *I* was using the caps. At least it wasn't pronounced in all caps, like when fiftysomethings or thirteensomethings got on social media for the first time and felt every post had to be a scream.

"Okay, so you always believed in Him, but before your— uh—unfortunate death—it was strictly faith. And I had faith without proof until my thirteenth birthday, when Mother appeared and explained my destiny. Then I knew. And we can help everyone know. We've time traveled, we've seen Hell; my mother was the devil, you're the *new* devil! We know the Bible's right; we can tell people! We can save everybody!"

"Why . . . why would we do that?" Was she talking about us going on some sort of . . . of lecture circuit of the damned? Would we be copresenters, or would it be her show and I'd be trotted out like the miniature elephant in *Jurassic Park*: *Look what we made! Give us money and we'll make more!* (The book, not the movie. I loved that stupid dwarf elephant. The scientists should have skipped the dinosaurs and just engineered a huge park of thousands of dwarf elephants. If they escaped, it'd be annoying but also adorable.) "Laura?"

"Why *wouldn't* we do that?" she replied, puzzled. She was leaning toward me; our hands were almost touching; she was as friendly and excited as I'd seen her in weeks. Our last meeting hadn't been so pleasant. Was she—was she trying to forge a new relationship with me? Was setting up the We Can Prove

God Exists lecture series her way of reconciling herself to what she'd lost? Was she regretting her choices less than a month after she had made them, or was this the plan all along?

"I've barely started, and I wanted to tell you right away—"

Really?

"—but you've been gone."

"Wow."

"I know!"

"You actually managed to make me being *in Hell*, doing *your job*, sound like a character flaw, or like I was rude to keep your Great Idea waiting. I can't even figure out the time thing between dimensions—"

"Conjure up a row of clocks, like in a brokerage firm."

"—when I was—well, yes, that was Marc's suggestion and it'll probably work, but it's not like I was off having fun!" Although listening to Dame Washington bitch about her kid *had* been pretty entertaining . . . and pissing off all the teens and twentysomethings with my No Tweets rule (and confusing everyone else over fifty: "What's *tweets*?") had also been fun . . .

I forced a calming breath (focus!), and decided to go with the least complicated objection first.

"Never mind where I was or for how long or why I had to be there in the first place; I'm here now, right? And the thing is, about your Great Idea, our word isn't proof." I said it as nicely as I could, and not just because showing the world our trials and tribulations had zero appeal. In a future that will never come to pass, I ruled the world. And it was a huuuge downer. What little I'd seen of the other, ancient, grumpy, zombie-raising, Sinclair-killing me had been more than enough. I wouldn't revisit it. And since I could time travel from Hell, I meant that figuratively *and* literally. There was no way to prove the good (Heaven a real possibility!) without dredging up the bad (vampires take over the world!). "People don't know who we are, and they shouldn't, Laura."

She ignored this, so the bright-eyed enthusiasm continued unabated. "There are enough of us who know the truth; if we combine forces we can reach millions!"

Sure, but so could Taylor Swift, and any Kardashian. In this day and age, reaching millions wasn't unheard-of . . . and oh boy, I hoped that wasn't her point. That if ordinary mortals

(sometimes I miss being an ordinary mortal)

could make their presence known with just a video or a silly trick on YouTube, if the "Leave Britney *Alone!*" guy and the ice bucket challenge could go global, the Antichrist and the queen of the vampires could, too. "Once we convince the rest of the world, things would change overnight! No more wars; no more murders."

Oh boy. She was less than a decade younger than me and I felt every day of that decade now. "People not knowing if there's a God is not what causes murders and wars," I said carefully, because she was glowing like a zealot turned light bulb. "At least, not all the time. Anymore. General dickishness causes wars. Money causes wars." I had a flashback to one of my favorite lines from *Gone with the Wind*: *"All wars are in reality money squabbles."* "I promise you, Laura. I promise. There will always be war and murder because there will always be assholes. They are not an endangered species. Even if every single person on the planet converted to Christianity, there'd still be crime."

She waved away war and murder and crime with a small long-fingered hand. "We can quibble about the details later. Say you'll help me with this."

"You mean in addition to being the queen of the vampires—"

"Sinclair is perfectly capable of overseeing the vampire nation."

"—and running Hell—"

"You've made a committee, and even if you hadn't, Hell will run itself if you leave it alone."

I— Wow. Okay. Wow.

"What's the pitch, exactly? Assuming you could prove God's existence? We somehow prove it and hey presto, everyone in the world becomes a Christian?"

"Sure."

When I was little I'd wait for the bus with a bunch of neighborhood kids. And after the first big frost, we'd kill time by easing across puddles that looked frozen but weren't—or at least, not all the way through. We'd inch across, freezing and giggling at every *crack!* Best case, you made it across and the kids gave you props. Worst case, you broke the ice and soaked your shoes, which was unpleasant but not fatal.

Well, I felt like I was inching across a puddle that was bottomless. Like if I put a foot wrong I'd fall down so deep no one would ever find me. It *looked* safe enough . . . but probably wasn't . . . and if I put one foot wrong . . .

"Hell being a thing doesn't mean every other religion is wrong."

Laura just looked at me.

I sighed. "I get it. You've decided Hell being a thing *does* mean every other religion is wrong."

"We know the devil is real, ergo God is real, ergo Jesus is real." At my expression, she plowed ahead with, "It's *not* arrogance. I'm not saying it's what I think. It's what we know."

"But that doesn't mean other things *aren't* real. You're like someone who's red-green color-blind: just because you can't see them doesn't mean red and green don't exist."

"Your analogies are starting to suck less," she said grudgingly.

"Thank you!" Ugh, I was always so pleased when she

complimented me. It was the dark side of being Miss Congeniality, the thing they don't tell you at the pageant rehearsals. "Listen, Hell and the devil being real doesn't disprove Allah and Buddha and—uh—Mohammed and Zeus—and—" Why hadn't I taken a single religious studies course before I flunked out of the U of M?

She shrugged off Buddha and Mohammed and Zeus. "They can't prove *their* religious icons are real. That's the difference."

"But what's the point of— Oh." I saw it. Finally. "Aw, jeez. This is about you bringing gobs of unfaithful into the flock. So if you get to Heaven—"

"When."

Oh Christ. "Fine, when you get there, you can tell your pal Jesus that you heroically avoided running Hell—through lies and trickery, but who cares about the details, right?—and that you disapproved of your sinful vampire sister but managed to recruit her into helping you bring millions into the fold so where's your Christian gold star already?"

Her pretty mouth (how does she not have chapped lips in a Minnesota winter?) went thin. "It's a far better use of your time than lolling around your mansion slurping smoothies and accepting blood orange offerings."

"First off, I don't loll." I was pretty sure. That means lying around, right? Lolling around? I rubbed my temples. *Don't beat the Antichrist to death with a hymnal. That would be deeply uncool.* "Second, if vampires want to stop by and bring me fruit and promise not to be assholes, what's the problem? It's a lot more than the previous vampire monarch did. His big contribution was starving newborn vamps until they went insane and making older vamps do all his murder-ey dirty work." Ugh, I hadn't thought of Nostril in years. Nobody talked about the undead-and-now-dead-forever wretch; he wasn't missed by anyone.

New as we were to the monarch thing, Sinclair and I were still loads better at it on our worst day than Nostril was on his best. Was it weird when vampires showed up at the mansion to hand me a bag of citrus and pledge eternal blood-sucking devotion and to seem relieved when all I made them do was promise to not be asshats? Yes. Was it a bad thing? Hell no! (Or just no.)

I scooted back a bit on the pew, away from her, and I wasn't aware I was doing it until I noticed I'd put another foot between us. "Y'know the difference between you and me, Laura? Other than the fact that you've never had a pimple? I never sat in judgment on you. You and our father like to bitch about the embarrassment of having a vampire in the family; how d'you think I felt when I found out my long-lost sister wasn't just prettier and smarter than me, but was the Antichrist? And what did I do? Huh? Whine? Yes. Feel incredibly insecure? Of course. Show you the door? *No.* Tell you that you were bound to turn evil because that's what happens in every single book or movie about the Antichrist? No."

"That's not—"

"Now let's talk about what I *did* do. Did I welcome you into my home? Yes. After you tried to kill me? Yes! You tried to commit fratricide, and I could have killed you for it but didn't, but *I'm* the Hell-bound bitch?"

"Sororicide. Fratricide is killing your brother. And we're not discussing your nature," she added, but she had the grace to look uncomfortable. "This is about the great thing we can do together."

"Ohhh." I saw it then. Her actual plan, and the plan beneath, the thing driving her to recruit zillions for the Lord's force, the thing she might not be consciously aware of. "So your life's purpose *wasn't* to take over for Satan. And me giving you the boot from Hell—and by extension taking away all your supernatural abilities—that's all fine, because *really*, your purpose was always to bring peace on earth, goodwill toward men by proving the existence of God. It's not you flailing around for something meaningful to do because you didn't think past getting out of your birthright."

"I hated my powers," she said to the pew in front of us. "They were proof of my sin, my dark nature. But . . . I liked them, too. And now I miss them."

"Tough shit." I couldn't muster even a shred of sympathy. She'd been able to teleport to and from Hell, and she could focus her will—which was considerable—and make weapons of hellfire, swords and knives and on one memorable occasion, arrows, that had no effect on "normal" people but were devastating to the supernatural. They made her remarkably skilled at killing vampires. "Like a hot knife through butter" didn't begin to cover it. "If you're waiting for me to go all 'there, there' for you, I hope you packed a lunch, because we'll be here for a while."

"You owe me!" she cried, and the hell of it was, she really believed that. I was the big bad vampire queen who'd cheated her out of what she wanted to give away.

"I don't owe you a goddamned thing," I snapped back. Her mouth popped open and I kept on. "I know we're in church! I think God would give me a pass on this one!" I was on my feet without remembering standing. "We're done. So sorry to keep you waiting while I was learning your job. I'm going now."

She sniffed. (I'd have snorted; did she have to be more graceful in *everything* she did?) Mumbled something that sounded like, "Typical," but I wasn't going to rise to the bait. (This time. Probably.) I heard her stand and follow me down the aisle like we were the Taylor sisters hanging out after church, just a couple of sisters disagreeing over matters that weren't life and death, instead of the Antichrist and the vampire queen arguing about the best way to prove God was real, or not, in order to demand the conversion of millions, or not.

The worst part? I still wanted her to like me. She was the only sister I was ever going to have, and I admired her when I wasn't thinking about puncturing her eyeballs with my stilettos. She was sneaky but brave, judgmental but unwavering, beautiful but bitchy when crossed. I'd been impressed and jealous since the moment we met. She was her mother's dreadful daughter in every way . . . and our father's . . .

. . . and I still wanted her to like me.

CHAPTER
ELEVEN

I yanked myself back to the present and reminded myself that Jessica was right—we had no idea how the mess du jour was going to shake out, and it was too soon to contemplate. I was opening my mouth to cough up the equivalent of "there, there, don't fret, want a booze smoothie?" when the kitchen door swung inward and Marc galloped in, hauling Will Mason in his wake like a kid dragging a blankie. It didn't help that the guy was wearing a pastel blue shirt and smelled like laundry detergent.

"Jeez, *there* you are!"

"Uh, I wasn't hiding, Marc. Remember when we both popped into the kitchen at the same time? And then you scampered off? Remember? Happened less than five minutes ago?"

"No jokes," he barked, "this is serious!"

"Actually, I usually joke *because* things are serious—"

"And now where's Sinclair run off to?" Tell you what, Marc could really hit high notes when he was upset. He usually saved the shrieks for whatever *Game of Thrones* nonsense he was enduring at the hands of the heartless boob-obsessed bums at HBO. "Where is he?"

"Dude, you're the one who keeps yelling and then leaving. And keep it down." I shifted the warm little football that smelled like milk and was named Elizabeth or Eric from one arm to the other. "You'll wake the babies. Theoretically." They didn't nap so much as hibernate for hours at a time. I was amazed at the things they slept through. I took another sniff (someone seriously needed to bottle *eau de bébé*), then laid Elizabeth or Eric down beside Elizabeth or Eric. "Hi, Will. Nice to see you again. Thanks for not breaking in this time."

"I didn't break in last time," he protested. He looked frazzled and wispy as usual, like he wasn't all there. Pastel shirts and jeans were his uniform of choice, and he smelled like Dreft and Suave. His hair was longish, over his ears, baby fine, and always messy. His eyes, behind wire rims, always seemed a little too wide and starey—you could see the whites all around. He was always like a horse about to bolt. "I just . . . y'know. Came in. You guys need locks."

"Yeah, because you walking in uninvited means *we're* the problem." I was needling him more for sport than out of any real ire. Look: if he was going to be anything more than a one-night stand for Marc, he needed to toughen up. So far his life had been smooth sailing. Except for being orphaned at a young age. And being terrified when he realized he could see ghosts. And struggling for his place in a world where the dead bugged him and the living didn't notice him. And referring to himself in all seriousness as the Freak. And being a huge John Cusack fan. And being gay on top of all of that. Or bi. I wasn't really paying attention to that part of it.

I couldn't imagine the hell of his lonely, terrifying childhood. No parents. Lots of ghosts. Cripes. I saw ghosts, too, but not until I was thirty. And they weren't bugging me so much lately. Probably because they knew plenty of souls in Hell were busy bugging me.

"Listen," Will was saying, all earnest and cute, "my sources—"

And I laughed. I couldn't help it; he was downright adorable. *Sources* was how he referred to the dead people who pestered him.

"Yeah, yeah, I'm aware you think that's hilarious—"

"You're adorable!"

"—but you've got a real problem." He was trying to stay stern, but a shy smile escaped anyway; he was like a little kid sometimes. Honestly, the mansion, our lives, the danger, the profanity—it was all no place for him.

"You had Sinclair haul me from Hell to tell me that? I've got about nineteen real problems."

"Darling." Speak of the devil, and there I was. Oh, and my husband, too, who'd just walked in holding my most precious, most treasured book. "How did you get the author of *Smoothie Nation* to sign this with that immature nickname you persist in using?"

"Isn't it nifty?" I cried. I rushed over to him, nearly knocking Will over. "Did you check out page sixty-three? Banana split smoothies!"

"I think that particular smoothie ventures into milk-shake territory."

"Never question *Smoothie Nation*, you ignorant bastard. Plus, pictures! I love cookbooks with photos." Truth! I liked knowing what the thing I was consuming was supposed to look like if a competent person had followed the recipe.[20]

"*You guys.*" From Will, and it got our attention, because that

---

[20] Cookbooks without pictures are lame. That is all.

guy never raised his voice. Probably because he was always running around whispering to ghosts so people wouldn't think he was insane. "My sources told me the Wyndham werewolves—"

"Oh, damn," I sighed. "You're right, that's a problem."

"Yeah, well, they're not pleased; that's for sure. I heard rumors so I canceled my meeting with Marc—"

"Meeting?" As opposed to date? Hmm. That might mean the Ant was going to win the bet. Did I care? Too early to tell.

"—and followed up and it's true. It's happening."

"A pack of werewolves is on their way to see us?" Jessica sounded as tense as I felt. She'd met several of them. Werewolves on their worst, weakest days were still nothing to mess with.

"No, I mean a pack of werewolves is *here*."

Which is, of course, when the doorbell rang. And when our puppies set up a clamor like I'd never heard. If puppies could scream, they'd have sounded like Fur and Burr just then.

Dammit.

CHAPTER
TWELVE

"Jessica, come on. I'll help you with the babies and we'll—"

"Mom, leave BabyJon where he is."

"—get out of— What?" She wasn't used to a calm tone from me, shrieking and bitching being my go-to emotions for pop-ins. It was the age of social media, for God's sake. You could call *or* text *or* e-mail *or* poke; there was no excuse for a pop-in these days!

"BabyJon stays here, Mom. But yeah, help Jess with her babies."

My mom started to reply, but Jessica cut her off. "I'll say hello to them. I've met Michael before. Then we'll go."

"But—"

"Dr. Taylor." Whoa. Jessica almost never called my mom that. Heck, sometimes she pretended to slip and called my mom *Mom*. "We moved out because of the people we don't know, like eight dozen reporters hanging out in front of the house doing God knows what. And nobody knows where Laura's devil-worshipping minions are—they could be on the block right now, planning to get in here and start some shit. So yeah, we moved out."

"Then why—"

"But I know Michael Wyndham. I've met him and his wife and his kids. I've been a guest in their home. So I'm going to say hello like a civilized person and welcome them to town and then I'll take my babies and leave. But I'm not scuttling off like some pathetic loser."

"Can *I* scuttle off like some pathetic loser?" Will asked, and whether he meant to or not, that broke the tension.

We heard measured footsteps—Sinclair and I did; the others probably couldn't hear anything—and knew Tina was calmly going to the door to let them in. Because Jess was right: we didn't hide. And we didn't scuttle. And also, *Smoothie Nation* was waiting for us to settle this and make smoothies. We'll never let you down, *Smoothie Nation*.

"I'll go through the mudroom and calm the puppies down," Mom said. "But, Betsy, I really think I should take BabyJon." She paused, then added wistfully, "Though it'd be fun to meet more werewolves."

Fun? Wasn't my mom adorable? "Trust me—that baby's in no danger from werewolves." Or vamps. Or witches. Or ghouls. Or mermaids.

"I don't see how—"

Sinclair, who'd already scooped up our dozing boy, turned to my mother. "He is impervious to paranormal harm."

"What?"

"Nothing paranormal can hurt—"

"No, I heard what you said, I just— What?" She turned to me. "Since when? I spend more time with him than you two; why wouldn't you tell me this?"

"When the hell would it have come up? 'Hey, he's getting

another tooth and by the way, a werewolf tried to bite him and BabyJon thought it was hilarious.'"

My mom stared at BabyJon. "Well, that's pretty interesting. It must be the link to your father."

"Let's leave Dad out of this. And everything else. All the time. Forever."

Disobeying me yet again, she continued. "He's had three children—"

"That we know of," Marc piped up. "What?" In response to my aghast look. "Your dad's kind of a slut."

"We're not going to talk about my dad being a slut, either."

"—and one of those children was the prophesied vampire queen, one was the Antichrist, and now his youngest can't be harmed by any means paranormal." Then: "You still should have told me, and we're not done discussing this."

"Of course, Dr. Taylor."

"I'll leave, though."

"As you like, madam."

"And this explains why almost overnight our boy went from being a pain in your ass to 'our boy.'"

"You should have seen those other werewolves," Sinclair said, tenderly patting BabyJon's back and definitely not bragging. "They were terrified. Of an infant! Think when he's in his prime."

"Hmph. See to your guests. We'll talk later. Jessica, I'll be glad to stay here with the twins while you pay your respects."

"Thanks."

"And I'll stay with you while you stay here with the twins while Jessica pays her respects," Will piped up. "If . . . y'know. If you want me to."

"You don't have to stay," Marc pointed out.

"No, no . . . I mean, I want to. I'm not the kind to scuttle off, either. Usually. I'll, uh, hold my ground. Help you hold your ground, I mean." He didn't look like he could hold his own urine, but whatever. But he'd come on the run to warn us. A lot of people would have just kept their heads down and waited for the storm to break.

"It'll be fine," I assured him. "We know these guys. They're probably here to bitch about something, and then they'll do some posturing, and then we'll decide everyone's going to keep being friendly, and then they'll go back to the Cape and do whatever it is they do when they're not bugging me. Just give us five minutes with them."

"Well, you sure sound confident." Will let out a nervous laugh. "Gotta admit, you guys can be a little unnerving."

"Well, it's what we do."

"It was kind of you to warn us, Mr. Mason." This from Sinclair, who had nudged the kitchen door with his foot and was now holding it open for us to precede him into the parlor.

"Yeah, well." A shrug. That bashful smile again. "That's what *I* do."

Adorable!

CHAPTER
THIRTEEN

NOT EVEN TWO MINUTES LATER . . .

"Listen up, Windup!"

"That's *Wyndham*."

"Do I go to your mansion and insult you and criticize your process and tell you what to do?" Oh. Wait. That's actually more or less exactly what I did when we went to Cape Cod. A werewolf had died saving me—Antonia, in fact, the asshat who'd called right after my TV interview—and we'd escorted her body back to Massachusetts.

I got staked. BabyJon scared the shit out of a bunch of werewolves. I figured out how to bring Antonia back to life. Back in Minnesota, Laura led a devil-worshipper-staffed revolt. (Yeah, she's kind of always been a problem for me, now that I think about it.) Other stuff happened. Then we went home.[21]

But that was then, dammit, and this was now.

---

[21] Soooo much stuff happened: *Undead and Unwelcome*.

"I know this is overused," Marc commented, "but that escalated quickly."

It sure had. Never should have let them into the Peach Parlor. Bad things almost always happen in the Peach Parlor. Starting with the fact that it was called the Peach Parlor. It was hard to take me as an authority figure in there; I was bathed in tones of flattering pastel. I looked terrific, but not especially intimidating.

The first minute was all hey, how are you doing, nice to see you again, are all your cell phones broken because we had no idea you were in town, ha-ha-ha but no big deal, always a pleasure, you guys look great and what the *fuck* do you mean, I never should have done an interview with Diana Pierce? You don't even know Diana Pierce! Diana Pierce was a consummate professional and I wasn't bad, either!

Sinclair was just sitting back and enjoying the show, still giggling to himself at how the werewolves reacted to seeing BabyJon

("Yeow! What—what *is* that?")

in his arms.

Meanwhile, Michael "My shit smells better than yours" Wyndham and I were eyeball to eyeball. Well, eyeball to chin. He was pretty tall. "You told me," I reminded him, "you said just last month that you thought everything was fine and there were no problems between us."

"Yes, and then the story went viral, you refused to deny anything, and then you as good as exposed werewolves."

"None of that is true! Okay, two of those things are true."

Glaring up at Michael Wyndham was like glaring up at a hawk. He had, I shit you not, golden eyes. Not brown. Not hazel. The color of old gold coins, and those strangely gorgeous peepers brought out the golden glints in his dark brown hair. He was easily a head taller, powerfully built and as fast as he was strong. An alpha in his prime, but as impressive as he was, his wife, Jeannie, was equally intimidating. All the more so because she was human. With naturally curly hair. I mean, come on—who finds cute curly-haired blond women intimidating? She was like a tall Shirley Temple, if Shirley had been terrifying and considered a Beretta M9 an indispensable accessory. (In Jeannie's defense, that was—literally—a killer accessory.)

Also, I was trying hard not to melt at the sight of the king of the vampires holding BabyJon while answering Lara Wyndham's many, many, many whispered questions. Lara was next in line to lead the werewolves and was born fearless. She'd sidled up to my husband so she could sniff BabyJon over and pepper Sinclair with questions: "Why's a baby so intimidating? Is he supposed to smell like that? Are you supposed to not smell like anything? Oh, look, he smiled at me—he likes me!"

"What should I have said?" I asked. We'd all started off the meeting sitting down, but now Michael and I were toe-to-toe while Jeannie and Sinclair sat across from each other, and Tina and Derik sort of prowled the perimeter of the room while Lara's whispered questions ("But *why* is everybody scared of your baby? I don't want to turn my back on him but I can't figure out why. Ooooh, he needs a diaper change! Yuck!") went on and on.

"'Hmm? Oh, werewolves? I'm glad you asked, Diana Pierce, of course they're real! There's one living just down the block from my house.'" (This was true, by the way.) "'And a buttload of them hang out on Cape Cod. I can draw you a map if you want.'"

Michael rubbed the bridge of his nose. I considered the "ugh, here comes the migraine" expression to be the signal of my eventual triumph.

"But I didn't do *any* of that, did I? No. I took the high road

and reminded her I was there to talk about vampires and that
was that."

He stopped rubbing his nose and looked up. "A more de-
finitive no would have been better."

"Thanks, Captain Toldja So. That's very helpful."

Derik snorted and got a "whose side are you on?" glare
from Michael for his trouble. Derik was Michael's second-
in-command; they'd been friends all their lives. You hardly
ever saw one without the other. They were like Mormons, if
Mormons were apex predators.

"So, what, Michael? Huh?" I had to actively restrain the
urge to kick him right in the ball of his ankle. I don't care who
you are: that always stings like crazy. "Are you here to critique
my interview technique or yell at me or pick a fight or all three
or what? What inspired you to hop on a plane and say howdy
to the Twin Cities?"

"Yes, Michael," Sinclair replied in a voice of pure silk.
Their gaze met over Lara's small dark head. Sinclair had let
her hold BabyJon. And really, that was Lara right there. Baby-
Jon freaked her out, and instead of being scared, she wanted
to spend time with him and figure things out. She was more
or less the embodiment of the best qualities of both parents.
"What *does* bring you to my home?"

"My home"? Knock off the caveman crap, I thought to my
husband. *Don't even think about undermining me in front of these
dickbags.*

Check the mortgage paperwork, darling. It is *my home.*

Oh, very funny.

"What makes you think it's anything to do with you?"
Michael countered.

"Besides the fact that you're in our house? Right now? Where
you came straight from the airport, I'm guessing, since you all
still look travel mussed?" And frankly, at least two of them

needed to brush their teeth. "I bet if I went outside and checked your rental car, it'd be full of suitcases but no room keys."

Silence. Derik looked impressed in spite of himself, though he might have been stifling a sneeze. Our mansion was old, and dusty, no matter how often we cleaned. I zeroed in for the kill. (But not really.) "What, you got lost? You just happened to be in the neighborhood? 'Why, Betsy, I had no idea you were here even though I've been here before.' You meant to go north to Rhode Island but took a right instead? You're throwing the lamest surprise party ever?"

"Rhode Island is to the south," Lara—*Lara!*—pointed out. Geographically shamed by a middle schooler. In the god-damned Peach Parlor.

Michael sighed. "At the risk of alienating you—"

"Too late, bright eyes."

"—not every werewolf visit revolves around what you've been up to."

Well, that had to be a lie. "Yeah? Why else are you here?"

"To visit with other Pack members." They all pronounced it like that, so you could hear the capital letter. Ugh. You'd never catch me going on and on about Vampyrs. "I have family scattered all over the Midwest."

"And you decided the perfect time to visit them was within days of my TV interview? Come on. Do better."

"I don't have to 'do better,'" he snapped. He took a step forward, but I knew this game. You can't step back from a werewolf. Not even once. "I believe you're the one who owes *me* an explanation."

"Yeah? Why?"

"Didn't you tell me your half sister is causing all this trouble?"

"Yeah, she's got dad issues, and she decided to cope by try-ing to get me to help her prove Hell was real so everyone would convert to Christianity, and when I wouldn't she outed vampires for spite." Huh. I hadn't known I could compress the whole mess into one sentence.

"Good God," Derik said, appalled.

"Right? This is what I've been putting up with."

"No, I mean—why didn't you destroy her rebellion before it could take root and endanger your people?"

Because I'm not a hairy sociopath? "Look, Laura and my dad are both dead to me, okay? Yes, she's a pain in my ass, but I'm not about to kill her for it. One way or the other, we'll straighten this out." Most likely.

They didn't have to say anything, but I could feel it: total puzzlement from the werewolves. *But—the solution is so simple! Just fight to the death. Problem solved.* Yikes. Not for the first time I remembered Jeannie's warning: werewolves weren't human; they were an entirely separate species. Expecting them to behave like humans who occasionally turned into wolves was always a mistake.

"Anyway," I said to break the silence, "Laura and my father are out of my reach now. And it's our job, mine and Sinclair's, to deal with the fallout. We're basically letting the vampire nation be dragged into the twenty-first century. I'll do my best to keep you guys out of it, like I always have. That's all I can promise."

"Your blundering has endangered every one of my Pack members and I expect you to make amends."

"Reconsider your tone, Michael."

Whoa. When had Sinclair stood? And crossed the room so he was standing right next to me? Nobody had seen a thing.

"That's a fair request," Jeannie said quietly, and hey! How'd she get BabyJon? Oh, right. Because Lara had moved when Sinclair did, and now she was standing next to her dad, staring at my husband. Hopefully Jeannie had taken BabyJon as opposed to Lara pitching him at her like a basketball from half-court. "We're in their home. Uninvited."

"Yeah, but in Michael's defense, Betsy's really annoying," Derik drawled. Marc made a really weird sound, and I realized he was trying to turn a laugh into a cough. Tina and Sinclair remained like stones, though. Gorgeous, humorless stones. Lara stood to her dad's right, small hands curled into claws. Waiting. Whatever he did, she'd back him. She wouldn't even think about it. She was the scariest, cutest middle schooler in the history of middle schoolers. Well, maybe not *the* scariest. Madonna was probably pretty intimidating when she was a kid.

"Okay, maybe everybody take a breath," Marc suggested, which was hilarious coming from a zombie soothing vampires. "Not to be out of line here or anything, Michael, but I think maybe you forgot how unnerving vampires are—you can't smell them, right? Which makes you nuts?"

"That's true," Jeannie replied, amused, "but it's considered rude to point that out."

"Well, that's fair, and I don't mean to offend, but I think it's left you short-tempered. And the media zoo has left *us* short-tempered. Nobody's having a particularly good week. I think we all need a nap."

"Not me," Lara whispered to her father. "I slept on the plane."

"We're not too keen on how you smell, either," Derik Gardner pointed out. "If you don't mind my asking, what are you?"

"It's a long story," Marc hedged.

"And he comes off really dead in it," I added. So think *that* over, you hairy chumps. "But he's fine now." More than fine, according to Will Mason. Who was probably still cowering in the kitchen with my mom. Jessica, after a quick greeting, hadn't lingered. She was going to be mega-pissed she'd missed this.

"So how about you guys head on out and find somewhere

to sleep and have a good meal and everybody can get some rest and get their heads straight and we can all meet up again tomorrow. Or whenever."

Michael arched a dark golden eyebrow. "We?"

"If you're meeting in my home, yes," Marc replied in a pleasant, even tone. "I'm for Team Betsy. Always have been."

I made a mental note: get *Team Betsy* T-shirts made. Like, yesterday. In every color and every size.

"That's good advice," Jeannie said. "Don't you think? Michael?"

He let out a breath. "Yes. It is. I'd like to talk about this later, if—if you can accommodate me." He almost bit the phrase out; you could see he was practically chewing on the words. I knew what it cost him to stay polite.

"Of course. You're always welcome here," I replied, and it was almost the truth. "And it really *is* nice to see you again, no bullshit. All of you." To Lara: "What are you, a junior now?"

"No." She was a vicious werewolf cub, but she loved being mistaken for older like any kid. She smiled and looked down, and I realized with a start she was dropping eye contact for a moment to be courteous, something her grown-ass dad hadn't been able to do. Have I mentioned I friggin' love this kid?

"So we'll see you later?" I asked, and two minutes later they were pulling out of our driveway, heroically resisting the urge to plow over some reporters on the way.

"Okay, well. That wasn't so bad." And I was right. Our next meeting was going to be much, much worse. Like, call-an-ambulance-and-then-a-lawyer worse. I'm really glad I didn't know that then.

CHAPTER
FOURTEEN

Cathie and the Ant were waiting for us in my office in Hell, which was exactly as alarming as it sounded.

"Welcome back!" my stepmother said with a big too-much-lipstick smile, and I thought I'd known fear before? Any fear I'd known in the past faded to mere concern as I watched my stepmother projecting warmth. Bonehomie? Is that the word? She was just spewing bonehomey everywhere.

"Thanks," I replied, already anticipating the body blow. Something horrible was bound to be coming. Then I realized . . .

"So, Marc. How's your new friend?"

. . . she wasn't talking to me. *Thank you, Jesus. I don't deserve it, but you did me a solid. Never hesitate to call in that favor. Love, Betsy.* (My prayers were mostly like notes between pals. If Jesus came here, we'd hang out. We'd go fishing, after I got him some decent footgear.)

"My new friend?" Marc's expression didn't change, though he raised his eyebrows.

"It's Will, isn't it?" This from Cathie, whose efforts to squash her natural bitchiness were probably giving her abdominal cramps. "The orphan boy you're into?"

"He's in his twenties," Marc said mildly. "I don't know that he identifies as an orphan boy."

"Well, you're going to reschedule your date, right? You're not going to let your Hell duties impact your love life. Right? Marc? You deserve a social life."

"Or you're a thorough professional and wouldn't dream of letting your love life impact your Hell duties. Right?"

"Yeah, I'm already sick of this," was his (wise) reply, and he shooed them away like ill-tempered ducks. In a few seconds we were the only ones in the office.

"The reason I'm here—" he began.

"I know, I appreciate the support."

"Uh. Yeah, that. I'm definitely all about the support. And also, you can find anyone in Hell, right?"

"If I know their name." One of the many dumb arbitrary rules. I careened from godlike powers (teleporting in and out when I liked) to rodeo clown (I tried to make it rain marshmallows, and it rained maple syrup instead and, oh my God, the screams). The only person who would have been any real help was banished after I beat the ever-lovin' crap out of her. "Who'd you have in mind?"

"David Bowie."

"The guy who invented hunting knives?"

Marc's mouth popped open. "Okay, even for you, that—"

"Mmph."

"Oh, you bitch, don't tease."

"Can't help it." I giggled. "Your face! Like you wanted to hug me, then hit me. Or hit me, then hug me."

"Those two options are always on the table. So: is he here?"

"I want David Bowie." I should start keeping a list: "Demands I Never Thought I'd Make in Hell."

We waited.

Nothing.

"Okay, great. Great! I think that's great." His smile faded. "Okay, I'm now a little bummed I won't get to meet him, but it *is* good knowing he's not burning in a lake of fire somewhere. Thanks for checking."

"Sure. Should have thought of it myself. But it's just one more arbitrary rule that makes no sense around here."

He sighed at the ceiling. "Oh, here we go."

"I mean—take Antonia, for example."

Marc made a noise like he was chomping on lemon rind. "Uggghhhyecchhh, why?"

"Not my stepmother. The other Antonia, the werewolf."

"I stand by my question."

"Well, that's fair." I slumped back in my chair—the only chair in Hell that was comfortable, because why the Hell should *I* have to suffer along with everyone else? "So, she died saving me. Took bullets for me."

"Yep. It was gross. Her brains were everywhere."

"You're a doctor; you can't use words like *gross* to describe medical conditions."

"She presented with multiple GSWs resulting in penetrating brain injuries including but not limited to brain parenchyma seepage from her skull and multiple intracranial fragments—"

"Never mind, stick with *gross*. Anyway, we escorted her body to Massachusetts and they had a funeral and buried her."

Marc plopped down in the chair opposite my desk, winced, tried to get comfortable, gave up. "Yeah, just because I didn't go to the Cape with you guys doesn't mean you didn't tell me all about it when you got home. I know all this."

"Shut up, this is my process." I swiveled in my chair and swung my legs up on my desk, and reminded myself that it would be sandal season soon enough. See ya next winter, red leather midheel Gucci loafers. Your time is almost up. "So fast-forward a few months, I'm in Hell by accident." Ah, the golden days when I thought just visiting Hell was the worst thing to happen to me. "And there she is: Antonia. And what with one thing and another, I bring her back to the real world. And so she's alive again."

"Right. Which is troubling you."

"Yes."

"Because it's weird."

"So very, very weird. I mean, she's alive now. She's got a body, a physical body, and she can die again. And if we went to Massachusetts and bought shovels and found her grave and dug it up—"

"If you're angling for company during this ghastly-sounding field trip, I'm busy. For years and years."

"—her dead body would be in there! So what the *fuck*?"

"It's confusing."

"Yes."

"Doesn't make much sense from any scientific standpoint you'd care to name."

"Right." I knew talking to a scientist about this was the right move. Hooray, physicians![22]

Marc leaned forward. "Want to know why?"

"*Yes.*"

"This isn't science."

"Argh!" I kicked out, frustrated, and there was a quick paper blizzard.

---

[22] No, really! Doctors and nurses are the *best*.

"You just booted over a ton of manila folders," Marc observed. "Do you even know what they're all for?"

"Of course not." Yes, Hell had manila folders. And not a single one of them was ever the right size for whatever project required the use of manila folders. Diabolical, really. "I'm so sick of that nonanswer."

"Any sufficiently advanced technology is indistinguishable from magic."

"And I'm not too fond of that one, either."

"Arthur C. Clarke said that."

"I know," I lied. Was he the guy who wrote about the Knights of the Round Table?

Marc's smirk told me he knew I was talking out of my butt. "It's from *Profiles of the Future*. And it means exactly what you'd think it means: no matter how smart you are, some things are so far beyond our grasp we'll never understand them." This from a guy who held two jobs all through undergrad and medical school, never missed a party, usually showed up only on test days, and still graduated with a GPA of 3.6. *Sure, Marc. Tell me about the things that are beyond your grasp. I guarantee I've got more of them.* "If you were to go back in time with a flashlight—"

"Oooh, oooh, I know this one! I've done that!"[23]

"—and showed it to a bunch of people at, say, the court of Henry VIII, and tried to explain batteries, they wouldn't get it. Does that make them stupid, or you a genius?"

"No," I said slowly. "And no." Unfortunately.

"I think it's like that with paranormal science."

"That's not a thing." Or at least it shouldn't be.

"Of course it's a thing; you come face-to-face with it pretty

---

[23] Kind of. She did go back in time, but she didn't bring a flashlight. Should've, though: *Undead and Unfinished*.

much every day. I mean, there are actual, scientific reasons why the Wyndhams change form once a month. It should be impossible, right? Well, for hundreds of thousands, it's not. It's obviously a perfectly normal function of their biology . . . that sounds impossible to anyone who isn't a werewolf. Can we explain it? Nope. Is it magic? Nope."

"So . . . what?" I swung my legs down so both feet were on the floor and swiveled in my chair. It was hard to sit still and have this conversation at the same time. I wanted to pace. And throw things. And kick the things I threw. Then pace more. "Keep blindly plunging ahead and hope for the best?"

"I'm pretty sure that's your family motto."

I laughed. "No, that's not it. Would you believe it's 'Salvation from the Cross'?"

"Wow." His green eyes went wide. "Whatever you do, don't read anything into that, O Chosen One of the Vampyrs."

"Ugh, don't pronounce it like that. There's no *y* in vampires."

"Mmm." I got a long stare, and then he said, "You're nervous about sending Jennifer back today."

"Guilty." Cindy had fulfilled her sworn buddy duties and talked Jennifer Palmer into agreeing to go back to the real world and make amends. Or just wore her out with every cheer she could think of until Jennifer begged her to stop. Either way: today was the day!

"You're doing the right thing," he added.

"You hope."

"Yeah." He shrugged. "If it doesn't work, it doesn't work. But it's worth trying. Hell's still in the business of punishing sinners. We've just also instituted a parole program."

"A mere trifle of a change!" I cried in a plummy British accent.

"Raw-ther. Hardly noticeable, dah-ling."

"And also, worth doing just because the original Satan hated the idea so much."[24]

"Like you needed another excuse?" He squirmed in his seat. "Dammit! Change this seat into something that doesn't make my lower back feel like it's on fire!"

I pointed. Smirked. "Be more comfortable." And the resulting bright purple beanbag chair, a good five feet in diameter, almost swallowed him on the spot.

"Jesus! I—c'mon, help me—don't just sit there and laugh—oof!—help me out of this thing! Oh, you awful bitch, I hate you so much right now!"

Ever laugh so hard your face hurts for five minutes afterward? Yep.

"Fine, fine, you big baby." I gestured and the beanbag chair sort of barfed Marc out. He wasn't free, exactly, but he wasn't being swallowed so much. The thrashing went on, though. "Let's get it over with. I want Jennifer Palmer."

"—don't even know how I'd do it." Jennifer cut herself off, glanced around the office, gave us both a tentative smile. "Hi, uh, Betsy. Hi, Marc. Are you okay?"

"Hi, Jennifer."

"I'm very fucking far from okay." Marc managed to wrench himself free, then offered his hand to Jennifer. She blinked at it, then tentatively shook it. "Never tell anyone what just happened here. And good luck. Hopefully we'll never meet again."

"Thanks."

I looked up at her. "Ready?"

"No."

"Going anyway?"

"Yeah."

---

[24] So. Much. *Undead and Unforgiven.*

I was on my feet by then, too. "Why?"

"Well." She spoke slowly, clearly choosing her words with care, a trick I should get around to mastering. "If it's a test of my obedience, to show I can obey. If it's a trick, to show I'm a good sport. If it's real, I owe them. The ones I left holding the bag."

"Good enough. C'mere, give me your hand." She tentatively stepped forward, and I took her small hand, which she offered with all the enthusiasm she'd offer a grizzly. "We're gonna take a trip. And hopefully, never meet again."

She licked her lips. "Okay. But if I screw this up, if I can't make it right, please remember that I didn't fight you. That I was willing to go. For when you see me again, and have to figure out my new punishment."

"That's the spirit." And away we went.

CHAPTER
FIFTEEN

"I'm not complaining—"

"Every time you say that, it's a lie," Marc said. "Every. Time."

"—but what's happening?"

It was two o'clock in the morning and for some reason, we were in our basement. The creepy, gigantic, horrible, right-out-of-every-horror-movie-ever basement. It wasn't so much the hour as the fact that, again: basement. I'd been living here for years and could count on both hands how often I'd been down here. And frankly, I was annoyed I needed both.

Sinclair had strolled to the far end while Tina, Marc, and I tripped along in his wake. His dark suit was impeccable and, even more annoying, didn't look out of place. Sinclair could wear a suit anywhere. *Anywhere.* Sometimes I forgot he started out as a farm boy who never wore shoes once the snow was gone for the year.

"The Wyndhams have requested a follow-up, Elizabeth."

"Basement."

"And then, in what I cannot imagine is a coincidence—"

"Basement?"

"The sensors tripped."

"But why are we in the basement?"

"The ones at the dock."

"So maybe we should be at the dock? And not the basement? Also, what dock? The biggest river in the universe is, what? Two miles from here? That same river comes with a zillion docks."

"The Mississippi isn't even the biggest river on this planet."

"It's still a bigass river, Marc! Why aren't we out freezing our asses on it, instead of freezing our asses down here?" A measure of my consuming basement hatred: I'd rather be on the Mississippi River in early spring in total darkness for who knew how long, doing who knew what, than be in our basement.

DARLING.

"Ow!" I rubbed my temple. Sinclair's exasperated thought had ripped through my brain like a fishhook.

"And obviously," he continued out loud, "the Wyndhams are coming through the tunnel, the entrance and exit of which, you'll recall, is in our basement."

"None of that sounds right."

The basement. The tunnel. Because there weren't enough clichés in life, ours was a basement the psycho from *Silence of the Lambs* would envy and it came with a secret tunnel leading to a moonlit dock on the river. Because of course it did.

We'd had to use it only once, thank God, because at the time we were running to keep ahead of the angry vampires on their way to kill me.

CHAPTER
SIXTEEN

ELIZABETH!

"What?"

"Stop doing exposition in your head," Sinclair ordered out loud.

"I wasn't!" When Marc snickered and Tina bit her lip so she wouldn't laugh, I corrected myself. "Well, maybe a little. Mostly I was reminding myself why I hate our basement."

"You hate our basement?" Marc asked, wide-eyed. "Really? Gosh, I had no idea. I don't think you ever mentioned it."

"Marc."

"Not once."

"Marc."

"Not even one time."

"Fine, I get it, I'll try to bitch less about the basement, okay?" I snapped. "I can't help hating it down here."

"Given the many times it has saved our lives, that is idiotic," my husband snapped back. Touch-*y*. I decided to let it go. Stressful week for everyone, and marriage to me isn't all sunshine all the time. Marriage to me was, in fact, occasionally typhoonesque, with a side order of shrill. Besides, I'd much rather passively-aggressively punish him for the next several days. Those were the ways of my love.

"My king, I am sure the Wyndhams won't—"

"Hush."

Tina hushed. Marc gave her a 'you gonna just let that one go?' look and she shrugged. I, in a moment of rare wisdom (or laziness), decided to keep my mouth shut.

He had his head down and every line in his body was tense as he listened. "They're coming," he said quietly. "Four at l— No. Five. That's . . . odd."

"How'd they even know about this tunnel?" I whispered. Then, duh, it hit me. "Dumb question. Antonia the Werewolf would have told him." She'd lived with us for a bit.[25] And I couldn't even get mad at her for it. Her link to Michael was through blood and family; of course she would tell him everything. I was just her landlord for a few months. A landlord who didn't charge rent. A landlord plagued with werewolf freeloaders. A landlord with the best shoe collection you've ever seen. "Though why they'd want to . . ." I stopped myself.

Duh, again. They *didn't* want to. They didn't want to drive through the media and knock on our front door in front of God and everybody. They wanted to come to us in a way where no one would see them. And maybe in a way they hoped *we* wouldn't see them, because the sensors had gone up *after* Antonia had been killed. She couldn't have told Michael about them, so maybe the werewolves didn't know they'd activated them.

That didn't bode well.

---

[25] *Undead and Uneasy, Undead and Unworthy.*

"At least they tripped 'em so we got a little warning," Marc murmured.

"Well, that and the phone call." It had been a weird call, though. Lara, of all people. I'm not one to tell people how to raise their werewolf cubs, but what's a kid doing up at that hour? After a three-hour flight halfway across the country? Tsk, tsk. You'd never catch BabyJon running around in the dead of night calling vampires and sneaking into tunnels. He'd have to get a lot better at walking first. And maybe grow more teeth. And learn how to use a potty.

And of course we had sensors, and cameras, and bugs tripped by movement, and more cameras. The best money could buy, in fact, so sleek and high-tech I forgot about them most of the time, and you'd better believe they were tough to spot. They'd been in place before my sister blabbed about vampires but after we started putting our address in the vampire newsletter.

Sure, Sinclair and I had a basic "You got a beef? Come and tell us to our faces, jerkweeds" philosophy, but that doesn't mean we didn't take precautions. There were sensors all over, and one of the parlors had recently been converted to a security room; it was positively *stuffed* with monitors. Tina and Marc spent a weird amount of time in there. I suspected strong voyeuristic streaks in both of them, the pervs.

We could all hear the footsteps approaching—well, maybe not Marc. Zombies didn't have enhanced senses. He was just really good at healing from horrific injuries now. He'd broken his leg hauling Will Mason's narrow ass out of the path of a truck a few weeks ago, and he was fine by the weekend. It's why Will had such a crush, I think. Marc was gorgeous *and* smart *and* funny *and* loyal *and* brave *and* he was now an unkillable paranormal doctor who hung out with vampires and werewolves and served on a committee in Hell. Who wouldn't have a crush? Poor Will: he never had a chance. Put it this way: I saw someone getting hurt in all this, and it wasn't Marc.

But Marc had tipped his head, listening, so we could all hear the steps now, and murmured voices, one high, two low. There was a click, and then the wall that looked like unmovable cement slid back. Not like the movies, either, all rumbly and slow. The cement wall that wasn't slid back without a sound, in just a couple of seconds.

So what now? A pissed-off werewolf? A vampire who felt betrayed? Both? Ugh, I really didn't want the werewolves teaming up with all the vampires who were super pissed at me right now. That could get messy. And inconvenient. And it would definitely cut into my Hell time. So, it wasn't *all* bad.

Or worse: an enterprising reporter. Yeah, don't worry, media, the paranormals lurking in the basement definitely aren't up to anything sinister. Oh, this? This is our secret tunnel leading to the river, which we use in darkest night— What, you don't have one?

Someone stumbled through the passage like they'd been given a shove from behind, and I caught the scent for the first time and nearly shrieked.

It wasn't a werewolf out to get me because I sucked at PR. It wasn't a vampire out to get me because he felt I'd exposed him to the world. It wasn't the media.

It was so much worse.

"Dad?"

CHAPTER
SEVENTEEN

You know how dogs like to fetch ducks and geese, and cats like to bring dead birds and mice to people? This was a zillion billion times worse, and I say that with a complete lack of hyperbole.

Lara had somehow tracked down my dad, grabbed him, and hauled him back to Derik. (I cannot even fathom how this happened. Someone should look into the schools on Cape Cod, because they're teaching some strange and cool stuff.)

Jeannie and Michael, like all parents staying in a nice hotel (the Saint Paul Hotel!) with an unexpected free evening, had been indulging in private time. (The Ordway Suite! Lucky jerks.) And Derik, formidable in a fight and never, *ever* one to mess with, was a great big blond marshmallow who would have killed or died for his best friend's kid. Luckily he didn't have to kill or die, just cover for her. He helped Lara bring my dad through the tunnel, and Michael and Jeannie weren't far behind them. And at the crucial moment, they basically all ended up in our terrible basement.

So much shouting.

"What have I said about running off without permission to trespass, break and enter, and then commit assault with a dash of kidnapping?"

"Leave a note," the feral child replied.

"*Leave a damned note.*" Jeannie was practically breathing fire. Never had curly blond hair been more intimidating. "And did you?"

Glumly: "No."

"What?"

"No, Mom, I did not leave a note."

I blinked. That's not how I thought the lecture would go. "Wait. What?"

"If Derik hadn't texted us, we still wouldn't know where you were!"

Lara flashed a golden glare at Derik: *traitor.*

Sinclair had been standing off to the side, hands behind his back, looking down at Lara.

(We were, of course, up in the Peach Parlor, because my life. The arguing only *started* in the basement.)

"May I address Miss Wyndham?" he asked politely.

"If *address* means *smack*," Jeannie replied, arms folded across her chest, "then yes." To Lara: "Thank heavens you didn't cross state lines. Then it'd be federal kidnapping instead of ordinary, run-of-the-mill kidnapping."

Yeah. Thank goodness for that.

Sinclair inclined his head in a sort of nod/bow to Lara, who was standing beside one of the couches, eyes on the carpet, the blush creeping up her neck to stain her cheeks. "Why have you done this, Miss Wyndham?"

She looked up, surprised. Probably figured he'd do the yelling thing. "You don't— I mean, you can call me Lara," she said shyly.

"Thank you. I am Sinclair. Why did you do this?"

"So B—so the queen of the vampires could clean her own house."

"Boy, have *you* got the wrong queen." I had no idea where we kept the brooms. If we even had brooms. Most of the house was carpet. I *think* we kept a vacuum in the mudroom closet, but that was more for the messes Fur and Burr delighted in.

"Clean her house?" Sinclair asked.

A low mutter from Derik. "Ohhhh boy . . ."

"After we left here and were driving to the hotel, Mom and Dad were saying you had to clean your own house and nothing could be fixed until you did. Nothing! And I asked what that meant and Dad said that meant Betsy had to track and punish her dad and her sister and if she couldn't, nothing would be fixed."

"That's, ah"—Michael coughed into his fist—"not exactly what I said."

"And you interpreted that to mean my queen was *unable* to 'clean house'?"

"Uh-huh." Earnest now, looking up at Sinclair, feet together, hands clasped behind her back like a kid competing in a spelling bee. K-I-D-N-A-P-P-I-N-G. F-E-L-O-N-Y. She had dressed in dark gray jeans and a dark blue, long-sleeved turtleneck for her evening of lawbreaking. Her hair was pulled back, showing her pretty, pointed face. She was like a golden-eyed fox. With a ponytail. "She said she couldn't get them."

"I did?"

"So I figured, *I'd* get them."

I shook my head. "That's not—I said they were out of my reach." Meaning things had gone too far between my dad and Laura and me. Meaning we couldn't chalk it up to a misunderstanding like we might have been able to do even a year ago. They did what they did specifically to hurt me. And I had cut them out of my life for that.

But I could see how a child would take that literally: that they were physically beyond my reach. And so I was unable to get my hands on them. And if the child in question has a keen nose, and an unusual mind-set . . . actually, gotta give it to her, the whole caper was pretty ballsy.

She was still earnestly explaining herself. "Sinclair, your queen said it was her job and your job to deal with her family. And my dad said nobody could go home until things got fixed. So I thought—"

"Produce the family, step back while Betsy does her bit, everything gets resolved, you and your family get to go home," Marc said.

The corner of Tina's mouth quirked into a half smile. "There have been worse plans." Unspoken: *some hatched in this very room.*

I glanced at my husband and, even if I hadn't known what he was thinking, I'd have known what he was thinking.

I know that look. You're already fantasizing about having your very own werewolf hitman. Hitgirl.

You must admit, she is an extraordinary child. She'll be an out-standing ally.

"Excuse me."

Jeannie was now in classic mom pose: hands on hips, scowl on face. "Lara, running off on your own is never acceptable."

"Excuse me?"

"I'm sorry, Mom." She certainly looked sorry. Look at that lower lip starting to quiver! "It's just you said that you and Dad were not to be disturbed; you said the three Bs were in effect."

Even as I tried to figure that out, Jeannie elaborated: "Don't bother us unless it's about blood, barf, or burns."

"Nifty." I made a mental note to implement that when

BabyJon got bigger. The three Bs and also, a few Ps and Zs. Maybe a Code Blue if it was anything shoe-related. We could do drills!

Jeannie, like all good moms, appeared unmoved. They key word being *appeared*, because let's be honest: you knew she was as proud as she was exasperated. A wimp who always does what she's told isn't much of a leader. But this! Michael could drop dead tomorrow and I'd be pretty confident the Wyndhams wouldn't have anything to worry about. "You still knew it was wrong, and there will be consequences. Starting with your apologies."

"Excuse me!"

I rounded on him. "*What*, Dad?" My father had been huddled in the easy chair by the window, as far away from the front door as he could get. We'd had them all come upstairs, and nobody had wanted a drink, and I wasn't sure if Dad was sitting over there by choice or if I'd subconsciously herded him into the corner. My subconscious was a murky wasteland, so anything was possible.

"Are you going to call off your pets and let me the hell out of here?"

I turned to Michael so fast I almost fell over. "He didn't mean you guys. My dad did not suggest or imply or infer or intimate or in any way mean that I think you guys are my pets."

For the first time, Michael smiled, which took years off his face. "It's fine. I know all about embarrassing relatives."

Because my father was an idiot who never, ever learned, he added, "And you'd better know I'm going straight to the police!"

"Oh, well, we should keep you our prisoner forever, then," Tina said with such indifference to his fate, my dad went pale. And he was normally pretty pale—golf season was well over a month away and that was about the only time he was outside.

"Relax," I told him. "Obviously we aren't going to keep you a prisoner forever. Ugh, who could stand it? But come on—telling us you're gonna run to the cops? How does that get you what you want?"

He glowered and didn't answer, and I couldn't blame him. And he was horribly mussed. Lara had snatched him while he was in pajamas and an old T-shirt. He had on boots and his coat, because she was a kidnapper with standards, dammit, and knew frostbitten victims were problematic. The Wynd-hams probably had a rule about making sure all their victims were appropriately dressed for the weather.

If I seem like I am about to laugh, kick me.

Don't you dare laugh! It's not funny! My poor dad must be terrifi—ugh, I can't believe I thought of him as 'my poor dad.' But come on. He must have been really scared. Well, maybe not at first. But eventually. Definitely by the time Derik showed up to help her.

Remind me to gift Lara Wyndham with several gold bars. Or a car. No, too young. A horse? Girls like horses, yes?

This one would eat *that poor horse.*

Two horses, then.

I shook my head to clear Sinclair from my thoughts. "Dad, just—give us a minute, okay? Let's get this sorted and then I'll get you a cab or a ride or what have you."

"It wasn't even my idea," he muttered from his corner. "The video, talking to the media, that was all your sister's plan."

That's it, can't bail on her fast enough, can you? I eyed him and decided, no, best not get into the "hey, jackass, she did it for you and who are you kidding? You bankrolled the whole thing" discussion in front of the Wyndhams. But it did get me thinking.

"Lara, Derik—how'd you guys even know he was my dad? You've never met him before, right? And you can't pick up my scent."

"No, but things in your house carry scents," Derik explained.

He seemed relieved to be answering a straightforward question. I didn't envy him being caught between Michael and Lara. Jeannie'd probably have some choice words for him, too. Which definitely didn't make me want to snicker. "And your mother and brother are frequent visitors here. We could pick up their scents, no problem, and that was half the battle."

"So family members smell the same?" Fascinating. And a little disgusting. Did that mean that I smelled a bit like Polo aftershave? And/or Laura's cheap sneakers? And that they smelled like cotton and Beverly Feldmans? Also, what were the odds that I'd have two Antonias and two Laura/Laras in my life?[26]

"Well, it's like lettuce leaves."

"Um." I took another look. Yep, Derik seemed serious. "What?"

He actually warmed to the topic. And keep in mind, the topic was lettuce. "There's all kinds of lettuce. But butter lettuce doesn't taste like radicchio and iceberg lettuce doesn't taste like romaine. Chicory endive tastes nothing like mizuna, and cress isn't at all like oakleaf."

"Okay, you know a lot about lettuce." Maybe too much. Although I'd never thought about lettuce as particularly sinister before now, no one could know that much about greens and not be up to something.

"He's a gourmet," Lara piped up.

I didn't smile, but it was a near thing. "Gore-*may*. The *t* is silent." That'll teach her to correct me on geography. And as strange as the family-as-salad analogy was, Derik had put it in a way I could grasp, which I always appreciated.

"*Lara*." Yikes. When parents snapped your name in unison,

---

[26] Author's note: I'm not great at thinking up names.

and italics, it was time to pay attention. "The topic under discussion is not Derik as amateur gourmet," Michael continued. Though maybe it should have been. Lettuce-sniffing weirdo. "It's that you have wronged our hosts and need to make amends."

Hosts. Aww, that's cute. Hosts who didn't invite you. Hosts you're not actually staying with. Hosts you overtly threatened before we encouraged your rapid departure. But sure, sure—we're their hosts.

"Yes, Dad."

"You need to ask forgiveness."

She nodded, clearly miserable. She'd probably expected praise, or at least a quick resolution to the vampire/werewolf spat. Instead she broke several rules, could have made the situation much worse, got ripped for it in front of strangers, and now she had to apologize in front of those same strangers. I hadn't been a kid in years, but I remembered that feeling perfectly well. Like there's something in your throat and you can't choke it down no matter how much you try. Knowing everyone in the room can see you're blushing, and not able to do anything about it, which made you blush harder. Knowing everyone in the room—especially the strangers—was almost as uncomfortable as you were, but nobody could move on until you forced yourself to talk. And talking, in that moment, seemed impossible. Like you'd never find the words, and everyone would stand around and stare at you until the end of time.

The worst.

I went to one knee in front of her. There really was something to that whole "get down on their level" thing. I had always liked being tall, starting when I was a kid. Being taller than my teachers by the time I was in high school cut *way* back on the condescension. But the reverse of that was sometimes I intimidated people when I didn't mean to. So: down.

"Lara, you are brilliant and brave and sneaky and a criminal genius and you should be grounded for a decade and I'm a little terrified of you right now. Of course I forgive you; you were trying to solve a problem, trying to help your Pack, and it wasn't your fault that—" I cut myself off. No point in piling it on; Jeannie *still* looked like a sentient thundercloud. "Next time—because I have every confidence we'll be working together in the future—just ask me what you think I'd want. Unless it's my birthday. Then just always assume: shoes."

She let out a shaky breath. "Okay."

"Okay."

She glanced at her mom, then back at me. "Thanks. Uh, 'bye?"

"*Lara.*"

She winced so hard her ponytail swung. "I'msorryforoversteppinginyourterritoryQueenBetsy. There."

"I understand why you did." I stood.

Most gracious, my own.

Enh, give her a break. It's not like my dad wasn't begging for it.

"That's kind of you," Michael said quietly.

"Oh, I'm sure one of these days I'll make some horrible blunder in werewolf etiquette," I replied, and the thought made me feel oddly cheerful. "If not this visit—which isn't over, so there's still time!—then maybe the next one. I'll probably need some of that leniency from your side then, right?"

"Right," absolutely *everyone* said in unison. Not cool, gang!

Lara apologized to Sinclair, who bowed and said, "The pleasure of your company is matched only by your courtesy. Perhaps before you and your family leave, you'll indulge me by telling me how you pulled off such a remarkable feat."

"You—really?" The blush was fading and her entire face lit up. "I thought you'd be—I mean, I know Betsy doesn't like her—um—I mean—he's your father-in-law. I thought you'd be mad."

"And did it anyway? Risking the wrath of vampires as well as werewolves? Commendable. Further, I have no regard whatsoever for Mr. Taylor," Sinclair continued, taking no trouble to keep his voice down. He smiled at Lara. "The only reason I haven't killed him is *because* he sired the queen."

And Lara smiled *back*.

Yeesh. Time to steer the subject away from killing my dad. "The irony is, this is only partially my dad's fault. If you really wanted to get the culprit who put it all in motion, you should've grabbed my sister. Oh, and by the way, that's not a suggestion."

"Um." Lara coughed. Looked at the floor again. "About your sister."

Which is when familiar fists hammered on our front door and a familiar voice shrieked, "You give me my father back!" and familiar feet kicked at the bottom of the door and that same familiar voice added, "Or I'll give these reporters an interview you won't *believe*!"

I stared at the world's most dangerous middle schooler. "You're unbelievable."

"Thanks!"

"Not a compliment." I was pretty sure.

CHAPTER
EIGHTEEN

"Are you all right, John? Did they hurt you?" Laura had stormed the Peach Parlor in a fury. Once we'd let her in, that is. Believe me, there'd been a couple of votes to just leave her out on the porch to let her squawk to the media. Marc can be *such* a bitch when he's aggravated. Sinclair, too. "Are you hurt?"

"'Mfine," my dad mumbled, shrugging back into his coat. He wouldn't look at me, but that had been his MO for years. "Ready to go."

"Don't worry, John. I've got some of my people outside and they'll make sure you get out of here safely."

"John?" I asked, mouth open. "You don't let her call you Dad?"

"That's how I show my respect!" she flared. She'd extended a hand to help him up from the chair, which he'd avoided as he clambered to his feet. And she couldn't see it. All the subtle tells that showed he wanted nothing to do with us. And the way he kept saying he wanted nothing to do with us. All whizzing over her head.

"That's also how his mailman shows respect. And his accountant. Because they're his mailman. And his accountant." Could. Not. Believe it. How long had this been going on? "You're his daughter. Jeez, just call him Dad already."

"I don't take orders from you anymore, Betsy."

"Did you ever? Honest question." I started tapping my foot as an alternative to daring Jeannie to shoot her in the face. "When, in the time we've known each other, when have you ever followed an order of mine? When did I even *give* you an order?"

She stopped trying to help our father, who was having none of it anyway, and whirled to face me. "Did you really think you'd get away with this?"

"Which part?"

"Don't play dumb!"

Play?

"Ms. Goodman, my daughter has already apologized to Mr. Taylor and the queen—"

At "queen," Laura made a noise like a cat that had been thrown into a bubble bath.

"—on behalf of our P—"

"You set your pets on our father," she said, aghast. "Had them *fetch* him to your command."

"Whoa!" I spun toward Michael. "Nobody fetched anything! Again: I have never, ever, in any way, *ever* referred to any of you as my pets, ever—"

"I think they get it," Marc said. "But maybe throw a few more 'evers' in there, just to be sure."

"—because first of all: rude. And second, super-duper inaccurate. And third . . . well, I'll need a minute to come up with another one, but once I do I'll definitely have more in reserve." I mean, Jesus. Were they *trying* to get me killed? Oh. Right.

"How'd you even fix it so Laura would show up here?" Marc asked, which was a wonderful question.

"Well, I took away his phone and called the last few numbers still in 'Recent.'" To my father as he inched ever closer to the front hall and sweet, sweet freedom: "Sir, you really should passcode your phone."

"Yeah, any rando werewolf could kidnap you and use it to trick the Antichrist into doing a pop-in," Marc added with, it must be said, vicious glee. "That's what would have solved all this: passcodes!"

"Anyway." Lara seemed a little irked at being interrupted. Oh, honey. Welcome to my galaxy. "I figured out which number was Laura's by process of elimination. The others were his accountant and some reporters."

"Tsk. Tsk. Tsk," I clucked, popping each *k*. "The paps, Dad? Really? Hope that whole you-faking-your-own-death thing didn't come up."

"Don't worry," Lara assured me, "I didn't tell the reporters anything."

"Bullet dodged. Good to know."

Now Michael *and* Jeannie were doing the "oh shit another migraine" temple rubs. Heh.

"Anyway, yours was the only number that called him that he didn't call back. He did call Laura back, though. The one who actually likes him."

"Ha!" From Laura, who was deluded enough to think that would hurt me.

"So I figured if I called her and told her exactly what I was doing—"

"Didn't even apologize," Laura said with an indignant huff. "Just called me up and confessed!"

"—I could get him as well as the *other* person causing all

the trouble over here so the whole clean-house thing could get under way."

"That," Sinclair said, "is an excellent story. Tell it again, will you, dear?"

"No, don't. We have long outstayed our welcome. And Lara and her mother and I still need to have a lengthy discussion about the events of the evening." And the smile just *dropped* off Lara's face. "Our apologies again. And our thanks. Again," Michael said.

I waved it off. "Nobody got hurt and your kid's heart was in the right place." Also her claws and teeth.

"You should all be ashamed." Because scolding people who had sincerely apologized always fixed everything. "Everything you do brings havoc and hurts innocents," Laura continued.

Lara blinked up at her. My sister was even taller than I was, which was probably God's way of compensating her for having shitty taste in clothes and also being a tight-ass. "Aren't you the Antichrist?"

Laura flushed so hard she actually swayed on her feet; that's how fast the blood rushed to her head. Also, ha! "That—that is irrelevant. You're just a child; you don't know what you're talking about."

"Doesn't the Bible say you're going to persecute the saints?[27] And names you the son of destruction[28] and says you're going to deny God and Jesus?"

Whoa. If Laura got any redder, I was pretty sure she'd faint. Just pitch face-first into the peach carpet. And me with my phone all the way upstairs! "I will never deny Them! That's

---

[27] You bet it does!
[28] Yep.

why I—" Then she snapped her mouth shut so hard we all heard her teeth clack together.

"Oh. Wait. This isn't some hugely pathetic bid for our father's love. Well, it is, but it's also about proving to God that you're not going along with the Antichrist agenda. Huh." This . . . explained a lot, actually. Laura had always been worried she'd be like her mother. I was only now realizing I had way underestimated her terror; she was a lot more afraid of turning *into* her mother. And then destroying the world. "Well, the Bible's not infallible. It's not a blueprint. It's—it's stories. They don't have to all come true exactly the way someone wrote them."

"Shut your mouth. You've never read anything more complex than *Vogue*. The complexities and messages of the Bible would be completely beyond you," Laura ranted.

"Hey! I don't even like *Vogue*; the thing's bigger than a phone book and the ads are weird. You know I'm an *InStyle* subscriber and that's plenty complex." They weren't just about clothes, you know. *InStyle* was about how anyone can come up with their own signature style and look great—any age, any size, any budget. Now, *there* was a message for all the people of the world. "And I'm trying to make you feel better, you beautiful moron!"

"Wow," was Michael's comment. Oh, right. The werewolves were still here. "You actually paid attention in Sunday school. Good for you, honey."

Meanwhile, Jeannie was studying Laura. "That's right. We were so focused on the vampires, we forgot about you." *Story of Laura's life*, I thought but didn't say. "You betrayed her secret to the world. And in return, she took pity on you and declined to tell the world that you're actual, literal devil's spawn. That's something actual, literal devil's spawn should keep in mind. You owe her."

Oops! Just when Laura's face couldn't get redder, she outdid herself. Purple was not a good look for her forehead. "I've got no interest in taking advice from some werewolf's bitch."

"Wonderful to see you all again!" Michael said loudly. "We'll definitely have to do this again sometime!"

"Really?" Sinclair asked, looking as delighted as I'd ever seen him. "Wonderful. Just wonderful."

"But, wow, look at the time!" Which was inaccurate, since he never looked at the time. Michael now had Jeannie by one elbow and Lara by the hand, and hustled them over to the door so fast they almost knocked over my dad. "Thanks again, Betsy, you've got our numbers, let's definitely get together before we have to leave town, good-bye." Then they were out the front door, Derik right behind them.

"You have no idea how lucky you just got," I informed the Antichrist. "Just so unbelievably lucky. You managed to piss off the second most dangerous person in the room." Lara being the first, naturally.

Laura opened her mouth (again), only to be interrupted by a soft, toneless, "Everything all right in here, Laura?"

We all looked. When the Wyndhams had gone out, followed by my dad, someone new had come in. Why couldn't the Wyndhams have left, and Laura and my dad left, and no one come in? Was that really so much to ask?

Because I didn't want to talk to this poor guy, but I didn't dare send him away, either. He was untouchable, and that was entirely on me.

CHAPTER
NINETEEN

*"Bring out the other one. Your assistant. Prove ordinary vam-*pires can tolerate sunlight. Not just the king and queen."

Whoa. Okay, I knew Laura's obnoxious campaign included snippets about our lives that were none of the public's business. Those snippets included everything that came out of her mouth while on camera. But these people were actually paying attention to the details! They knew Sinclair and I were special; they knew regular vampires were vulnerable to sunlight and fire. For the first time I was more frightened than pissed. Did today's media really have nothing better to do than troll YouTube videos put up by gorgeous blondes?

Don't answer that.

"I don't have to prove anything, pal. That's on you guys. Do *not* take that as a dare! Besides, you— Sorry, what's your name?"

"Ronald Tinsman."

"Right, Ronald Tinsman. Do you really not have anything

better to do than stand in my yard babbling about vampires and freezing your ass off?"

"No," he replied quietly.

"Oh." Well, *that* took the wind out of my sails. "Well. Okay, then."

Tinsman. I knew that name. I'd heard it in recent, unpleasant circumstances. He didn't look or sound familiar, and he was dressed in midwinter casual: jeans, boots, a partially unzipped parka revealing a green-and-black flannel shirt. He was pale and puffy, with thinning brown hair and an exhausted gaze. But there was something about his eyes . . . dammit, where'd I know this guy from?

Sinclair must have caught the stray thought, because . . .

I doubt Mr. Tinsman is interested in our condolences on the loss of his daughter to vampirism and beheading.

"Oh, *fuck*!" I managed, and the shriek of microphone feedback nearly deafened me. "Argh, sorry!" I shook my head like a dog at a whistle to clear the ringing. "Wait, I'm not sorry. You're all trespassing and this is a stupid story. Isn't there a war going on somewhere? I'm almost positive there's a war somewhere. It's not the war on drugs—we've pretty much given up on that one . . ."

"What do you have to say about your father giving sworn affidavits testifying to the fact that vampires exist?"

"My *father*?" Tilt! Too much to process. For the first time ever, I longed to be back in Hell. "You mean the asshat who faked his death to get out of spending time with his family because he didn't care for the paperwork that comes with divorce proceedings?" I glared at Laura, who just shrugged. Suddenly this was making a lot more awful, awful sense. The Antichrist, in her continuing efforts to find the adult equivalent of a Daddy and Me class, had teamed up with my dad to expose me and mine to the world. And for what?

Revenge for imagined slights. Both of them. Pathetic. Both of them.

"My father and my half sister have at least one thing in common," I said shortly. "They're both liars." This was technically true, though more so in my dad's case than Laura's. The Antichrist was a huge fan of lying by omission, then convincing herself it wasn't like that.

"But what about the allegations of—"

"This unscheduled interview with you pack of trespassers is over. And this is private property. All of you get out. Not *you*, Laura. We need to talk."

Understatement.

"What the fuck is wrong with you." I was so pissed, so shocked by what had just happened, I couldn't get any volume or inflection. My outraged question came out like a little flat statement.

Laura shrugged and leaned against the back of the love seat.

"Laura! Answer the question: what's wrong with you?"

"Nothing's wrong with *me*. Besides, I'm just doing what you told me."

"God, you're an *infant* sometimes—you know that? It wasn't a dare and you damned well know it!"

"It was a taunt," she replied. "You were taunting me. You're always taunting me."

"Taunting, huh? That word-a-day toilet paper is really working out for you."

"See?"

I was pacing back and forth in front of her, trying not to rip my own hair out. Harshing my highlights would help no one; looking less attractive would help *no one*. "And how the hell do you know Cindy Tinsman's dad?"

"We both volunteer at Fairview."

"Of course you do."

Of course they did. My entire postdeath life consisted of huge, life-changing pieces of luck: sometimes good, sometimes bad. This time it was definitely the latter.

"And don't get any ideas," she warned, looking far too comfortable for the trouble she was in. "My people have instructions on what to do if I mysteriously disappear. You can't do anything to me while the world is looking over your shoulder."

"You're definitely watching too much television." I rubbed my forehead and added, "Walk me through this insanity of yours. You and Cindy's dad know each other, and somehow you found out what happened to his daughter—"

"Happened to?" She snorted. "You're making it sound like she was caught in a thunderstorm. You decapitated her after turning her."

"I didn't turn her! And Sinclair didn't either, and neither did Tina—"

"One of your filth," she said with a flick of her fingers. "It's on you."

I ground my teeth. She had a point. With great blah-blah came great blah-blah.

"I was the only one who would listen to him. And together we decided to expose you. He's got media contacts, and I've got plenty of—"

"Satan-worshipping staff," I interrupted. "I'll bet you didn't mention to Mr. Tinsman that you're the Antichrist."

"I did, actually," was the calm reply, and I nearly walked into the wall (probably should slow down my pacing).

"You did? Really?"

"Of course. We can't be partners without transparency."

"And you think him being numb means he's fine with that."

For the first time, she faltered. "He's not— I mean, yes, he's grieving. But he knows I'm a force for good, despite my birthright, like he knows you're a force for evil, despite yours."

I stopped pacing and stood in front of her. "No," I said bluntly. "He's lost his wife and daughter in a very short time. His wife died of cancer while he was helpless and could only watch, and his daughter was recently murdered in a particularly nasty way, because a lifelong friend of his family happened to be a vampire. You could have set yourself on fire and waltzed with a grizzly bear and he'd have had the same reaction: 'yeah, okay, sounds good, I don't care.'"

"I don't—"

"Yeah, that's just right. You don't. Oh, say, where's our dear old daddy-o?"

"He—" She realized she didn't know, and closed her mouth. I was too irked to feel much triumph. *God, what an idiot. Both of them. Must be a genetic thing. Curse. Whatever.*

"You didn't even notice, did you? Too busy preening for the cameras. He slipped away the moment he realized I'd seen him. And that, little sister, is our father in a nutshell. All talk, no follow-up. He's made a career out of terrible choices that he can't stick with."

"He's scared of you! And he's right to be scared. I said I'd protect him—"

I almost giggled.

"—and when I told him my plan he thought it was a wonderful idea. He *wanted* to help. He helped finance the operation."

"With his ill-gotten gains. But hey, the ends justify the et cetera, right, Laura?"

"You just can't stand that he wants to help me expose you. He had to fake his death just to get any peace."

I sighed. Laura had an amazing ability to interpret all my

actions as evil, and all our evil dad's actions as good. And her own intentions were, in her mind, always golden. "Yeah, he committed fraud for the greater good. Except not really."

"And why do you suppose he did that?" she asked in an exaggerated let's-find-the-answer-together tone.

"Because he's a raging coward who thrives on ducking familial responsibility?"

She glared. "That's our father you're speaking of."

"I know." I could feel my shoulders slump. Exhausted and it was barely noon. "That's why it's so awful."

"He did it because he was afraid of you."

"Oh Jesus-please-us." I rolled my eyes hard enough to hurt. "He can't think I'd ever hurt him."

"You threatened to kill him!"

"Mmm . . . doesn't sound like me. No, I'm pretty sure I never—oh. Wait. Huh." It was all coming back to me, like those nightmares where you're naked and tardy and haven't studied for the test and everyone's throwing tomatoes at you. "Fine, I did threaten him. Don't look at me like that; it was a stressful couple of days, took me a second to remember. Do *you* remember every conversation you've had in the last two months?"

She took a breath and put her hands behind her back. I grinned; in her mind she was throttling me. I've been seeing that look on people's faces for decades. "So you admit it. You know he doesn't trust you!"

"Wait, the guy who *faked* his own *death* is the one having trust issues? Jeepers, who'd have thought?"

"He still wanted to help me. He was so happy to see me," she babbled, lost in the happy memory of our father pretending he cared. "He was on board from the start; he thought telling the truth about you was a wonderful idea."

"He thought revealing he'd faked his death and committed insurance fraud was a wonderful idea?"

"He— What?"

"Moron!" I'd leaned down and shouted it into her face, and watching her flinch was deeply satisfying. "He broke the law! It's a felony, dumbass! He'll be lucky if he's *only* sued. They could slam his ass into Stillwater for—for—"

"Up to twenty years and a fine of up to one hundred thousand dollars in the state of Minnesota," the doorway said, except not really.

"Oh, you might as well get in here," I said, resuming my pacing.

To my surprise, Dick led the charge: "You're pathetic." Tina stretched on her tiptoes to peek over his shoulders, and nodded in agreement. The others were crammed in behind them (narrow doorway).

Laura said nothing, just raised her eyebrows.

"She's only ever welcomed you," he continued, presumably referring to me, "and occasionally called you on your shit." Definitely referring to me.

"Not her job," Laura snapped back.

"It by God ought to be someone's job! Sorry, Tina," said Dick.

"It's fine," said Tina. The rest had come in and were glaring en masse at Laura, who should have been less irritated and more afraid. "Understandable."

"I can't wait until someone catches you flinching at the Lord's name on camera," Laura said.

"You underestimate our resources," was Sinclair's cool reply. "And you underestimate our queen, as ever." In small rooms he always seemed taller than he was, and if Laura wasn't exactly cowering (she got points for that, if nothing else), she was definitely in his shadow. In *all* ways. "You think you're the only person in ten thousand years to try to expose us? This is nothing new. You're nothing new. There's not one original thing about you, not a unique thought in your head. Everything about you is a cliché, including this childish resentment you have for your older sister. I'd pity you, Laura, if you warranted it."

Whoa.

CHAPTER
TWENTY

And just like that, my reverie was over—finally—and I was back in the present in the Peach Parlor. (Hmm, alliteration.) Unfortunately, that meant I now had to talk to *this* poor bastard. "Hi, Mr. Tinsman. How—" I stopped. I knew exactly how he'd been. Numb and miserable.

"Everything's fine, Ronald," Laura assured him, completely oblivious to the fact that she was (a) using him, and (b) adding to his pain in the long run. *Hey, vampires were being punished, so it's all good, right?* "I was just leaving."

"No, we were just kicking you out." She didn't get to take the credit for her departure. It was our idea!

"I'm going," she snapped, "and I won't be back."

"You're leaving, and you won't be *allowed* back!" Again: the credit was rightfully ours.

"Is he here?"

I stopped my side of the death glower to look over at him. "Who, Mr. Tinsman?"

"The vampire who murdered my daughter."

Annnnd just like that, I ceased caring about who got the credit. "Mr. Tinsman, he—"

"You protect him, right? It's your job? As queen." Tinsman was looking around with a vacant expression, as though Lawrence was behind the peach curtains, or the peach sofa. "He's under your protection. They all are."

Oh. So that's how it was. *I'm helping your sister expose you so vampires will have nowhere to hide.* Had to give it to him, it was clever. *His* motives were understandable, and no one with a conscience could doubt his sincerity. As a recovering Miss Congeniality, it was my fate to hope for the regard and affection of people who loathed me.

I turned so I was facing him. Everyone else was sort of frozen in place, caught in the act of leaving. Marc and Tina were probably off to the monitor room, Sinclair wanted to whip up a new batch of Bacon Cookies for Fur and Burr, and I'd love to get back to reading *Smoothie Nation* (chapter six: "Melon Mania!"). Laura? Who knew? Probably leafletting our bedroom with "Repent, for the End Is Nigh, You Whorish Moron" brochures.

But none of those things were happening. Instead we were all prisoners of the Peach Parlor, trapped by Ronald Tinsman's grief.

"Mr. Tinsman, *I'm* the vampire who killed your daughter," I said. Never had I been more tempted to use my vampire mojo on someone. Not to get myself out of this mess. To make him forget about his pain.

We cannot, beloved.

I know, I know. Can't help wishing for it. Vamp mojo, I had learned over the years, was a short-term solution at best, and often backfired. Or worse, you pushed a little too hard, and you drove someone insane. How do you make a man forget he's mourning his entire family without doing serious brain damage?

You leave him the hell alone. Because some things can't be screwed with, a lesson I wish my sister would just internalize already.

"Not Lawrence. In fact," I continued, "Lawrence refused to turn your daughter when she asked. Which, I'm sorry to say, drove her to desperate measures."

"So it was his fault." His tonelessness was as sad as it was creepy. He was like a mannequin who had learned to walk and talk and nothing else: no expressions, no humanity. "His inaction drove her to seek her killer."

Well, hell, anything sounded bad when you said it like that. "No, it's still my fault. But listen . . ." To *what*? What could I possibly say to this poor guy? There were only two ways I could think of to comfort a grieving parent: tales of vengeance, or assurance that their child was out of harm's way. *Yes!* "You don't have to worry about her. Cindy's totally—"

Elizabeth, don't!

"—fine where she is."

I caught on half a second too late. I didn't dare look at Sinclair. At any of them.

Tinsman blinked slowly, like an owl. I could actually see him processing. "She's totally what? What did you say?"

"Shit," Marc said under his breath.

"Agreed," Tina said under hers.

"Totally, um, doing well. In Hell. Where I recently saw her." *How do I get myself into these messes? Pure natural talent: I don't even have to practice.*

"She's in Hell?" he whispered, and I'd never heard so much anguish crammed into three words. This was—and I didn't think such a thing was possible—worse than the mannequin.

Okay, salvage it. Somehow. My big, flapping, unhinged, loose-lipped, babbling mouth got me into this; time for it to get me out.

"Yeah, she is, but it's not like it sounds. She's got a buddy—we have a system down there now. Not *down there* because it's not under us. She's even helped her friend get paroled. And she's—" *Making friends,* I'd been about to say. *Lawrence is sticking by her and looking out for her. She's not alone, she's with someone she loves, and she's not being tortured. And she did so great with Jennifer, I'm going to give her more responsibility.* Except maybe the thought of her spending eternity with Lawrence, and doing chores for the vampire queen, wouldn't make Tinsman feel better.

He gulped so hard we heard it. "My daughter went to Hell?"

Marc was making slashing motions across his throat. Tina had simply closed her eyes and was enduring. But I was in it now. Nothing to do but finish.

"The thing is—"

"My daughter went to Hell," he said again, and for some reason hearing it the second time was worse.

"Yes, but Hell's a lot like L.A. You only hear awful things about it, and when you get there, parts of it *are* awful, but some parts are pretty okay. Nice, even."

"You sent. My daughter. To Hell."

"No! That's just—"

Elizabeth, for the love of God. Just stop.

"—where she ended up," I finished, and it would be so great if this was a nightmare. A nightmare would be good. Let me look down and realize I'm naked and haven't studied for the history test.

I looked down. Fully clothed. Nuts.

"C'mon, Ronald." Laura was back from wherever and now she sort of steered Tinsman toward our front door. "Let's go. You've done your part, and they'll all pay for what they've done."

Well, at least she doesn't sound like a Bond villain knockoff.

"And you, Laura?" Sinclair asked gently. "When will you pay for your sins?"

She snorted, gave Tinsman a gentle shove out the front door, and said, "You almost sound like you know what you're talking about. By the way, I let your puppies out of the mudroom. Hope they haven't gotten into any mischief."

Ack! Fur and Burr, unsupervised, having the run of the mansion while we were all stuck in the Peach Parlor with Ronald Tinsman as he tried to process the fact that his daughter was in Hell! Did I leave my bedroom door open? Was my *closet* door open?

I ran, and behind me I could hear Marc bellowing, "And stay out, you passive-aggressive cow!"

My sentiments exactly.

CHAPTER
TWENTY-ONE

They didn't speak until they were in the car, ignoring the reporters who asked questions and wouldn't take "No comment" for an answer. Why were they bugging *her*? The story they wanted was squatting in that mansion. That's why Laura hadn't told the world who she was when she exposed the queen of the vampires. Her status—the Antichrist who'd been demoted—would have just confused the issue.

The media, who were supposed to be the weapon Laura wielded to take down her idiotic sinful vampire whore half sister, weren't the avenging sword she'd envisioned. They were more like a kid's toy lightsaber. Flashy and cool in the box, not worth much when you had to actually work with it.

When she'd thought this up and discussed it with her father, he'd kindly written her a sizable check to help with expenses. Waging a one-woman campaign against vampires was surprisingly pricey, and *she* didn't have an indulgent rich husband.

They assumed Betsy would deny-deny-deny, be exposed,

be humiliated, slink out of town, or, even better, be run out of town. And/or play dumb, something she more or less had a doctorate in. She hadn't expected Betsy to *own* the truth. She'd never dreamed the queen of the vampires would go on camera and tell the world: "Yeah, we're real. So?"

Laura had waited for the uproar.

There was no uproar.

Oh, sure, things had "gone viral" and "blown up." But those were just words; they didn't mean change, or progress, or a revolution. There were fewer and fewer reporters at the mansion every week, because social media stories had the shelf life of dairy products. The emerging narrative seemed to be, "Yeah, vampires are real, that was *last* month. What's going on now?" Plenty, she'd wanted to scream. Werewolves, too! Ghosts! Hell! Heaven!

Listen to me!

Betsy's world hadn't been torn asunder. Her world had barely wobbled. She hadn't been run out of town; she was making *new* friends. There hadn't been a vampire revolt; the vamps were pissed, some of them, but most were taking a wait-and-see attitude. She was too strong to challenge openly just now. Because of her *friends*.

So no vampire revolt. There hadn't been any kind of revolt. Laura had showed the world exactly what Betsy Taylor was and the world kept spinning.

Unacceptable.

But her followers had sources. An assembly of vampires was coming to town. The rumor was there would be an election, but animals didn't hold elections; the idea was laughable. No, they were coming to oust Betsy and her disgusting husband. They certainly weren't coming in from all over to say, "Hey, great work not heading any of this off and not standing up for us!"

And since they were no better than bloodsucking beasts, it would be bloody and violent and would take place in their seat of power, the beautiful mansion Betsy lived in and didn't appreciate. And the media would have a front-row seat.

Then she could get on with things. With no Betsy and Sinclair, dead or dethroned (and on nights like tonight, Laura didn't care which), with vampires exposed as the animals they were, Laura and her followers could get back to proving to the world that Hell was real, and God was real, and vampires were real . . . so who did good people expect to save them but the Lord? Crosses and holy water were their weapons, even better than the hellfire weapons Betsy had taken from her.

(She had no right!)

(But it's what you wanted . . . You were scared of turning into—)

(SHE HAD NO RIGHT!)

Now here was poor Ronald, a reporter who looked bland and boring but wasn't, a man in mourning who had been a combat engineer. A sapper, he'd said, like his father, who had accidentally blown himself up in Vietnam. "That's sweet," had been all Laura managed say to *that* heartwarming family tale.

Poor Ronald had taken a clock and something he called mechanical fusing and magnesium powder and a few other odds and ends and built a cunning incendiary device. Laura had gone into the mansion under the guise of rescuing her father

(not a guise—she would have killed him or the wolves would have, but I saved him!)

(he left town, gone forever, Betsy's fault again)

and planted the bomb in the one room where it wouldn't be found, while Ronald kept the vampires busy in the parlor. Talk about Cindy, she'd advised him. They'll all feel too guilty to walk out on you. I just need you to keep everyone in the room for a couple of minutes.

"Oh, excellent idea! Using their empathy and compassion to trick them," a random follower had added, and she'd frowned and banished him from her sight. Empathy? *Compassion?* If those were the qualities he thought vampires evinced, she couldn't have such a fool on her side, someone so easily tricked.

That's what Betsy did. She kept the monster tucked behind the sweet, silly face she showed the world. It fooled almost everyone. Never Laura, though, not even from the first.

If all else failed, the mansion would burn, and the world would watch.

It was only a last resort.

Really.

CHAPTER
TWENTY-TWO

"When did it all go wrong for us, Sinclair?" I asked on my knees while scrubbing puppy pee out of the carpet.

"There's no denying it has been a stressful month."

"When I died? When I died again? When I didn't set Laura's hair on fire the day we met? If I can pinpoint the exact moment things went to shit, I can . . ."

"Yes?"

"Go back in time and make everything so much worse." I sighed and wrung out the sponge over the bucket. If you had to sponge up pee, puppy pee wasn't the worst. Their tiny bladders filled (and, alas, emptied) so quickly, their urine barely had any color or odor. "The good news is, Fur and Burr seem really healthy. And really hydrated. The bad news is, everything else. And why am I down here scrubbing while you watch?"

"You know why."

It was true. But I was in a stubborn, pissy mood. "Enlighten me."

"When you wish to punish yourself, you give away shoes to the disadvantaged or take on your least favorite household chores."

That was also true.

"If I were to get down on the floor with you, it would accomplish nothing."

"Except to get pee out of the carpet faster."

"Yes, except for that."

"Dick." But there was no heat in it. He was right, the bum. I had earned this punishment by pee. The only thing for it was to scrub.

Technically I didn't have to do a thing. We could hire a platoon of housekeepers; we could hire a dozen people whose only job was pee patrol. And now and again we did get a housekeeper in here, sometimes human, sometimes a random vampire. But we all liked our privacy, and with so many people living here, and most of us neat by nature (or at least not slobs by nature), the workload wasn't out of hand. So we divvied up the chores based on individual specialty or preference.

Sinclair loved making homemade dog treats for the li'l monsters, so he was in charge of making sure they had sufficient food and water, kept their mudroom lair as clean as possible under the circumstances, walked them, and took them to the vet for checkups and shots. Oh man, the day the tech slipped with the needle

("Sorry, I'm new at this.")

and Burr let out a pained howl . . . let's just say it was fortunate I'd happened to come along that time. I had to pry Sinclair's fingers from around the guy's neck, then use vamp mojo to make the terrified tech forget the whole thing. And that was *after* I tackled Sinclair to the ground.

Marc was in charge of fixing things: loose hinges, sticky drawers, the occasional boo-boo, maintaining the cars ("If I

learn how to do oil changes, I can save us over a thousand—"
"Don't care."). He needed to keep his zombie brain active or
he'd start to deteriorate. As usual, the movies had the concept
right ("Braaaaaains!") but the details all wrong. Marc needed
brains, all right: his own. He no longer had to sleep, so he had
to fill that time with thinking and learning and doing. Recently he was a car guy. He'd mastered oil changes and was
moving on to . . . I dunno, spark plugs or something.

Tina was in charge of— Actually, I had no idea. At all. I
should probably spend a week just following her around: take
your vampire queen to work day.

Me? I was in charge of ice and groceries, and the care and
maintenance of my shoe collection, which, believe me, was
close to being a full-time job.

Also, now and again I got the urge to organize and clean.
(What? Just because I didn't like cleaning didn't mean I didn't
know how to do it.) Sometimes, and I don't know why this is,
sometimes manual labor just made me feel better.

Which is why I was on my knees on pee patrol.

"I hesitate to add to your burdens—"

"Oh God, what? *What?*"

"—but our out-of-town guest is nigh. She advises via a
rather curt e-mail that she'll be here tomorrow."

"Of course she does." Curt e-mail. Yep. Sounded about
right.

"It will be interesting."

"Yeah, that's definitely the word. I wasn't thinking of any
other word but interesting." I scrubbed harder, a beleaguered
vampire Cinderella.

"And an assembly of vampires would like a formal meeting
with us."

"Assembly?" That sounded official.

"Yes, as you'll recall"—I loved when he assumed I remembered stuff—"an assembly of vampires consists of several local citizens and out-of-state representatives, usually coming together to discuss matters of policy. Or policy changes." Gosh, had there been some sort of policy change? About vampires? Jeepers, I had no idea. "There will be about twenty, and they'll represent anywhere from two hundred to two thousand vampires."

"So they're like city councilmen."

"If that enables you to grasp the concept. Yes."

I wrinkled my nose at him. "Asshat. So what you're saying is a whole bunch of pissed-off vampires want to come over and yell at us."

"Yes."

"And maybe have an election?"

"Likely not. I suspect that idea was quashed rather quickly."

I had to laugh. "You sounded so smug when you said that. What, was Lawrence right? Nobody wanted to take me on? No one was up to putting on a cross and learning how to teleport to another dimension?"

"Precisely."

"*So* smug."

"I take pride in my wife and queen," he replied with simple dignity, and for a second I thought of my parents' ill-starred marriage. Had my dad ever taken pride in anything my mom did? If he had, I couldn't remember. Sinclair and I were in love, yes. And in lust, oh, you bet! But we also respected the shit out of each other, and that was the part that took years.

"Goody." I put my hands on the small of my back and stretched. Undead stamina was great, but scrubbing carpets was, apparently, a literal pain in the back whether you were alive or other. "Can't wait. Bring it on. I'm sure nothing terrible will come of it."

"Enough." Sinclair had put his phone away, stepped behind

me, and picked me up by the armpits. That shouldn't have been sexy, but it was—everything he did seemed effortless and sexy. He took my sponge and my bucket. Still so sexy! "I will dispose of these. Shower?"

"Yeah." And bed, pretty soon. The sun was coming.

"Start without me. We'll finish together."

See? Perfectly innocuous comment on mutual hygiene and I was *still* dizzy at the thought.

"Um. Okay." Good Lord. We'd been together how long, and I still got tongue-tied. Oooh. Tongue. The things that man could—

"Are you all right, my own? You look somewhat . . . glazed."

"Shut up, you know why I'm glazed." I started past him toward our bedroom to strip, then turned. "I'll tell you what, though—nobody's having a weirder day than we are. No chance."

TWENTY-THREE

It took Jennifer Palmer twenty minutes to move. Betsy
(she expects us to call her that!)
had brought her from Hell to downtown Cannon Falls, given her a perfunctory "Good luck!" pat on the back, and promptly vanished. That had been how Jennifer had realized she wasn't entirely jaded, because she still found everything about any encounter with Betsy to be surreal.

She still couldn't believe the twentysomething woman with absurdly high heels and virtually no short-term memory had defeated Satan. Twice. Then took over Hell and made all sorts of changes, and now here she was back in Cannon Falls, and fuck, none of this could be real, could it?

Could it?

Jennifer had been born and raised in the small river town about fifty miles south of Minneapolis, attended CF Elementary and graduated from CFHS, worked part-time at the bakery, and mourned the town's lack of movie theaters. She'd passed the army reserve recruiting station every day, conveniently placed in front of the high school. Her mom had cracked up every time she'd driven by. "They've really got all their bases covered, don't they? All that's missing is a community college in the back. But that's not your plan, is it, hon?"

Once, a thousand years ago, she'd wanted to graduate high school—she'd killed herself halfway through her senior year— and get a bachelor of science in nursing at the U of M, and then her RN. Her mother had thought this was an excellent plan ("There's a zillion baby boomers, and a lot of them are going to need medical care."), and had been putting money aside—not that there was much on an office manager's salary—since Jennifer was a first grader.

Mom.

Would she still be here? Jennifer was a third-generation CFer; her mom had been here all *her* life as well. Dad had vamoosed before Jennifer's sixth birthday and just as well. Even now, she associated the stink of Budweiser with her father. Yes, there was every chance her mother was still here. But Jennifer couldn't stand on the corner of Mill and Fourth and ponder. She had to find out.

That was part of it. Her parole—cripes, she could *still* hardly believe it. Thirty-one years of damnation and then . . . back in Cannon Falls in the literal blink of an eye, and with a mission, no less. She had to find those she'd wronged, however she could, and make amends, however she could. If she did those things, she could live out the rest of her life in the real world.

(Doing what? And with whom? I still look like I'm in high school . . . Should I go to college? I didn't even finish high school. Maybe I should do whatever women who look seventeen but are really almost fifty do. What would that be, exactly?)

Never mind, focus, stay focused. Way too early to think about the next fifty years. Worry about the next fifty hours.

If she failed, she went back to Hell. To, she presumed, more damnation. And even worse: the new devil's fury. Jennifer wasn't so dumb as to miss the fact that she was the test case. How she handled this would have a lot to do with whether or not more souls would be able to leave. Hell would be even *more* unpleasant if she had to face souls who wouldn't be able to leave because she'd screwed up.

So: the house she'd grown up in was up the hill on Mill Street, not more than six blocks from here. Time to get hoofing.

Oh God. Tammy used to say that. Jennifer shivered and took a step forward—and jerked back when a car that looked like a big blue electric shaver nearly clipped her as it went through the intersection. The driver—no one she recognized—could be seen visibly rolling his eyes as he blipped his horn at her in rebuke.

Stupid, stupid, stupid. She was mortal again. She could be hurt. She could be killed. Injuries wouldn't heal overnight so she could be hurt all over again the next day. And if she got killed on parole, she seriously doubted her chances of making it to Heaven.

Also, cars looked strange now. Like they could probably fly, all sleek and rounded curves. Even the horns sounded different.

She took care to check for traffic this time—it was a little heavier than when she'd last been here, and the stop sign was now a stoplight, which was why she'd nearly gotten smeared into the crosswalk. She hurried across the street, feeling exposed and vulnerable and alive.

Alive.

Cannon Falls looked mostly the same, for all it had been thirty-one years. There was another stoplight, yes, she'd finally noticed that, thank you very much. And a McDonald's. Brewster's was still there, and the bakery, though the clinic had moved. And there was a winery, of all things. Right downtown. No vineyard, but a winery.

Strange.

Even stranger, Jennifer checked a store window and confirmed that, yes, she looked the same, looked exactly as she had the day she'd chased a bottle of Valium with a fifth of vodka. In those dark pre-*Wikipedia* days, she'd had to go to the library—the one not even a block away from where she was standing, in fact—to do her research. She'd found articles explaining benzos and booze were painless and even caused euphoria as you nodded off, but that had been a lie.

Not about the pain—the articles had been right about that. But euphoria? No, she'd definitely been in a euphoria-free zone. In fact, she'd been uneasy throughout, struggling not to vomit—she'd had very little experience with booze; the one good thing her father had left her was an aversion to alcohol. Toward the end, she'd started to think that perhaps she was being hasty. The fire was an accident. She hadn't meant any harm. Maybe it wasnnnnnn't

tooooooooooooo

laaaaaaaaaate.

She woke up in Hell.

Up, up, up the hill, and now she was glad for the coat and boots Betsy had given her. She'd looked Jennifer up and down in her office, said, "Well, jeez, you can't atone if you've got frostbite; talk about setting you up to fail!" and just like that, Jennifer had a new coat, gloves, and boots over her outfit of a Madonna T-shirt and acid-washed jeans. It was technically spring, but: Minnesota spring. So she was glad for the layers.

The best part about Betsy making things appear out of nowhere was how surprised she looked each time. There was already a betting pool in Hell over when that would stop. Or if it would stop. Jennifer had declined to participate, but if she'd taken a date it would have been at least ten years in the future. Betsy struck her as the type who took a while to get used to new things. Like, a *long* while. And would complain the whole time she was adjusting. Constantly.

But who was she to judge? Having been judged, Jennifer was careful to avoid any appearance of siding with any judgments. No better way to piss off fellow Hell residents than by implying (a) they deserved to be there, and/or (b) if anything, they hadn't been judged harshly enough.

She had, though ironically it could be argued the judgment and punishment she'd handed down to herself

(death penalty)

were worse than anything the devil had cooked up

(food court duty).

Tammy's lungs had been crisped. She hadn't died of smoke inhalation, but from trying to breathe the superheated air. Jennifer had discussed her sins

(in Hell, even confession is seriously screwed)

with a man who'd been an arson investigator in life (and who liked to spend his spare time crisping the neighborhood cats in his broiler). He'd happily explained that the air in a house fire can reach eleven hundred degrees Fahrenheit. Just one breath of that air could kill someone. Then he'd pinned her down and masturbated onto her stomach, which wasn't important to the story except to say that at that point, Jennifer could still be shocked by the things people did in Hell as a matter of course.

Tammy'd had to take more than one breath while she waited for Jennifer to bring help. And she'd had to wait a long time, struggling to breathe air getting progressively hotter with every second.

Thinking about her best friend's last moments of terror and agony—and she had, almost obsessively, for decades—had been worse than anything Hell could put her through.

The only thing worse would be admitting what she'd done. Parole, Jennifer feared, was just another way to torment the damned. And she didn't know what was more frightening: if Betsy knew that . . . or if she had no idea.

CHAPTER
TWENTY-FOUR

If the speech team had made state, Tammy might have lived to be a grandmother. Unfortunately, they got stomped. For want of a nail, a kingdom was lost.

So they were home that weekend. Tammy's parents had gone to Vegas but didn't mind if Jennifer came for a sleepover, since she was a notorious virgin who didn't drink. "Isn't it great how usually when a father abandons his family it screws up the kid, but that didn't happen in your case?" Tammy's mom had burbled on more than one occasion. "I mean, you really learned something!" *Oh yes, definitely, my dad leaving was a wonderful learning experience and worked out great for us in the short* and *long run. So, 'bye.*

A notorious virgin, yes, but not because of abandonment issues. She was saving herself. For Lars.

He'd moved to Cannon seven months ago and his name should have been stupid. A blond, blue-eyed guy named Lars

Gundersson who lived in Minnesota and loved lutefisk?[29] It sounded like what someone from Hollywood thought a typical Minnesotan would be like.

Not only was Lars all those things and more; he was popular! She was sure with a name like Lars he'd be doomed to marching band, but nope. Because he was also beautiful and athletic, played b-ball and football and had the build of a running back: fleet and strong.

Tammy had invited him over to her house on Jennifer's behalf. So Lars was coming over. Tonight. And he could stay as long as he—and she—wanted. Tonight! Tammy, giggling, offered the use of her parents' room.

"Whoa," Jennifer had said, putting her hands out as if to physically rein in Tammy's enthusiasm as a matchmaker/pimp. "We're not even going together. We haven't even been out. He only just broke up with Amy last month."

"So? You can just snuggle."

Well. That sounded like a plan and a half.

So she went over early and Lars called and said *he* was coming over early, so she and Tammy did the teenage girl squealing/yelling thing

(*"OhmyGodohmyGodohmyGod!"*)

and Jennifer went around and lit candles in every room, then went to the basement and stoked up the woodburning furnace, something she'd done in that house at least a dozen times over the years. She'd been so excited

(*he said he was biking that means he'll be here in ten minutes*)

she hadn't latched the door after tossing in several logs, and some coals had spilled out onto the floor. In her panic

---

[29] Anyone who loves lutefisk might be a sociopath. Just sayin'.

(where's the shovel WHERE'S THE SHOVEL gotta get these picked up oh shit it's catching)

she'd made it worse. And Tammy's folks kept five cords of nice dry wood right there in the basement where it was convenient. Tammy's dad hated scrounging around outside for wood, even if it was stacked neatly behind the garage.

Even now, she couldn't believe how fast it had gone up. Masturbating Arson Investigator Guy told her that the time between the fire light point and total engulfment of the structure was two minutes.

She knew. She saw.

She hadn't even tried to help her friend. Well, she had, but not very hard. It was just—smoke was everywhere and it was so *fast* and she had to get out so she started up the basement stairs and couldn't get past the fourth step

(I thought smoke was supposed to rise can't see I can't see can't BREATHE)

and finally she had to turn and stumble through the opposite hallway to get out via the garage door and when she opened the double doors a ton of oxygen-rich air rushed in, which fed the fire, and two minutes? If anything, it hadn't even taken *that* long.

Of course Lars saw the smoke and rushed in and tried to help them. As she was leaving by the garage, he was running through the front door, for all the good it did Tammy, or him. They never saw each other.

The police had been right behind the fire trucks.

They thought it was on purpose. Apparently, teenage boys and fires went hand in hand sometimes, and the investigators decided Lars had a crush on Tammy—his call to her house just before the fire looked bad—and set the fire so he could be a hero and rescue her. This sounded exquisitely stupid to Jennifer, but she was in no position to argue.

Incredibly, she was safe, and not just from immolation. She wasn't supposed to be at Tammy's until after supper; no one knew she'd been in the house that afternoon. And Lars didn't know about her crush; he'd thought he was just going over to hang. Everyone thought he was going over to have sex with Tammy, because parents forgot that kids almost never turned down invites to parent-free houses. It could be someone you didn't even *like* and you'd still go. Lack of supervision was like any drug: once you got a taste, you always wanted more.

The sympathy. That was the worst part. Everyone in town knew she'd loved Tammy, that they'd been best friends since sixth grade. She got almost as many thoughtfully sympathetic looks as Tammy's folks did. Hell, Tammy's parents tried to comfort her: "Thank God you weren't there; you could have died, too!"

Then, the indictment, and she said nothing.

The trial. She said nothing.

Guilty of felony arson and involuntary manslaughter. Tried as an adult, of course—why not? It was a heinous crime, one that bought him twenty years. *'Bye, Lars. I loved almost going out with you.*

She said nothing. She said nothing. She said nothing. She was too busy researching methods of suicide at the library.

CHAPTER
TWENTY-FIVE

"This might be the dumbest thing we've ever done," I announced.

"Ha!" Marc stuck a finger in my face, which was just as annoying as you'd think it would be. "You've got nothing to back that up and you know it. This isn't even *close* to the dumbest thing we've ever done."

"The most annoying, then," I countered. I was tired of holding the bag, so I dropped it on the dock at my feet. "Or idiotic."

"Well, you might have something there."

"Children," Sinclair murmured. Usually he'd be glued to his phone, but we were outdoors and it was a sunny spring day, so not this time.

It was still super cute to see Sinclair luxuriating in sunshine. Most vampires burst into a cloud of fanged, wailing ash if exposed to sunlight, and for decades Sinclair had to work to avoid that sad, ashy fate. But the devil owed me a favor, so I asked her to fix it so he could bear sunlight, handle holy water, et cetera. She knew she owed me for killing her (long story[30]), and granted my wish, because nothing about my afterlife makes any sense at all.

This, as anyone could have foreseen, led to lots of alfresco sex (Between Sinclair and me. Not the devil and me. Obviously.) and Sinclair joining the church choir. It also led to Sinclair taking Fur and Burr outside for walks about seventeen or eighteen times a day.

Now he had his hands stuffed into the pockets of his black greatcoat, head tilted back so he could close his eyes and turn his face up and just soak in the sunshine like a sexy sponge. He occasionally hummed and rocked back and forth on his feet because now and again he was the cutest thing ever.

"Am I the only one who thinks it's weird that we haven't even talked about the dock or the tunnel in years—"

"*We* means you, Betsy. Just you."

"—and now we're in the tunnel twice in twenty-four hours?"

"Yep. You're the only one."

"Also, we've got an Assembly of vampires about to descend on us in all their fang-gnashing rage."

"Are you pronouncing *assembly* like it's capitalized on purpose?"

"Yes. Murder of crows. Pack of wolves. Flock of geese. Assembly of vampires."

"Asshat of vampires," Marc suggested, and I giggled like a kid—couldn't help it.

"Nice to see you lighten up, Betsy. You've been pretty grim lately. Well, grim for you."

"Well, weird shit is happening. More so than usual, even.

---

[30] *Undead and Unstable.*

Perfect example: we're hanging out on a dock waiting for a mermaid to swim up and say howdy."

Sinclair glanced at me. "Undersea Folk, my queen."

"Sometimes she's got legs; sometimes she's half fish." At all times, she's a grump. "Mermaid."

"You can't use that word!" Marc faux snapped. "That's *their* word!"

"Oh my God."

Hours. Hours we'd been waiting on a dock in the chill when I could be running Hell or doing something to ruin Laura's life or sitting for another disastrous TV interview or reading chapter eight of *Smoothie Nation*: "All Things Citrus."

It's been eleven minutes, my own.

"Why are you talking like everyone doesn't carry clocks?" I took out my phone and waved it at him.

"Oh, just another of my idiosyncrasies. But you need fret no longer, as Dr. Bimm approaches."

"No."

"Beg pardon?"

"That's not Fred Bimm." I pointed. "That is an angry coconut that has been steadily bobbing closer because of the current and not under its own power. And the reason it's a coconut and not our out-of-town guest is because there's no way in hell someone is swimming in the Mississippi River in March. There's also no way she's going to dog-paddle right up to this dock and either flop out of the Big Muddy on her own like a fish deciding to evolve or wait for us to haul her out like the world's biggest smallmouth bass."

"Now, there's a mental image," Marc said, equal parts disapproving and impressed. "A couple of them."

"Indeed."

"Although"—I nudged the bulging bag at my feet—"that

would explain why the text she sent to let us know she'd arrived consisted of 'bring towels.'"

"Unreal," Marc breathed, watching the coconut. Then: "My God. I'm seeing it and I don't believe it. That is definitely a person and she is definitely swimming this way. And she doesn't appear to be in any sort of stress. Also she appears to be naked, because why the heck not?"

And a shameless exhibitionist on top of everything else! Mermaids: nature's hussies.

She can hardly be expected to swim with a tail while fully clothed, Sinclair pointed out, which was just annoying.

I take issue with that. I absolutely can expect her to take a cab from the airport and not swim UP THE DAMNED RIVER LIKE AN UTTER WEIRDO.

"Where d'you think she went in?" Marc speculated, never taking his gaze from the angry coconut moving closer. "What, she took a cab from the airport to the Highway 5 bridge, stripped, and just dove in? 'Here's the fare, keep the change, see ya.'"

Actually, yes. I can see her doing exactly that. Fred wasn't much for social conventions. Or long cab rides.

The coconut raised a pale arm and waved, so yeah, probably not a coconut, probably Fredrika Bimm waving at us and swimming closer. I'd seen her in action before, and I didn't think I'd ever get used to how quickly her kind could move through water. I mean, you knew intellectually they were like sharks, but seeing it was always startling. And, to be honest, a little frightening.

Then she was at the dock reaching up, and Sinclair courteously bent, took her hand, and hauled her out of the river in one swift, easy motion. She had a waterproof bag on a string slung around her neck and was otherwise totally naked. Not even a ponytail holder in her hair.

"Welcome to St. Paul, Dr. Bimm." Once both her feet were on the dock, Sinclair politely turned his back. Which was dumb. Not only had we both seen her naked before, Bimm didn't give a shit about stuff like that. Because, again: nature's exhibitionists.

"Thanks, Eric. And it's Fred." She accepted one of our giant towels and started drying off. And because she was a huge show-off, she wasn't even shivering. Totally pretending it wasn't cold just to spite me.

"Oh my God you're real I can't believe it your tail just disappeared retracted whatever and how are you not deep in the throes of hypothermia?" Marc rushed out in one breath. "Please don't be offended I'm not staring because I'm a perv actually I'm gay so you don't have to worry about me creeping on you my curiosity is strictly professional I used to be a doctor and how did you do that? Any of that? How? Dr. Bimm? Hi?"

"I don't care if you look." But she cracked a smile, and who could blame her? Fascinated Marc was fun Marc. "And I'm biologically engineered to withstand extremes of temperature as well as water pressure, so. That's why I'm not dead. Or tired. Or frozen."

"It is *so* nice to meet you! Can you stay until Christmas?"

Don't even joke about that! My thought was so strong and horrified, Sinclair had to fake a cough to hide his chuckle.

Fred Bimm had unlooped the bag from around her neck and was rooting through it while smirking, because she was big on multitasking. "Hear that, Betsy? Your nice friend would like me to stay with you for nine months. Doesn't that sound grand?"

I made a sound. Some sound. It wasn't a word, unless "Ggrrbbl" meant something. Meanwhile Fred had towel-dried her hair and wrapped a towel around her head, spa-style, then used the other towel to rub herself dry.

The hair on her head was deepest, darkest auburn (from a box, I knew), and her pubic hair (which—ahem—could have used a trim) was green. Apparently Fred's natural hair color was green. Or blue, depending on whether you were in love with her or not. I'm not making this up, by the way.[31] That's her deal: hair color dictated by love, or the absence of same.

While I pondered the riddle of her pubes, Fred stepped into black hipster underwear, pulled on white athletic socks and a pair of battered jeans, and shrugged into a New England Aquarium sweatshirt. No bra, BTW. And no wonder—she didn't need it. Neither did I, but only because I'd died with perky boobs; the twins would be thirty forever. Fred had tried to explain about gravity and water and pressure and centers of gravity, blah-blah . . . bottom line, mermaids had naturally perky boobs, because it wasn't enough to be super strong and fast and blessed with unfathomable stamina, I guess; they also had to hog all the good boobs.

She finished by stepping into and tying sneakers that looked like they'd rolled off the assembly line the day Kennedy was shot.

"Ggrrbbl." I'd forgotten about her horrible taste in clothes. The first time I saw her she was wearing flip-flops. And she denied it was punishment for losing a bet, which, let's be honest, had to be a lie.

"Thanks for offering to come."

"Thanks for taking me up on it." Fully clothed save for a heavy jacket—which she clearly didn't need—she balled up her now-empty bag and stuck it in her pocket. I saw she'd also brought a small battered purse, probably to hold cash and ID. "I wasn't sure you would. We got off to a bit of a rocky start."

---

[31] She's not. You can catch Fred's backstory in *Sleeping with the Fishes*.

"Still holding a grudge, huh?" I found out the hard way that vampire mojo didn't hold mermaids very long. Fred had expressed her severe displeasure by hitting me hard enough to knock me out of my Alice + Olivia Devon floral pumps, then throwing me across the room, and that had been just the warm-up. What can I say? She got my attention. "How many times should I apologize?"

"The last time was the magic number," she conceded. "I'm here, aren't I? And I'll bet the Wyndhams preceded me by . . . I'm going to guess twenty-four hours."

Have I mentioned Fred's a bright cookie? I didn't even know she knew the Wyndhams existed—I sure hadn't told her—and how could she guess they were in town? She was a little like Sherlock . . . stuff nobody else noticed was like a road flare to her.

"I saw you on the cover of *Time* and I know this is irrelevant but you're much prettier in person." This from Marc, who was still fangirling all over the place. *My God, man, where is your dignity?* Or was I just jealous? He used to fangirl all over *me.* I had pretended it was annoying and oh my God, he was still burbling away. "They had a picture of your mom, too, in the article—you don't look much like her so I guess you take after your dad? He was full-blooded USF, right? I'm sorry, I'm babbling." Babbling, burbling. Tomato, toe-mah-toe.

He sure was. But it was good that he said what he did, because it reminded me that Fred Bimm was a busy woman. On top of her genius marine biologist duties, whatever those were, and giving talks at aquariums all over the world, and talking all things Undersea Folk on the news (CNN *loved* Fred), she was the liaison between the Undersea Folk and, er, all of humanity, apparently. Because as Marc had reminded me, her mom was human, and her late father had been all merman. Fred was half 'n' half, though she preferred the term—

"I prefer the term *hybrid*."

Bottom line: she had stuff to get done. But she'd come to town anyway. That counted for a lot with me. Especially since if our positions were reversed, I don't know that I would have reached out and offered help. Not until I knew her a bit better.

Which made me wonder: what did Fred need from me? Probably nothing right now. So: what did Fred think she might need from me in the future?

No idea.

I whined about a lot of things in general, and (today) Dr. Bimm in particular, but if I have to be honest, I will always cut that bitch some slack because a slave trader used his ill-gotten gains to build a meeting hall in 1743, which resulted in the best food court ever: the Nathanial Hall Marketplace.[32]

That place. I can't even tell you. So many food choices. It smelled like your grandma's kitchen had a baby with Christmas. And they had not one, not two, but three smoothie bars. *Three*. Monkey Bar. Cocobeet. The Juicery. The best trinity ever.

The marketplace alone was worth the trip, which was a good thing since we'd almost died. The whole thing turned out to be super dangerous, not least because that was how I found out Fred Bimm didn't like hippies. Also, a wheelchair-bound bad guy tried to kill a bunch of people, but that was after Fred tried to kill me. Fun weekend![33]

"We have a car waiting, if you would come with us? Your room has been made ready if you'd like to"—a pause so teeny I was probably the only one who caught it—"freshen up."

---

[32] It's actually called Faneuil Hall. I'm embarrassed to tell you how long I lived in Boston before I realized that. It was more than a year. That's how dim I am.

[33] Stressful, but in a good way. Except for the attempted mass murder. *Undead and Underwater*.

Translation: wash some of the mud and crud from your leisurely spring swim through the Mississippi out of your hair and other, um, places.

Fred's smirk just got wider. "That bad, huh?"

"Not really," I replied, because Sinclair was too polite. "I told you when we met, you guys don't smell bad to vampires. Just different. But you don't have to shower. If you don't mind smelling like mud, we don't."

"Well, then, lead on." She fell into step behind Sinclair as he climbed the bank leading to the side road. Because—yay!—we weren't taking the tunnel home. I'd decided a tunnel-free day was a good day.

Dr. Bimm probably wasn't out to get us, but that didn't mean we should make it easy for her if she—if any merjerks—were.

TWENTY-SIX

Exactly the same. The house Jennifer had grown up in, and killed herself in, was unchanged. Even the Christmas lights were still there (her mother kept them up year-round).

The place had been painted every five or six years, she knew, or it would have looked a lot worse: white two-story house, green shutters and trim. Built in 1940, and when Jennifer lived there she and her mom had the run of the downstairs and rented out the upstairs, which had a separate kitchen, bathroom, and entrance.

The large yard—their house was on a corner lot—was still pretty dead; it'd be another month before everything was green. She didn't recognize the car in the driveway, which was still gravel. And why *was* there a car in the driveway? It was Thursday afternoon. Why was Mom . . . ?

Stupid. She was retired, of course. Mom would be in her midsixties now.

Stop staring. Get moving.

She got moving: walked up the sidewalk, opened the porch

door, and was instantly soothed by the sight of lawn chairs and a small table stacked for winter at the far end of the porch. The same chest freezer was still right by the door, no doubt stuffed with venison and trout and beef and pork and pudding pops and Klondike bars. They still made Klondike bars, right? Yes. They'd been her mom's favorite when she'd been a kid; they both loved them. Klondike bars were eternal. She didn't even have to look. She knew they'd be in there. No need to pause to check. She could keep going right into the house, see if the door off the porch still opened into the living room.

She wasn't stalling. She was . . . reassuring herself. Not that there was any need for reassurance. Because they still made Klondike bars. Sure they did.

She popped open the freezer door and gasped. S'Mores Klondike Bars! Cookie Dough Swirl Klondike Bars! Oreo Klondike Bars! Rocky Road! Double Chocolate! Reese's! Oh, what a glorious world the future was!

She closed the freezer—gently; her mom hated it when Jennifer would drop the lid with a bang that could be heard all through the house—then opened the front door and walked in, and cursed herself pretty much immediately.

Should have knocked. *Stop acting like you belong here.* Then: *at least Cannon Falls is still a town where people don't lock their doors 24/7.* Rediscovering that was likely to be the best part of parole. And the many, many varieties of Klondike bars.

She heard steps in the kitchen and a familiar voice. A little rougher, but undoubtedly her mother. "Hello? Whoever you are, I have a ferocious guard dog I keep next to a loaded shotgun and they're both here in the kitchen with me, so if you're up to no good, prepare to embrace your violent death."

She made a sound that was new to her, sort of a sob turned into a laugh, or vice versa. Mom's habits hadn't changed. Jennifer hurried through the living room as her mother came through the kitchen and they caught sight of each other at the same time.

She felt dizzy and realized she'd been holding her breath. *I forgot what being short of breath felt like! Breathe, moron. The one thing that would make all of this worse is if you come back from the dead, then pass out at her feet.* "Mom? I know this is going to—"

"Oh my God!"

"—seem incredible, like a dream—"

"Jennifer Bear!"

"—but I promise it's—" Jennifer Bear, God, how could she have forgotten? *Don't cry. Don't cry.* "—really happening."

Her mother took a step, stumbled, pitched to the floor. Jennifer lunged and missed, so they both collapsed in a heap together on the faded kitchen tile. She could feel her mother's hands on her, touching her hair, her face.

"You're real! You're warm and—and here! You—oh Lord, I can't believe it, I can't *believe* it. This is really happening, this is actually taking place in our house right now and you're back, how did you come back? Where have you been, oh my God, forgive me, forgive me, please, please say you forgive me."

"What?" She jerked back, grabbed her mother's wrists. "No, Mom, you've got it wrong, I'm the one who—"

"You couldn't tell me. You were in the worst trouble of your life and you couldn't come to me." Her mom had put on about ten pounds but smelled the same: Crabtree & Evelyn's Summer Hill perfume, and Cheer laundry detergent. "I did something, said something, to make you think death was the better option. I'm so sorry, Bear. Please, whatever it was, however I screwed you up, I swear it wasn't out of malice, I—"

"*No.*" Jennifer climbed to her feet, helped her mother off the floor, marched her into the living room, gently pushed her into the easy chair. Hmm, that was new. The old one had been black. This one was navy blue. And her mom preferred slacks to skirts these days.

She knelt before her, took the older woman's hands. Oh. *Her hands. They got older, too.* She looked up into small, dear, dark eyes overflowing with tears. "I was selfish, and cowardly. I let them punish Lars for what I did to Tammy. I didn't say a word when they sent him to Stillwater. I couldn't bear to tell you, but that was *my* failing, not yours. It was entirely on me and not even a little bit on you. Please forgive me."

Her mother's grip tightened. "You didn't leave a note."

"No." The coup de grace of her cowardly act: she knew she wouldn't be around to face the consequences of her actions and *still* couldn't admit what she'd done, even in a suicide note. "No, too chickenshit, even at the end."

"I knew. Not before. After. There was only one reason you would have . . . hurt yourself like that. Killed yourself." Her mother's grip hurt, felt like fleshy clamps grinding the frail bones of her fingers together. Jennifer didn't say a word. "I spent the next few years blaming myself for not seeing—"

"No, Mom. You did nothing wrong. Nothing."

"I—I can't believe you're here."

Tell me about it. She shrugged and managed a smile.

"Are you a vampire?"

Her smile dropped away. "What? No." Was her mother slipping into shock? "What in the world made you ask that?"

"They're real, I guess. Vampires. It's been all over the news the last few weeks. When I saw you standing there, looking exactly the way you looked on that last day, that was my first thought."

"Well, I knew vampires were real, but no, I'm not one." Was this a good time to mention that the queen of the vampires was running Hell, and Jennifer was on a first-name basis with her? No, her mother had never been impressed with name-dropping.

"Then where have you been all these years?"

"In Hell," she replied without thinking, and her mom's grip, which had been loosening, tightened, *clamped* down on hers again. "Youch!"

"Hell's *real*?"

"Well, yes. You sound surprised. You're the one who made me go to Sunday school," she teased. "Sunday school, Easter, and Christmas: holiday Christians, that was our th— Oh. Oh, don't. Mom. Don't cry."

"Did—did they hurt you?"

Oboy. Jennifer had thought this would be difficult, but as happened so often, the reality was much worse. How to explain Hell to someone who had never been there? "No, not really," she said gently. "It's not brimstone or lakes of fire." Unless you needed it to be. "It wasn't my fate to be physically tortured. Mostly I was bored and the only thing I could do was think about why I was in Hell. Thirty-one years of that was worse than torture, I think."

"I don't understand."

"It was more boring and frustrating than anything else— my last job was working in a food court."

"But you hate food courts! Ever since you were little and gulped that Orange Julius too fast and threw up all over yourself in public."

Jennifer smiled. "Guess *where* in the food court."

Her mother blinked and swiped at her eyes. "You worked at an Orange Julius?"

"For years." Or a few weeks. Time was strange down there. But this was better, much better . . . her mom was still crying but was now trying to smile, and Jennifer would take a watery half smile over sobs. "So gross."

"But, Bear, why are you here? Are you supposed to take me to Hell? Is it my time?"

"*What?*" She jerked back so hard she almost fell on her ass. "No! Christ, of course not, oh my *God!*"

"Language," Mom snapped, then clapped a hand over her mouth. When she lowered her hands, she had a sheepish expression on her face. "Sorry. You still look like my girl—but you're forty-eight now." Of course her mother would know her real age, probably to the day. "Old enough to decide when it's appropriate to blaspheme."

"Don't worry about it. And—I can't emphasize this enough—I'm not here to take you to Hell like some kind of morbid Angel of Death. Gross."

"Then why are you here, Bear? Here, sit up here with me." They moved to the couch, which was fine with Jennifer. Her mother couldn't stop touching her, patting her back, holding her hand, and that was fine, too.

"It's a long story, but the quickie version is, Hell is starting a parole program. The new devil—"

"Oh, my."

"—yes, it's complicated, but there's a new boss, and she's trying—"

"She?"

"—yes, there's never been a glass ceiling in Hell—anyway, she's instituting parole for some of us. I'm the test case. She let me come back to confess my sins and make amends."

"So you're back for good. You're . . . alive again?" She squeezed her hands again. "You feel alive."

"Yes. But, Mom, I have to warn you . . ." Ow! Her mom might be a retired office worker quietly living in a small Minnesota town, but she still had quite a grip. ". . . if I screw up, if I can't make it right, I go back to the food court."

"In Hell."

"In Hell." She took a breath. "Mom, where's Lars? I know he was sentenced to—"

"They let him out after twelve years, Bear."

"Okay." That was something. At least he hadn't done the whole twenty. "Do you know where he is?"

Mom nodded and wiped her eyes again. "After his dad died, he moved into their old house."

"So out by the fairgrounds?"

She shook her head. Mom was still a brunette, which was kind of cute. "They moved after the—you know. The trial. They had to, because of all the—anyway, they ended up moving to Burnsville, and when they died a few years ago, Lars inherited the house. I can dig up the address for you."

"Okay. And Tammy's parents? I have to find them and explain . . . No?" Her mother was slowly shaking her head. "Oh. They're dead, aren't they?"

"Yes. She died of cancer about ten years ago, and he went in a car accident a year later."

She was relieved; how was that for cowardly? "Okay. I can't do anything for them, but I still have to go to Lars. Can I borrow the car?"

Mom giggled, which was understandable. It was giggle or scream. "I think your license might have expired."

"That's the least of my problems." But she saw the humor in it, too, and smiled. "I'll be careful, I promise. And what's this?" She reached up and tugged softly on a hank of her mother's hair. "My, my, still a brunette, hmm? If I checked your bathroom I wouldn't find any L'Oréal products, would I?"

"Old women are allowed their vanities," she said with the acerbic tone Jennifer well remembered.

"You're not old," she lied. She tapped her mother's knee. "Keys, Mom? Please?"

"You have to go right now?"

"Yes, I have to go right now. It's what she let me come back for. I can't let her down."

"The—the new devil?"

"Yes."

Her mom had gotten up, gone to her purse, rooted around. "You don't sound . . . afraid of her, exactly."

There really wasn't a word that described how she felt about Betsy. "I'm done letting people down," was all she said, but it seemed, by some miracle, that her mother understood.

"How will we explain this? How do we explain you? If the new devil lets you stay? What would we say to people?"

"I can't think about that now." Truth. Because those problems, in the face of what she had to do to earn her freedom, didn't really sound like problems. Golly, what will the neighbors say? *Who gives a damn?*

But facing Lars? Confessing? Bracing herself for whatever came afterward?

What if he hurts me? Hits me, beats me up?

Well. What if he does?

Her mom, though. She was thinking about the things she could help with, the way she always did. "You'll need a new social security card," she was muttering, and Jennifer knew by her expression that she was already making lists in her head. "Your old one wouldn't work, obviously. If you looked your age—your *real* age—we could say it was all a mistake, that you faked your suicide and, I don't know, fled the country but now you're back because reasons."

"Because reasons?" What the hell did that mean?

"Something the kids say. If that was the case, you could use all your old IDs and just get a new driver's license . . . but you don't look your age." Her mother reached out, tucked a hank of hair behind Jennifer's ear. "My Bear. Pretty as the day you d—as when you were a girl." She paused. "We could move.

Get a new start somewhere. Or stay put and just say you're a grandniece or something. My sister's daughter's girl."

"You don't have a sister," Jennifer felt compelled to point out.

"Oh, who cares? Then we can put any comments on your looks down to simple family resemblance."

"Mom, I have to focus on you and Lars. I'll worry about making a new life here *if* I'm allowed to stay."

"And if you're not?"

"Then it was still worth it, if only to see you again, and tell you how sorry I am." Mom looked like she smelled something awful, which was what her face did when she was about to burst into tears. Jennifer rushed to head off more tears. "So find Lars' address and then let's dig up a paper and pencil so I can write down the directions."

That made her mom laugh, for some reason. "Oh, honey. You're going to love MapQuest."

"What?"

"Come with me to the office . . . I've got things to show you."

Ten minutes later, Jennifer was carefully pulling out of her mother's driveway. Driving her mom's new car, a burgundy Ford Fusion, was like piloting the space shuttle. And it was a hybrid! Which meant it ran on gas *and* electricity. Unreal! And MapQuest! Wow.

Mom had made her a sandwich and insisted Jennifer take it with her for some reason. It was on the passenger seat beside the printout of directions to Lars' house. Her mom had tried to give Jennifer her cell phone, but Jennifer politely refused. That thing *also* looked like some futuristic space mechanism to her uneducated eyes.

She resolved not to eat the food. Perhaps one of Betty Palmer's world-famous club sandwiches would at least get her in Lars' front door. Stranger things had happened. That very day, in fact.

CHAPTER
TWENTY-SEVEN

"I'm not saying you don't have any problems, obviously you do, and I'm not just talking about the way you dress—"

"How could I have forgotten your essential vacuous nature?"

"—I'm just saying I've got a buttload of problems, too! My life has never been easy." Okay. Exaggeration. Looking back, pre-death, the Ant was my biggest problem and, ironically, I saw a lot more of her now that we both hung out in Hell. And even when *Time* and *Newsweek* and MSNBC and the *Pioneer Press* were speculating about vampires, I still had a husband I adored and lived in a mansion with the coolest people ever.

But we'd barely gotten in the house before Fred was grouching about how my problems were making her life difficult. When, if anything, my problems were making *my* life difficult. "I don't expect you to get it, by the way." Why was I in such an ugly mood? Why was I picking a fight? Other than the fact that Fred was smarter than me, handling infamy better than me, and about a zillion times more respected than me? "I'm just saying things aren't all sunshine all the time around here."

Fred's eyes rolled so hard, she could probably see her big fat brain. Wow. Being on the receiving end of an epic eye roll was kind of annoying.

"Do tell me about your insurmountable stack of first-world problems."

"My father divorced my mom for the worst person in the world. I say that totally without hyperbole."[34]

"I was raised by hippies."

"I had to get nibbled on by feral vampires."

"I walked in on the hippies having sex."

"Then I woke up dead."

"I can only swim with my tail, never my legs."

"I had to kill a Big Bad who was a thousand years older than me."

"I had to put down a revolt virtually single-handedly."

Damn. Impressive. "Yeah, well. I'm having dad issues."

"My father led that revolt, the end result of which was we fought to the death. And since you've likely noticed I'm not dead, you can probably deduce how that turned out."

". . . I think we should be best friends forever and ever."

Then: the impossible of impossibles. Dr. Fredrika Bimm burst out laughing. "Ah," she said when she finally stopped chortling like a hyena. "Now I remember why I don't completely loathe you."

"Well, good." I'd take what I could get. And who knew? Maybe she had some dad-killing tips I could use.

I couldn't believe I just thought that.

---

[34] It's true. The Ant is literally the worst. And I say that in a book stuffed with plotters, killers, and devils.

Progress, my own. You must know that you'll likely have to kill him. Soon.

Stay out of my head, Sinclair. That was just for me.

If you would merely allow me to kill him, everything would—

Not better! Oh my God!

"Hi, Dr. Bimm," Jessica said, and where the hell did she come from? "I'm Jessica; I used to live here."

"Fredrika Bimm." They shook.

"Yeah, I know. Thanks for coming to help us." *Us.* Fred was hot shit, no doubt, and there were probably more Undersea Folk than vampires, but Jessica's love and loyalty were worth a dozen brainy mermaids. "It's nice to meet you."

Jess put the baby toter on the counter, where Eric or Elizabeth was inside, sound asleep.

"Hey, you're short an infant. Where's Eric or Elizabeth?"

"Elizabeth's got a minor cough, so Dick took her to the pediatrician today." Jessica was unhurriedly taking out the good blender, fruit, yogurt, ice. "I wanted to swing by and pick up some of our stuff from storage."

"Storage?"

"The basement."

"Ugh. Have fun."

Jessica shrugged at Fred. "Betsy's got a thing about our basement."

"You didn't put 'dark, spooky basement' on your list of woes," Fred pointed out. "If only you had, I might have mustered sympathy from somewhere."

I snorted. "This is me, not holding my breath."

"Also, you probably hear this all the time, Fred, but I've got to ask—"

"Yes, I'm really a mermaid." Fred had perched on one of the barstools around the big butcher-block counter and was looking around with an expression that was almost pleasant. "No, I don't grant wishes."

"Don't start with the pestering, Jess," I warned. "Marc scampered off to change his shirt, for God's sake, though there was nothing wrong with the one he had on, and that after he fangirled all over her all the way here. It was awful."

Jessica giggled. "Don't deny it, Marc fangirling is a beautiful sight."

"When it's *Game of Thrones*, sure. But he blew off Will Mason so he could keep bugging Fred." Which . . . huh. Was weird. Maybe Cathie was onto something. Marc *talked* about how much he wanted to spend time getting to know Will, dating, maybe canoodling, maybe beyond canoodling. (Marc's sex life was none of my business and that had been the case since day one. I was careful not to inquire. And I definitely never wondered about Cathie's hideous invasive blood-flow "can you even get it up as a zombie?" question.)

"He knows I'm a zombie," he'd whispered to me while we were binge-watching season four of BBC *Sherlock*, "and he doesn't mind! He thinks it's *cool*. It's not cool, of course. But it's nice that he thinks so."

"It's a little cool," I suggested. Marc wasn't gross or shambling or dripping. He was cute as hell, like always.

"It's . . . handy," Marc conceded. "Especially if I'm going to be running around with you guys, facing lethal danger often before lunch. And after lunch."

"Martin Freeman looks like a sad potato," I announced, which sparked a long, long, long argument.[35]

For a lonely guy who put in too many hours at the ER for a long-term relationship, and hadn't been on a date in the last

---

[35] He does! But in a cute way. Look, I'm from the Midwest; I *like* potatoes. It's not an insult.

year and a half, Marc was sure finding it easy to keep putting Will off. I needed to start taking Cathie's theory more seriously.

"Betsy!" Jess snapped her fingers right under my nose, because she's horrible. "Come back to us. Stay away from the light."

"Yes, are you all right? You look like your dinner disagrees with you." Fred added under her breath, "Whomever that might be."

"Don't worry about my dinner, you—you vampirephobe." Actually, I hadn't fed in three days. Queen perk: I didn't have to glug-glug blood as often as other vampires. To Fred: "Don't be one of those awful, awful vegetarians. 'Oh, you eat *meat*?' And they say it in a tone like 'meat' is code for 'kittens.'"

"Fair point," Fred conceded. "The tight-asses give us all a bad name."

Well, amen to that. I'd take that as a minor victory and decided to be generous in the face of her concession. "Sorry again about Marc. He's very immature."

"Yes, that must be maddening."

"Are you messing with me?"

"Yes. May I have a smoothie?" And, when Jessica nodded, Fred added with—I hated to admit it—a charming smile, "Maybe a few more strawberries to go with the bananas?"

A vegetarian mermaid, and you only had to look at her teeth to know why. Fred had inherited her mom's teeth: the flat grinders of landlubbers. Her dad and his kind had what looked like a mouthful of needles. They needed them; think about how tough it was to get through a piece of octopus sushi. Now think about having to do that just about every time you ate. The Undersea Folk needed the strength and speed and stamina and sharp, sharp teeth to catch and eat any manner of deep-sea creatures. Humans? We just needed cash. Or access to a pantry and stove. Or even a gas station. If you had to, you could get a sandwich there. It wasn't pretty, but people did desperate things to survive.

So, Fred "No meat" Bimm. No fish, even though fish made up something like sixty-five percent of your average Undersea Folk's diet. One of many reasons she had trouble fitting in. Killing her dad? Probably another reason.

Hmm, empathy for Fred Bimm. Was I maturing? Or just really, really tired?

"One of the times you were almost bearable in Boston was how much you enjoyed Faneuil Hall," she announced out of nowhere. "You were almost charming."

"How much I liked what?"

Fred closed her eyes to slits and the slits glared at me. "You pronounced it Nathanial Hall."

"Oh, *that* place. Yum."

In next to no time, Jessica had given us all glasses full of dark pink liquid and walked off, basement bound, leaving her baby snoozin' away on the counter. The nice thing, when they were that age? They stayed where you put them.

Sinclair walked into the kitchen, BabyJon slung over one shoulder; BabyJon was out of the stay-where-you-put-them stage, alas. "This child is getting tired," he said by way of greeting, gaze glued to his phone. Just like a man, or a monarch: make an announcement and wait for everyone around you to scramble to fix it.

"Thanks for the update," I said sweetly.

"And the Wyndhams would like to stop by."

"Well, that could get awkward." That brought the score this evening to at least three werewolves, two dozen vampires, a human/USF hybrid, Jessica, Eric, other Eric, a zombie, and whatever the heck BabyJon was.

"No, my queen, this is good for us. We can have all our

problems in one spot at one time." His dark gaze flicked over to Fred, who was gulping her smoothie like her life depended on it. Guess a leisurely swim down the Mississippi made her hungry. "I was not, of course, referring to you, Dr. Bimm. You are many things, but a problem is not one of them." *I think.* Crafty!

She flapped a hand at him, finished her smoothie, then nearly dropped her glass. "It's no concern of mine, but—where is the baby?"

We looked.

The baby carrier was empty.

Okay, complicated. "It's not a big deal," I began.

"Excuse me, but it is," she corrected sharply. "Your friend didn't take the baby with her. No one has touched the baby. People are very likely spying on you. Your sister and father are definitively out to get you. You have out-of-town guests who may or may not be allies."

"Hey," I pointed out, "you're on that list."

"So where is your friend's infant?" Fred was on her feet, like she was going to start checking cupboards and peeking behind furniture. "We need to find it right away."

"Oh hey, Fred Bimm! Wow. So, you were always kind of bossy, huh? Even in your youth."

I pointed to the teenager standing in the mudroom doorway. "He's right there. Eric Berry, Fredrika Bimmm."

Jessica's newborn let out a deep chuckle. "We've met."

"When?" Fred still sounded sharp, and now looked bewildered and suspicious. Annoyingly, this didn't impact her looks in a negative way.

"Another place and time." His big brown eyes lit up. "Any strawberries left?"

"Sure," I said, and made room so the baby could saunter over and take a seat.

CHAPTER
TWENTY-EIGHT

"I don't understand," Fred said flatly. *"You are not an* infant."

"That must be why you're *Dr.* Bimm. Nothing gets past you." Petty, yep, but for once, I knew something she didn't. I was gonna enjoy it, dammit. And big surprise, Sinclair had left the explanations to me, since he'd wandered off with BabyJon. Typical: once again, the burden was mine. Case in point . . .

"It's a long story," Eric Berry said, snatching my half-empty glass without shame and draining it.

"Oh you little shit!" I yelped. "You know where the glasses are and the blender's sitting *right there.* You only did that to bug me."

"You know you're the one I love to bug, Onnie Betsy."[36]

---

[36] Onnie Betsy is baby talk for Auntie Betsy, as close as the twins could come to saying that when they were toddlers. As with many unthinkable, annoying family nicknames, it stuck. Signed, MJ "Daddy Long Legs" Davidson.

Because I am a shameless compliment whore, this worked on me. It didn't hurt that the punk was gorgeous.

Jessica was cute, and Dick was handsome, but their kids were living proof that every redneck bigot got it wrong: biracial kids were the best-looking kids on earth. Eric had his mother's luminous brown eyes and his father's pale skin, except Eric's had gold undertones. He had Jessica's pointed chin and broad forehead, and Dick's swimmer's shoulders. His hair bristled out in a proud Afro; you looked at him and all you could think was, *Is it as soft as it looks? Let's find out!*

I'd seen newborn Eric and toddler Eric, and first-grade Eric and sixteen-year-old Eric; this one was the oldest iteration, probably eighteen or nineteen. Not drinking age, but not far off, either. He was in what I called jean-colored jeans, because I'm not creative, and an orange T-shirt with white lettering: *World's Okayest Brother.* He was sockless and wearing the shoes from the future I'd noticed on other visits, narrow black shoes that looked like a sneaker and a loafer had a baby.

And the best part? The twins' beauty was the least interesting thing about them.

"Excuse me," Fred said. "Explanation still required."

"Well, we need a minute," I pointed out. "It's hard to explain. See, when Jessica was pregnant, some days she was only a month along and some days she looked ready to pop. But none of us noticed except my mom, because she didn't live here. And where is my mom? BabyJon's here; is she? Because this place is gonna be Defcon 5 for weird pretty soon; maybe the kids should scram."

"That's actually the least severe Defcon," Eric pointed out helpfully.

I turned to him. "What, so Defcon 1 is more terrible than Defcon 5?"

"Nailed."

"Stop with the future slang; I can't always figure it out even with context. Also, starting at five makes no sense."

"So what am I supposed to do about it? Bring your grievance to the USAF; they're the ones who thought it up."

"You're saying that like you think I won't. And a little respect, please, for your honorary aunt."

"Nuh-uh." But he grinned at me, a sweet smile that made the sarcasm more cute than irritating. A good trick. Maybe he could teach me.

"Will you two stop it?" Fred cried. "Betsy, stay focused. Although since the two of you seem singularly unworried, I'm not sure why I'm fretting."

"Fretting?" Couldn't resist the poke. "Is that what you call it?"

"Get back to the story," Fred managed through gritted teeth, and thank goodness she didn't inherit her dad's choppers; she'd have bitten through her tongue by now. Blurgh.

"Okay, so, Jessica's pregnancy was all over the place; it was just like her tie-dye phase except—if you can imagine—even more worrisome."

"Oh good Christ," Fred muttered.

"I'm telling it! So after a while we realized it was because her babies were shifting between parallel timelines, even before they were born! And that's because—oh, I forgot to tell you that I accidentally changed the timeline since before I did that she and Dick had broken up because he was terrified of me, but when I came back not only were she and Dick together; she was pregnant and also I didn't skin my husband and turn him into the Book of the Dead."[37]

"*What?*"

"I warned you it was complicated."

---

[37] *Undead and Unfinished.*

"Complicated I can handle. Learn to tell a story in a linear fashion."[38]

I set my (empty!) glass down so it wouldn't shatter in a zillion pieces when I clenched a fist. Oh, I was going to give this uppity jerk-ass *such* a—

"Fred, I'm a version of Jessica's son from another timeline."[39]

"Oh?" Fred turned an inquiring gaze toward him. I loosened my fist.

"Yes. For reasons I can't go into, all versions of my sister and I have access to this house. And I'm vastly superior to the infant I've temporarily displaced, since at this stage of my life I've stopped shitting my pants." He paused, then muttered, "Mostly, but in my defense, that was a completely out-of-control prom."

"I thought you said it was complicated. That wasn't complicated." Fred extended a slim paw, totally showing off how quickly she caught on to all the weird around here. "Nice to remeet you, since apparently you know a version of me from your own timeline."

"A wonderful version," Eric replied at once, shifting into Shameless Flirt without a pause.

"Ewww. She's old enough to be your mom."

"Yes, but I know what a lovely person she is, and not that I place importance on physical features"—said the teenage boy—"but USFs age beautifully. You don't ever appear to get wrinkles," he continued, still holding Fred's hand and ignoring my subtle retching. "Must be all the time in the water."

"Nope. You're not going to sit here and flirt with Fred Bimm. You're just not."

---

[38] Never!

[39] *Undead and Unwary.*

"Agreed," Fred said with a grin, the finned hussy. "But I must say, it was fascinating to meet you." She turned to look as Sinclair came back in.

"My own, the Wyndhams are here. Ah. Eric." He nodded to Jessica's baby, who was topping up *my* glass with *his* smoothie.

"Hey, Sinclair, howzit?"

"Ah, fine." That was another annoying thing: future slang was almost incomprehensible. "Standing perm" and "snatch" and "howzit" and "zup." I missed the subtle, classier slang of the past: "as if" and "lame" and "doy."

"Intriguing." Yeah, well, Sinclair would have to narrow that down a lot if he wanted us to have any idea what he meant. "Your mother only brought one twin over . . . and only one of you shifted from your time stream to ours."

"Yeah, well." A cheerful shrug from the twin in question. "It is what it is. Or what it will be. What year is it today again?"

"You are of course welcome anytime, child, but I must warn you, we have quite a few outside—"

"Undersea/human hybrid, more werewolves than usual, more vampires than usual and—let me guess—the press?"

"Quite."

"I'll 'moose pretty soon. Promise, chief. Gimmee."

"Eh? Oh." Eric had held out his arms for BabyJon and a bemused Sinclair handed him over. "Carry on."

"And on, and on! Sorry, but I'm giddy—it's so *nifty* being bigger and older than this guy for a change." He scooped BabyJon close and held him with careless confidence, then brought him within nuzzling distance. "Yes it is. Yes it is!"

BabyJon had been eyeing the older boy with fuzzy bemusement, which turned into giggles as the kitchen filled with the "bbbblllllzzzzztttt!" of a raspberry to the belly.

Sinclair was lingering, which was odd. Not that he had anything against homey family scenes, but he had a houseful of werewolves to worry about, and the press outside. And an assembly of vampires was on the way. And other stuff he said.

"I don't suppose you would care to enlighten—"

Eric cocked a dark brow at the king of the vampires. "You know the rules, O chieftain my chieftain. Sorry."

"Mmmm."

The rules. The twins had made it plain that they wouldn't give us any hints about our (possible) future. For one thing, there was no guarantee they were right. Who was to say the past they remembered had anything to do with *this* timeline? For another, even if they were right, giving us foreknowledge of events might affect how those events unfolded. For a third, ow, it all made my brain throb.

Fred got up to go with my husband—apparently she wanted to meet werewolves, *yawn*—and Sinclair departed in the closest thing to a snit I'd seen in a while; unlike me, he *loathed* not knowing everything all the time about every situation. When I'd tease him about his inner (and outer) control freak, he'd smile and say, "Is such behavior not the reason I was able to survive two lifetimes before meeting you?" Well, jeez, when you put it that way . . . Me, I figured that mind-set was a setup for a daily nosebleed at the very least.

But that didn't mean I couldn't relate.

"So," Eric the younger was saying. He'd looked outside and observed the weather, then glanced at the calendar on the fridge. "The 'rents have moved on for a bit."

'Rents? Oh—Dick and Jess. For a bit? So they'd come back?

I'd hoped/suspected they would. Every iteration of the twins who showed up knew the mansion and everyone in it. Knew where the glasses were, the spoons, knew who everyone was all the time, teased Tina about her absurd vodka collection, complimented my shoes, were respectful and sweet to Sinclair, and Marc was apparently some kind of super-uncle in their eyes. When Jess and Dick had moved out a few weeks ago, even then part of me knew that one way or the other, they'd return. Maybe not this year, or next. But they'd be back, would raise their children here. Knowing that had been one of the reasons I'd been able to let my friends go.

"I think it will be fine," the boy said carefully, and I appreciated his effort.

"Yep, I think so, too." Y'know, eventually. Probably. Good thing there weren't any rules about me telling *him* stuff. I couldn't see the harm in confirming what he'd deduced . . . or remembered.

"It'll work out, Onnie Betsy," he said, and his eyes were his mother's—dark and kind.

"Well, I hope so. Your mom hasn't said much, but I feel bad that your dad had to quit his job because of all this."

"Oh. That. Don't fret, li'l fretter."

"I'm thirty-some years older than you are," I reminded the whippersnapper.

"And an inch shorter . . . so far. I'll *tower* over you, ha!"

"You're barely cute when you sneer like that." This was a total lie. *Little jerk.*

He shrugged off my objective criticism of his shit-eating grin. "Not to worry, Onnie. One way or the other, Dad's always fuzzy."

"That's a load off." Always fuzzy? What, like a grooming thing? Gross. Didn't I have enough to worry about? Now I had to picture Dick's intimate landscaping needs?

"And you're gonna be fine, too, little big brother." Eric pretended to nibble on BabyJon's fingers, which the baby thought was just the best game ever.

"Hope so." I sighed. "He's one in a sea of weirdos. At best, he'll *only* be lost in the crowd. Which sucks. At worst? Doesn't bear thinking about."

Eric laughed at me, but he had such natural charisma it didn't make me want to punch him in the throat. "BabyJon is the *only* one you don't have to worry about. You'll come to harm before he does."

"That's a nice thought." Wait, was it? Yeah. Yeah, better me than him, definitely. "But I worry about everyone. You, your sister, your folks, Sinclair, Tina, Marc. Even—"

"Laura and your father."

Whoa. Did he know them, in his timeline? Were they alive? Were we in touch?

Had I killed them?

"Well. Yeah, them, too." And I could never admit it out loud. The whippersnapper was wise and cute! "And sometimes myself even."

"Just remember when things seem like an enormo pile of tiger droppings: BabyJon's the last one you need to obsess over."

"Isn't this cheating?" I asked tentatively. "Not that I mind. But the rules you guys set in place—"

"Telling you is safe enough," he assured me. He was so nice! The girls and/or boys must go nuts over him in his time-line. "You're not known for your memory retention."

Nice, and also awful. "That's one way to put it."

"No need to perspire over it, Onnie; it works for you. You're the only person in the world who has somehow turned a case of the stupids into a superpower."

"Chronic stupids," I agreed glumly. Then: "You little prick."

He laughed at me, and before I could come up with something appropriately devastating, the kitchen door swung open and there was Derik, the blond werewolf obsessed with lettuce who looked like an escapee from the pages of *Martha Stewart Living: Kickass Gourmets*.

"Hey," I said, because I had to say something. "Welcome back." *I guess.*

He didn't reply. He wasn't even looking at me. He'd stopped still and was staring at Eric.

I forced a cough. "Helloooooo?" It's not that I needed the queen kudos. I hated the bowing, in fact, and the "Your Majesty" this and "dread queen" that, had put as much a stop to all of it as I could (though some of the oldies, like Lawrence, persisted). But returning my greeting would be nice.

By way of response, Derik scraped his hands through his short blond hair so it was standing up in spikes. He definitely seemed like he had something on his mind, and it wasn't me. Good thing or bad thing?

He cleared his throat and managed a faint, "Hello?" Again: not looking at me. Or talking to me. Or responding to me in any way.

Eric saluted him from his spot on the barstool. "And to you, fuzzy sir!"

"Are you okay, Derik? You look weirded out." *Like you don't know if you want to bite or bolt. Don't bite!* Then I got it. "Oh. It's prob'ly the baby, right?" I gestured at BabyJon, who was giggling in Eric's arms while the older boy blew on BabyJon's fat, flat little feet. (My mom called them pork chops with toes.)

"Good guess, Betsy, but it's not entirely the baby," Eric said with a sly smile.

"He's right," Derik replied. He took a careful step closer and I could see his nostrils flaring wide as he tried to catch Eric's scent. He was . . . *straining* toward the boy—that was the best way to put it—using every sense he had to perceive what was in front of him. "You're . . . not really here, are you?"

"Now, that," Eric said, and gave BabyJon a raspberry just above his belly button, "is pretty astute, fuzzy sir; full marks to you."

"*She's* here," he said, pointing (rude!) to me. "And her baby-son is here." Babyson? That . . . actually wasn't terrible. Better than sonbaby, which made BabyJon sound like some kind of a demigod.

"What are you talking about?" I wasn't shrill—just a little loud. "Everyone here is here." Hated, *hated* being the last person in the room to get what was going on.

Derik had zero interest in my output. His gaze never shifted from Eric, who was as placid as a pond. If Jessica's baby was worried about being the focus of a nervous alpha werewolf in his prime, you sure couldn't tell. Which probably also un-nerved Derik. They were uninvited, and quick to think the worst of me, but in that moment I couldn't help but feel a bit sorry for him. A Wyndham got hurt, or frightened, or at least rattled almost every time we crossed paths. No, *every* time we crossed paths, now that I thought about it.

"They're here; everyone's here but you," Derik said slowly, obviously figuring it out while he talked. "You're more like a photograph. Like a trace of something, not the actual thing itself. How can that be?"

"Oh, that's excellent." Eric slung a yawning BabyJon over his shoulder and rubbed his little back, which was striped be-cause my mom was a believer in fat babies flaunting horizontal stripes. "That's the perfect way to describe that; gotta trap that in my brain to tell the sis when I get back."

"Back from where?"

"Long story." He handed BabyJon to me and stood. "Can I see the Fur and the Burr before I bolt?"

"Sure." We never saw the iterations arrive, or leave. They were just suddenly there. Or not there. I didn't question it.

"'Kay. Later, prognosticator."

"Wait—" Derik began.

Eric ignored the werewolf, which was impressive. "Nice to

see you," he said with casual courtesy, and stepped past Derik to open the mudroom door. Fur and Burr had set up a clamor, which lessened only a bit when the door closed behind him.

Nice to see you. Not *nice to see you again*, which was interesting. It didn't necessarily mean Eric had met Derik in his own timeline. It did mean that Eric knew a werewolf when he saw one. He also wasn't remotely worried about it. That was interesting, too.

Derik looked at me and I liked him a little more just then, because I could relate to the look of complete bewilderment on his face. "What just happened?"

"Same old, same old. Which I think is nice." I shook the almost empty blender at him. "Smoothie?"

CHAPTER
TWENTY-NINE

Lars had grown fat.

Jennifer realized her first thought on seeing her high school crush was as accurate as it was unkind. *Did you expect him to go into stasis for thirty-one years? Not everyone was lucky enough to be damned, then return to the real world still looking like a teenager.*

Did I just classify my situation as "lucky enough"?

Finding the house had been easy. She'd known Burnsville well before she'd killed herself. (She never referred to her situation as "died." She always said exactly what happened: "killed myself.") Before the Mall of America, there was the Burnsville Mall. She and Tammy went every weekend they could, and when they couldn't shop for clothes, they hit Baskin-Robbins. Tammy always had some kind of chocolate; Jennifer stuck with daiquiri ice. It was pale blue, a cloud on a cone, and deliciously tart and cool. It even *tasted* pale blue.

Lars lived in a three-garage house on Nicollet Avenue South, and other than the paint jobs and the cars, it all looked as it had the last time she'd been in the small city. Jennifer piloted the Ford space shuttle right up the small hill into the driveway—3923 was prominently displayed on the front porch as well as the mailbox. Hooray, they still had mail! Jennifer decided to find joy in the small things. Especially since she might be back in Hell by the end of the night.

She hopped out of the space shuttle and rushed up the sidewalk, but she wasn't eager. All her life and death, she had rushed through things she couldn't bear, so she wouldn't chicken out. If she took the coward's way out today, if she chickened out about not chickening out, the pain wouldn't just be hers. Her mother would pay the price, too. She'd spend the rest of her life in the house on Mill Street, listening for Jennifer's footsteps.

No.

She knocked on the door and heard a faint, "Yeah, c'mon in, Pete!"

She opened the screen door, then the front door, and walked in. Lars—like her mother, he sounded essentially the same, just a bit rougher—kept yelling from the back of the house. "Hey, you're early, buddy! Be right out!"

Okay. Lars didn't sound mad, or sad. Whoever Pete was, he was a welcome guest. Or at least not overtly unwelcome. His parole officer, maybe? Lars had been set free early; would he still be on parole?

His house looked nice—nicer than her mother's, in fact. Two stories, three-car garage, sunken living room. A little cluttered inside, and the blankets on the couch were rumpled, but there weren't any dirty dishes in the living room, the bookshelves had been dusted, the newspapers were neatly folded and had been carefully placed back on the coffee table. There were vacuum tracks on the tan wall-to-wall carpet.

Lars had made a life for himself from the ashes of Tammy's demise.

She cleared her throat, sounding, to her ears, like a dying goose. "It's—it's not Pete," she called.

"Eh? Oh hell, Renee, is that you? Did I forget to leave your check yesterday?"

Check. Vacuum tracks. Cluttered but clean: cleaning lady.

"It's not Renee, either."

"Um . . . Tara?"

Are we going to go through every woman he knows? The thought was hysterical, but not in a good way. *It's not Tara or Jane or Susie or Carol or Mindy or Barbara or Debbie or Fiona or Lisa or Kelly or Penelope or Roberta or Anna. It's no one living.*

She heard heavy footsteps approach; it appeared the kitchen connected to the dining room, which connected to the living room. She could hear him but not see him until he turned the corner and—

Saw her.

Lars had gotten fat. The blond teenager she'd crushed on the moment she saw him was buried, *swallowed* in the older man before her. His complexion was florid, dark pink and getting darker as he looked at her. His hair was brutally short, a buzz cut that made him look like a retired soldier. His blue eyes were small, like raisins pressed into dough. He was wearing olive green work pants and a green-and-white plaid flannel shirt, sleeves rolled to the elbow. Athletic socks, no shoes. He was holding work boots in one hand, unlaced and ready to be pulled on.

Fishing opener, maybe, she thought. *What's the date?* Whatever he and Pete were going to do, it was probably outside. *Hope he doesn't have to climb a lot of hills.*

Why was she so obsessed over his weight gain? She couldn't

believe that's what she was focused on, kept going back to again and again. Then she figured out the problem.

This is what it's like to go to your thirtieth high school reunion, she thought. *You don't recognize anyone because you haven't seen them since they were teens. And in your head, and theirs, you're still teens.*

Except in her case, she really *hadn't* changed a bit.

"Lars, it's—it's me. I'm back."

He just looked at her.

Okay. That was okay. It had been decades. She shouldn't expect him to remember her; *she'd* had the crush, not him. He'd barely known her before the fire. She would have to explain who she was and hope he didn't think it was some cruel prank, that someone hadn't figured out why he'd gone to prison and cooked this up solely to mess with an old fat man living by himself in Burnsville, with a friend named Pete and a housekeeper he occasionally forgot to pay.

"Jennifer Palmer back from the dead, oh Jesus-please-us," he breathed, and then fell down, and she realized he knew exactly who she was, and had the moment he'd lumbered into his living room.

CHAPTER
THIRTY

The cherry on my nightmare sundae: we were all screaming at each other. In. The. Basement.

"It's the only part of the house that can hold everyone," Tina had explained, because the Peach Parlor was sadly insufficient. Even our huge kitchen—back in the day the kitchen had pumped out meals that fed twenty or thirty people a day, every day, multiple times a day—was too small for all the "visitors" (as polite a term as I could manage).

Worse? Worse than being here? It had been cleaned! The basement ran the width of the mansion, which meant it was as long as hell and almost as wide, with lots of rooms off the main area. It was basically a dark, underground mansion with a tunnel leading to the river. Someone had been down here dusting and scrubbing and mopping, and brought lots of big tables and all kinds of chairs, from folding ("Poker, anyone?") to overstuffed easy chairs ("Football game, anyone?"). Here I assumed we were just between housekeepers, cleaning up puppy pee without complaint, when Tina had hired an army of them and they'd spent the week making the basement slightly less revolting.

I felt tricked.

"It's not about tricking you," Marc soothed while I'd stomped down the stairs. "It's about not wanting to hear all the whining for a week beforehand. Now we just have to hear the whining now."

"Not better," I growled.

"Depends on where you're standing."

So we had vampires interrupting each other in their rush to complain about Laura exposing them, and Sinclair just letting them vent, and now tromp-tromp-tromp down the stairs, here came Derik and Michael and Lara and Jeannie, and I knew damned well at least three of them didn't have to make a sound when they moved; they just *wanted* to be noisy. *Hey-ho, the werewolves are here, sorry we're late, U mad, bro?*

"Oh, check this," I muttered. "Something jerk-ass this way comes."

Marc, who'd been leaning against the wall watching with an avid gaze, pretended to stagger. "Whoa. I—whoa! Was that a literary reference?"

"Shut up," I snapped. "I read." It was true! Though I'd never read that book. I just really loved the title. C'mon, how badass is a title that basically tells you bad shit is en route? Hey," I said a little louder as the Wyndhams approached. "Grab a seat and get ready to bitch." I remembered the world's most terrifying middle schooler was there and added, "Sorry about the language."

"'Sfine," Lara said with a giggle.

Normally I'd say something dumb and tiresome like "are you sure this meeting in a spooky basement packed with pissy vampires is an appropriate hangout for your child?" except, again: Lara Wyndham. She'd probably handle it better than

I did. She *was* handling it better than I was; she at least had a smile on her face and seemed genuinely interested in the goings-on.

"This is amazing," Marc murmured. "I can't believe Sinclair isn't just telling them all to shut up and fall in line."

"That's the plan. Y'know, eventually. But I asked him to let them have their say first. What, bored already? Play with your phone."

"Definitely not bored. And I forgot it upstairs."

"Yeah, me, too." It was in my bedroom. Tina and Sinclair probably had theirs; they were famous for taking their screens to bed long before taking screens to bed was considered acceptable twenty-first-century behavior. In fact I almost never had my phone on me because whoever I was with nearly always had theirs. "No big."

At least people were only yelling. No one was punching. Or biting. Nothing was on fire. It might not end horribly for all involved.

Ha.

CHAPTER
THIRTY-ONE

Laura was back at the mansion, the place she hated to be but couldn't stay away from. She was getting a little worried about Ronald Tinsman. Not much, just a bit. And not because she was starting to wonder if Betsy had been right. Betsy *wasn't* right. It was statistically impossible.

Laura was back and the mansion was looming in front of her like the Bates Motel and she was just . . . concerned. As a friend. A friend Ronald had known less than a year and never socialized with either before or after his daughter's murder. A friend who had told him she was the Antichrist and he hadn't blinked. *Because he was open-minded*, not *because he was numb, Betsy, thank you very much.*

The irony, given their mission to expose vampires, was that these days Ronald was the walking dead. But despite his deep personal grief, he'd been integral to the plan, had helped her expose vampires, would help her keep manipulating the media until the world rose in righteous fury and destroyed every bloodsucker they could find.

None of this would be happening without Ronald. It was almost as though Cindy had been murdered for the greater good. Perhaps in time, he would come to see it that way. That her death was necessary. Perhaps even a blessing in disguise.

You think him being numb means he's fine with that?

Even when Betsy wasn't there, she was there. Sometimes her half sister babbled on and on and on in Laura's mind until she thought her brain would burst.

He knows I'm a force for good, despite my birthright.

That was right. That was just right. Laura had been nervous about revealing her dark genetic legacy to Ronald, but he'd been fine with it. With her being the Antichrist. Totally fine with it. Not numb—accepting. Like a friend.

Besides, she wasn't anymore. Betsy was the Antichrist. If not the daughter of the Morningstar, then her heir. And Laura was—was—

(trapped)

free.

Anyway, here she was, worried about Ronald, and Betsy was probably wrong about him

(wrong about everything)

because Ronald wasn't numb to the world, he was *mourning*, there was a difference, and she didn't expect Betsy Taylor of all people to see the nuances. To understand anything beyond her own nose.

But still: troubling behavior. Ronald almost never went home. He spent hours and hours on the sidewalk in front of the mansion. He was the first reporter there and the last to leave. Everyone knew his story, and after the first few days, the other journalists left him alone. He made them all uncomfortable—men and women whose job was showing people's pain to the world were getting creeped out by Ronald Tinsman.

Once he'd gone thirty-seven hours without a trip home.

Laura had intervened then, had asked a couple of her followers to *make* him go home, make him eat and rest, and they had; they were anxious to do anything she asked; they would have *eaten* him if she'd asked, but of course she never would; she was good, and she would make her followers be good, and anyone who couldn't fall in line could leave, or die, or both.

Six hours later, he was back.

The meeting was tonight. Two dozen (maybe more!) vampires were in that house right now, and because they were animals there would be blood, and there were half a dozen reporters here and finally, *finally* the world would have to acknowledge Betsy Taylor was an animal who should be put down or at least run out of town, *thrown* out, not given a loving husband and buckets of money and a mansion and friends and her very own kingdom on earth *and* in Hell.

Finally.

"It's almost over," she whispered to Ronald. She thought about gently bullying him to go home and rest. But what she'd started with a few YouTube videos would be finished tonight. He would rest tomorrow. She would see to it. She'd show him that she *was* a friend, not someone who manipulated his grief and used it to her own end.

"You've got a lot to be proud of, Ronald. Cindy would be proud, too." Probably. Hadn't she been a cheerleader? Well, perhaps she would have shaken her pom-poms and cheered for her father if she could see him avenging her. Something like that. Sure.

"Yes," he replied with all the animation of—it must be said—a corpse. When she'd met him at Fairview, her first thought had been, *What a sad gray man.* But *sad* wasn't the word. Not even close.

"Is it true?"

Laura looked around at the unfamiliar low-pitched voice

and felt her eyes narrow. She knew that man. An overgrown boy, really, the skinny guy in his midtwenties, the blogger who claimed to see ghosts. The one who looked at Marc Spangler like he could eat him alive, the one Marc Spangler was careful not to look back at. Too often, anyway.

Another person who, by rights, should be scared to death of Betsy and her ilk but was too dumb or infatuated to keep away from here. He'd met Betsy's mother and her friends. He was a welcome visitor there. And Laura was out here on the sidewalk.

God, she hated the mansion.

Will something. Something to do with cooking, or kitchens. Will Pot? Jar? No. No, that wasn't it.

Mason.

"Is what true?" she asked, not bothering to keep the irritation out of her tone. If she hadn't been raised to be a good person, she'd tell him to get the hell away from her, couldn't he see there was important work to be done?

He wasn't speaking to her, she realized, irritated all over again. He was pestering poor gray Ronald. "My sources told me you lied to Laura about the bomb."

!!!!!!!!!!!!!!!!!!!!!!!!!!!!!!!!!!!!!!

No. No. No. Will Mason, puny infatuated faggot, did not know about the incendiary device Ronald had built as an absolute, total last resort. As a tool there was a ninety-five percent chance they wouldn't even use. It was . . . was . . .

Just in case.

Right. Insurance. People bought insurance knowing the chances were good that they'd never, ever need it. The bomb

(don't call it that sounds scary it's a device just a device like an alarm clock or a kitchen timer just a tool)

was like that. Hardly worth the trouble to assemble and plant, because they likely wouldn't use it.

God, he was *still talking*. He'd sidled close to them and was almost whispering. He didn't want the other reporters to hear him, which was a relief but also puzzling. Why was he confronting them? Had he told Betsy? Was this a trap?

Of course it's not a trap. It was my idea to come here, like it's always my idea to come because my darling sister can't be bothered to invite me. I'm the one who set the trap. The trap I can spring whenever I want, but I won't. Because I'm not like that. That's something she would do.

"You told Laura you could trigger it remotely as a last resort. But that you probably wouldn't have to."

"Yes," the gray man said.

"But my sources say that really, your bomb's on a timer, and the clock's been running for two days." Pause. When neither of them said anything—Ronald too gray, Laura too horrified—Will asked, "Is that true?" And his voice. His tone. *It's not true, right? You didn't really do that, right? My sources got it wrong. I'm almost sure. That's why we're out here having a quiet, civilized conversation. Because you wouldn't have done that to your own sister. Even if you secretly hated her. Even if you've thought about killing her since the week you met.*

Oh, it was awful. So thank God he had it wrong; his stupid little ghosts were lying to him and stirring up trouble because anyone not in Heaven or Hell was clearly up to no good, vampires and werewolves and now ghosts, treacherous, not to be trusted, they fell outside the natural order of things and ha! *Your ghosts got it wrong, Will!*

"No," she said, triumph ringing through her voice; oh, wouldn't he feel *stupid*. Betsy's friends were as dim as she was and it was pretty funny when you thought about it. "No, of course not; I'd never—"

"Yes," Ronald replied absently, almost indifferently. "The clock's almost run down. Not long now."

"Wh-what?"

To Laura: "Why do you look shocked? You know what they did to my girl. Did you think I'd be satisfied with a *meeting*? What do I care if they've come over to yell at the king and queen of the vampires? What do I care if they're fighting? Or if they kill one or none or some or both? None of them can live. They have to burn, Laura. They have to and anyone who would help them. We all have to burn."

Her mouth had gone so dry it took her a few seconds to speak. "Ronald, that's—that's not the plan. That was never the plan."

Wasn't it?

He laughed at her.

And here was Will Mason, pulling out his phone and hitting a number he clearly called a *lot*, probably had Dr. Faggot on speed dial and now he was half-turned away and muttering, "Come on, pick up," and that's when Ronald pulled a gun from somewhere and shot him in the back.

And then himself, in the head.

CHAPTER
THIRTY-TWO

Jennifer had managed to get him up off the floor

"Unnnnnnffffffff!"

and staggered into the living room, Lars hanging heavily on to her shoulder. Arrghh, sunken living room, the step had nearly had her buckling under the weight. She'd carefully shoved him off her, onto the couch, and they both breathed out relieved sighs when his butt hit the cushions. "Jesus Christ, Jennifer Palmer," he kept saying. "I can't fucking believe it. Jennifer Palmer."

She'd brought him a cold can of Coke, which he cracked open and drank half of in three monster swallows. His hands were shaking.

She knelt before him and she saw his small eyes widen; then he hurriedly took another drink of his pop.

"Lars, I'm back—"

"From *where*? You look exactly the same. Jennifer Palmer. I can't believe it. Where'd you come from?"

"Hell."

"Jesus Christ, Jennifer Palmer. I can't believe it. Jennifer Palmer."

"Yes, yes, it's me." She rushed ahead, not sure she could handle another five minutes of the "Jesus Christ/Jennifer Palmer" chant. "I've been sent back to atone for my sins. I set the fire, not you. I killed Tammy, not you."

"Yeah, I know."

"Oh." Doy. Of course he knew.

He cocked an eyebrow at her and she saw a glimpse of the boy she'd loved in an age when people thought puffy wide shoulder pads made women look feminine. "Well, I knew *I* didn't do it," he said dryly, "so that narrowed the field a little, y'know? And then you killed yourself. So. Wasn't hard to figure out what happened."

"Right. Okay. So, yes, I set the fire. Not on purpose."

"No, I didn't think you did it on purpose."

"Oh, I didn't!" She rushed ahead, leaning forward in her urgency to tell her tale and be done with it. "It was an accident. I wasn't paying attention because I was so excited. And the reason I was excited was because I, um—" She couldn't believe it. It was harder telling him *why* she'd done it than it had been telling him she *had* done it. "I had a crush on you and Tammy knew so when her folks went out of town she suggested we invite you over and I was hoping you and I would, um, spend the night together."

She'd died a virgin but hadn't stayed one. Out of curiosity and boredom four months in, she'd let the arson investigator fuck her. It had been an anticlimax, pun definitely intended. He'd died at forty-two and had been in Hell for fifteen years. An old man, and not very good at sex. Quick, though, she had to give him that. It hadn't hurt, either, so she had to give him that, too. Frankly, she figured losing her virginity in Hell had been better than, say, losing it in the backseat of her mom's car, which—until Tammy had her great idea—was how Jennifer assumed she'd give it up.

"Oh. You liked me?" Lars swallowed hard. "I didn't know that."

"Right. Well. Why would you?" Her face felt funny. Was she sick? Getting a fever? Oh. No, much worse than any fever. *Stop blushing like a teenager, you idiot.* "That's why I was there. And that's why you were there, though you didn't know it at the time. And I'm sorry I didn't have the courage to leave a note exonerating you."

"Well, y'couldn't. What if you hadn't taken enough pills? What if someone found you and they pumped your stomach? Then they'd know you failed at killing yourself *and* you'd killed Tammy."

Hearing his precise summary of the extent of her cowardice made her throat tighten. "Yes, that's—that's exactly right."

"Was Tammy there? In Hell?"

Fresh horror surged up her throat; for a long, dizzying moment she was afraid she would vomit. Finally she managed to blurt, "No! Oh God no, of course not! No, Hell's not for—people like Tammy. No. She wasn't there. She wasn't."

Jennifer had made sure of it. She'd asked around and, when told the most efficient way of getting the correct answer, didn't hesitate. It was the occasion of her first and last meeting with the original Satan.

The devil, she'd been surprised to discover, had taken the form of a beautiful older woman with thick dark hair shot with gray. She was slender, with long legs her beautifully cut black suit showed off to great advantage. Not a pitchfork or pair of horns or forked tail in sight. Her voice was low and pleasant,

and if she wasn't matronly, exactly, she was sexy and approach-
able, and Jennifer had found her courage and asked about her
dead best friend.

The devil had given her a long, considering look and had
waited just long enough for Jennifer to get nervous about the
delay before replying. "No, she's not here. Heaven, I suppose,
or reincarnated, or nowhere—whatever she was taught." And
then, when Jennifer had let out a relieved breath, Satan had
sweetly added, "Of course, seeing how relieved you are, I'm
sorry she's *not* here."

"Excuse me?"

"Wouldn't it be something to watch her burn over and
over and over? See it and *smell* it? Smell her? It's true what they
say—people smell like the most succulent pork roast you've
ever had." She leaned in and took a big whiff. "You're *delicious.*
Your little dead friend could call for you—just as she would
have in life. And you could do nothing. Just as you did in life."

And she had laughed, a cheery sound that was as jarring as
it was frightening.

Jennifer shook off the memory, the worst, the very worst
day she'd endured down there. "You've got no reason to believe
a word I say about anything, but I promise you, Tammy is not
in Hell."

"Okay. That's good. She was a nice kid. She didn't deser—
Well, that's good."

"Yes." Jennifer waited, but it seemed he'd said his piece.
*What now? Do I ask him to forgive me? Officially? Or do I talk
more? Or let him talk?* "I have to say, Lars, you're— I can't
believe how calm you are."

"Uh-huh." He belched, the sound so sharp and loud it was
like a gunshot. He made a fist, thumped his chest, belched
again. Looked at his fist. Started rubbing his arm.

"Lars?"

"I think. I need." He paused. "An ambulance."

Then his eyes rolled up, and he slowly, grandly toppled over on his side like a blond mountain that smelled like flannel and Coke.

Jennifer ran for the kitchen. *I hope he has an old-fashioned phone*, she thought, shoes skidding on the tile as she looked around wildly for a telephone. *And I hope the number for an ambulance is still 911.*

CHAPTER
THIRTY-THREE

Laura screamed and screamed and it wasn't like the movies.
The pistol, so small, had made more of a sharp *pop!* than a
deafening bang. Only a couple of reporters even looked over.
And it was full dark, and cold, and people wanted to go home,
and who cared if vampires were real, what's new *this* month?
Of the few reporters still hanging around, more than half were
wrapping up for the day, walking to their cars.

She had no way to stop the bomb.

She had to stop the bomb.

"Call an ambulance!" she shrilled. Ronald was gone; his
brains were on the sidewalk, slowly swallowed by the spreading bloodstain from his head. She dropped to her knees beside
Will Mason and flipped him over on his back.

He cried out—in her adrenalized panic she'd been rougher
than she intended—and then his gaze found hers. He was still
clutching his phone. His lips were moving. ". . . ering."

"What?" She bent closer.

"He's not answering. They don't know. Clock's . . . been running. Time's . . . almost . . ."

Then, of course, because that was the week they were all having, she heard the low boom of an explosion. When she looked up she couldn't see much, just the glow of what she assumed was a spreading fire.

"Get going, you silly bitch," Will Mason said, and died.

CHAPTER
THIRTY-FOUR

"Wait, Will Mason called you earlier and you blew him off again?" I couldn't believe what I was hearing! And not just because I had no interest in joining the vampire bitchfest taking place ten feet to our left. This was way more interesting. "Dude! You see what you're doing, right?"

Marc didn't say anything, not even, *Don't call me "dude."* For Marc, that meant, *Yes, you are absolutely correct, and I am too embarrassed to admit it, so I will remain mysteriously silent and leave you to draw your own conclusions.*

"Oh my God!" I pushed away from the wall and glared at the bridge of his nose, since he wouldn't make eye contact. "You *are*! You're blowing off this perfectly nice kid—"

"He's twenty—"

"Shut up! You're pushing him away because you're scared shitless to start a relationship with him!"

"With anybody," Marc admitted in a low voice.

"Ohhhh, you dummy," I moaned. I grabbed him by his scrub shirt and tugged him to the right a few feet. Probably a waste of time, since everyone in the basement had super hearing, but I felt better anyway, even if it was just the illusion of privacy. "Marc, he doesn't just like you. He likes you *and* he knows you're a zombie *and* he's an orphan so he's fine with you not dying and leaving him *and* he's helped us! His ghosts tell him useful stuff all the time . . . the ghosts who bug me only ever want favors. 'Tell my wife the money's in the Swiss account under her mother's name.' Jesus, who cares? *His* ghosts are helpful. Sure, he's a scrawny pathetic little dork who needs to leave the basement more often—"

"He's not scrawny!"

"Aha! I knew you liked him!"

"He's *slender*. Not scrawny." Whoa, my plan worked a little too well. Now I didn't have to look at the bridge of his nose, because Marc's eyes were locked on mine. "And his office isn't in the basement; it's upstairs! And he's beautiful!"

I just looked at him.

Marc groaned and dug the heels of his hands into his eyes. "I'm an idiot."

"Well, yeah, but Will's into it, so." That got him to laugh, which I'd been hoping for. "Listen, take a break, go get your phone, call him back, make a date, *keep* the date, fall in love, live happily ever after. Or if that's too much, just have a nice time and see where it goes. Okay?"

"Well . . ."

"*Okay?*"

"But what about . . ." He trailed off and gestured at the group several feet away.

"We've got this handled." And it really seemed we did. That (probably) wasn't a lie to get rid of him. The raised voices were calming, and Fred was having a bit to say, too. Even better, people were listening to her. I should probably get over there and find out about what. For all I knew, mermaids were great at instigating basement brawls. "I think it's going to be—maybe not fine, but . . . doable."

"Then there's no reason for me to be here."

"What have I been saying?"

"Ugh, you're so shrill." But it was halfhearted, more to save face than score points, and he said it while moving toward the stairs.

Shrill. Heh. No, that would be the Ant when I informed her she'd lost the bet and had to say three nice things about me every time she saw me for the next hundred years.

Man, I couldn't even imagine the uproar. I had to make a concerted effort not to rub my hands together in glee, and that's when I heard something

(aw no)

that sounded

(no, it can't be)

like gunshots.

"Everyone shut up!" I yelled, and what do you know, they all did. My husband had his head cocked to the side, and suddenly we were all listening for . . . what?

Sinclair! I think someone's shoot—

That's when the ceiling fell in.

CHAPTER
THIRTY-FIVE

The emergency room—everything about the hospital, in fact—was fluorescent and bewildering.

Jennifer had called an ambulance (luckily, 911 *was* still the number to call for such things) and then followed it to Fairview, less than two miles away. She'd been terrified the entire drive; her hands still ached from her white-knuckled grip on the wheel. *What if I get pulled over? What if the hospital needs to see my ID? What if I get arrested? Or Mom gets in trouble for lending a car to her dead, license-less daughter? Will they let me call her? What if Lars dies?* "Great to see you again, sorry I ruined your life and let you rot in prison for a crime I committed, and wow, I did *not* see the heart attack coming! My sad." That's what the kids said, right? My sad?[40]

The attendants had hustled Lars right through the ER and several nurses and doctors had descended upon his gurney.

---

[40] Yeah, no.

She'd been politely shunted off to the side and began a small season in purgatory (so to speak) waiting for news in a small side room filled with chairs, a watercooler,

(oh good they still have those whew!)

and several low tables with stacks of magazines.

At first she drank cup after cup of water. Then she paced, but when she realized she was irritating some of the others, she sat and flipped through magazines. Apparently, "apps" were very, very important. So were Kardashians. And Oprah's TV show had been so popular, she had her own magazine now. Tylenol was still in business and Elizabeth Taylor was still selling perfume. Maybelline was still making makeup, though Jennifer didn't recognize any of the models. Pale blue eye shadow was either back in style or had never gone out of style.

She'd whipped the magazine at the wall before she realized she was going to do such a thing. *You are not in Hell, moron! This behavior will be noticed and perhaps even commented on. Stop it!*

All the magazines did was emphasize that she wasn't a teenager and never would be again. She had no ID, no driver's license, no high school diploma. When asked, she'd identified herself as a friend of the family, then bit her tongue to keep the hysterical laughter from spilling out.

She had ruined her chances. Did they still play Monopoly in the twenty-first century? Do not pass Go, do not collect two hundred dollars, just go straight back to Hell.

"That's okay," a stout older woman with reddish gray hair told her, getting up and picking up the issue. "All those ads make me nuts, too. What's happened to journalism? D'you mind if I read this?"

Jennifer shook her head and that was when the nurse came to fetch her.

* * *

So now she was sitting beside a hospital bed, Lars in a drugged sleep beside her, his belly making a great white mound in the middle of the bed. Good health insurance ensured a private room, and the nurse had told her she could stay until the top of the hour but would then have to leave.

And go where, exactly?

She was mechanically flipping through channels with the remote, something small and sleek that she first thought was an incredibly advanced electric shaver. She was looking at the television without really seeing it, and wondering how the end would come.

Would Betsy just pop into being? Appear from nowhere and grab Jennifer's hand and haul her back to Hell? Would she let Jennifer call her mother first? "Sorry, Mom. I failed. I loved seeing you today and I won't ever see you again, because you aren't going where I'm going."

Then a thought so horrible struck her that for a long moment she was paralyzed with horror: what if her mother did something terrible to end up in Hell, so they would never again be apart?

No. No. *Focus on what you can control.* She could do nothing for Lars beyond what she already had: called an ambulance, stayed with him in the hospital. Her only option now was to wait, and so she would.

She clicked through more channels and wondered when she'd be hearing from the new devil. Then she realized what she was looking at—for the first time she really paid attention to the screen—and realized Betsy had her hands full and wasn't coming for anyone anytime soon.

The picture was of the mansion in flames, with a publicity

still of Betsy in the corner of the screen while red words streamed across the bottom.

BREAKING NEWS: Mysterious explosion at so-called vampire mansion.

"Oh shit," she managed, and groped for her mom's car keys.

CHAPTER
THIRTY-SIX

One minute I was patting myself on the back for saving Marc's relationship and maybe even getting him laid, and the next I was shoving hot chunks of ceiling off myself. Because the basement sucks, okay?

Elizabeth!

I'm fine, I'm okay! But Jessica and the babies are upstairs!

The basement was filling with smoke—had something caught fire? What? *Oh please not my shoes.* And what was with the gunshots I'd heard before everything caromed into the crapper? Related? I couldn't see a thing but could hear too much—vampire hearing was definitely a liability now. Shouts and screams and the roar of flames and thuds and just a cacophony of crap everywhere, no escaping it.

I'll help people on this side up the stairs and out one of the doors! You guys go down the tunnel!

Understood. Be careful, my own.

The basement fucking sucks, Sinclair!

Dark laughter in my head. Oh, he'd pay for that. Later.

I beckoned to several deeply confused and agitated vampires. I could practically read their minds: what was the etiquette when you were taking issue with your sovereign's new policies and the ceiling fell down? Remain until dismissed? Flee politely? "You guys, up this way, c'mere. Get going. If you see someone who needs help, scoop 'em up and get 'em outside. Now, go."

"Yes, ma'am."

"Majesty."

My, so polite as they practically broke their legs thundering past me for the stairs. Respect for their monarch? Or the fact that vampires were completely terrified of fire? Yeah, not much of a mystery. I was shooing the last of the vamps up the stairs, heard the crack, and jumped back before another chunk of the ceiling could clip me. "God *damn* it!"

Now the bottom of the stairs was blocked, though I was pretty sure everyone on this side of the basement was out by now. But I had to get my ass upstairs—the others might need me.

"Betsy!"

I looked around.

"It's me!"

I caught on and looked down. Lara Wyndham. Probably should have picked up on that earlier. I seized her by the wrist and hauled her over to one of the annoying, small, teeny-tiny basement windows that were useless for everything: a pain in the ass to unlock and open, too small to let in light, too small to squeeze out if you were bigger than a middle schooler, absolutely useless for any purpose for which windows were invented.

"My parents and Derik—"

"They're on the other end; they'll be going down the tunnel." I was pretty sure. But I didn't need Lara running around our scarier-than-usual basement in a blind panic. "Don't be scared; I'm going to give you a boost and you're going to wiggle out the window and be safe, okay? Don't worry. Won't take a minute." I reached up and yanked the lock so hard the metal twisted off in my hand. I could hear Lara coughing behind me—unlike me, she had to breathe. Me, I probably stank of smoke, but at least there wasn't any in my lungs.

I wrenched the window open so hard it separated from the hinges with a low groan and a shower of rust, letting in a small amount of chilly spring air. Then I bent, picked her up, shoved her through.

"You're safe," I called up to her. "Wait in the yard, okay, hon? Your folks will track you down pretty soon. Stay where they can find you."

She was crouched on the ground outside, peering down at me. "What about the babies in the house?"

And then she darted off. Because of course she wasn't scared. Had never been scared.

I cursed under my breath, looked around the smoke-filled hellhole, hoped for inspiration, then remembered the small door off one of the side rooms that led up to the mudroom. We never used it; it was inconvenient, small, the stairs needed repair, and they were off a tiny windowless room. Also, argh, Fur and Burr!

I ducked under the main stairs and grabbed the door handle, moved through the darkness—thank you, vampire eyesight!—and found the smaller, creakier stairs. I was up them despite the creaking and trembling and into the mudroom in just a few seconds, ran to the porch door and opened it. The puppies raced past me into the yard. Excellent.

"Betsy!"

Jess. In the yard, holding baby Eric. Thank God. Thank God.

"Stay outside," I shouted back. "Don't come in the house!" Jess needed to breathe, too, had no equipment or training, but was so loving and loyal she'd run into a burning house if she thought I needed her. "Stay there!"

"BabyJon's in the kitchen! The port-a-crib!"

Fuck.

"Stay there!"

I turned, felt the doorknob to the door leading to the kitchen—room temp, not too hot, so I opened it, and though there was smoke, nothing seemed to be on fire. But BabyJon wasn't crying.

I rushed to the crib, so terrified I'd find a small, limp, dead baby that at first I mistook the crumpled blanket for a body. But there was nothing there, and I wasn't sure if that was good or bad.

Sirens, finally. But where was Marc?

Sinclair! Wait. Wait. If you call for help, he'll come back through the tunnel, wade through smoke and fire and fight his way up the stairs to find you. He was immune to sunlight, not fire.

Beloved?

I think—I think everyone from the basement got out!

I concur; we're almost at the dock.

Okay! Come back to the mansion quick as you can!

Yes.

I heard the front door slam open, heard running, so I shoved open the kitchen door. And there was Laura at the other end of the hallway. She saw me and started screaming.

"I didn't know!"

"Oh no," I whispered. "Oh, Laura, what did you do?"

She screamed something else—I caught *Marc* and *Will* and *Ronald*, for some reason; what was that about? She took one step and then smoke just *boiled* through the wall and the floor disappeared and she did, too.

And then I heard BabyJon crying. I'd like to say I had a moment of indecision, that in my compassion I struggled to decide what to do, but it would be a lie. I went for the kid. What do you call a decision that was never truly a decision because there was only ever one choice?

It sounded like he was in the Peach Parlor, which meant jumping over the six-foot-by-four-foot hole that had just opened up to swallow my sister. I backed up, ran, and jumped—there was no good time to end up in our basement but never more than this moment. Unlike every movie ever, I made it with a foot to spare—it wasn't at all suspenseful, not that I'm complaining—and tore down the hall, skidding and lunging to the left when I got to the entryway.

The Peach Parlor was enveloped in thick smoke; at first I couldn't see a thing. If my eyes could stream, I'd have tears running down to my belly button. I'd never been gladder to be dead; a live person would be useless in this mess, would have succumbed to the smoke, probably wouldn't have gotten out of the basement in the first place.

I could still hear BabyJon and followed the sound right over to the big windows overlooking the front yard. The glass had been shattered, I realized, but not by the fire. Someone had broken them out, because there were scuff marks—no, I had it wrong; someone had kicked the glass out. Someone short.

I looked out and grinned at a glorious sight: Lara Wyndham standing in the yard, dirty and sooty and probably stinking of smoke, her jeans ripped and her pretty pastel sweater so dirty it'd never be clean, holding my babyson. I'd heard crying, all right: BabyJon was howling at being roughly yanked from a port-a-crib by a feral middle schooler who'd hauled him outside and was holding a onesie-clad toddler in the chilly spring air. I'd have been yelling, too. Maybe even rage pooping.[41]

I dove out the window like they do in the movies, though instead of rolling into an efficient somersault and popping up ready for battle, I just sort of flopped out onto the grass. "Are you okay?" I cried, staggering to my feet. "God, you're a mess; your mom's gonna kill me."

"It's okay. Don't worry—the baby's okay; he's cold, I think. Here." Lara handed him off and BabyJon started to calm down, recognizing me even in my wild-eyed state. Lately, wild-eyed was kind of my norm, so maybe he even took comfort from my stress. Glad it was good for something.

"I was worried about you, too, Lara. Well, a little. Actually, in retrospect, worrying about you is just a waste of time."

I realized she'd given him to me so she could take off her sweater, which she then wrapped around BabyJon, who was starting to calm down. She didn't even shiver, though she was down to jeans, tennis shoes, and a thin T-shirt, which (weird coincidence) matched Fred's New England Aquarium sweatshirt. I must have looked puzzled, because Lara said, "Dr. Bimm gave it to me!"

"Of course she did." Came to town to meet werewolves and vampires, brought gifts. But only for the werewolves, apparently? Must be a mermaid thing. "Lara, are you sure you're okay?"

"Uh-huh. And Mom and Dad and Derik are coming. I can smell them. They're okay, too."

I knelt and enveloped both of them in my arms. "Thank you

---

[41] Babies do that. I'm sure of it. Malicious pee and rage poop.

so much. Lara, I'm even more scared of you than I was yesterday and also I love you now. Thank you for saving my baby."

She hugged back with panicky tightness and I realized that for all her innate courage, she'd been—maybe not frightened, but tense, certainly. Worried. Fretful?

"I can't wait to tell your folks how brave and clever you were, but right now I have to go back inside and get my—"

"Betsy!"

Marc. Screaming.

CHAPTER THIRTY-SEVEN

I picked up Lara and BabyJon and ran with them through the front yard, plunked them down the minute I felt the cement driveway under my feet. "Stay here. Wait." Then I hurried to the sidewalk in front of the mansion, where Marc was kneeling over a body, reporters trying to talk to him while the cameras rolled. And Laura was still in the basement. Sirens were getting closer, but no one was on the scene yet. How to explain any of this to the authorities?

Explaining is the last thing you should be worried about.

"Help me," Marc panted, and I could see he was performing CPR on—oh God—Will Mason. Will's gaze was fixed and unblinking. I felt him. Cool and getting cooler. No pulse.

"Marc."

"Help me, I said! Breathe for him! I think I cracked a rib but we can worry about that later."

"Marc. *Look* at him." I wasn't a doctor, but I knew dead when I saw it. I'd heard the gunshots more than fifteen minutes ago. There was no bringing him back. Marc knew this.

He just couldn't—well. You know. "You have to stop; there will be others who need you."

"Can't. He died trying to help us." Marc was weeping as he pressed Will's unresponsive chest, forced that dead heart to beat. "It's not gonna be for nothing. That bitch. That jealous fucking bitch."

That jealous fucking bitch was in my basement and hopefully still alive. I decided not to mention this to Marc. "Sinclair and the others are coming. They had to get through the tunnel and then run back here. Lara's got BabyJon and they're just over there on the driveway. And the fire trucks and ambulances will be here any minute. You might want to . . . um . . ." Scuttle off like a zombie. Hide in the shadows like a creature of the night. "Help with a head count?" Far, far away from reporters?

"I'm not leaving him," Marc said, and he felt Will's cooling throat for a pulse. Then he leaned forward and eased the man's eyes closed with a sweep of his palm. He was still crying. I doubted he knew and, if he did know, doubted he cared.

"Okay. Forgive me for leaving *you*."

I got up and ran back to the mansion, which was now belching black smoke into the night air. It wasn't completely on fire—if the trucks got here in the next minute or so we might not lose everything—but I couldn't worry about that now.

What about my shoe—

And I couldn't worry about those, either.

I was through the front door in a blink, peering into the hole in the hallway in another. I couldn't see anything, had to jump and hope for the best.

I nearly fell on the Antichrist, who had landed badly, impaling herself on twisted metal and chunks of wood. In an exquisite, awful irony, she was dying from what would have killed

a vampire. There was a two-by-four sticking out of her stomach, and that was just one of many.

I dropped to my knees, felt the skin on my knees tear.
Didn't care. I grabbed up her hand, thought, *Easy, don't break
the bones, don't squeeze too hard.* "Laura, you gorgeous idiot, look
at this meth." Fuck, fuck! *Not now,* I raged at my treacherous
disobedient fangs. I wiped my face, furious. *Not now with this,
just stop it! The last thing my sister sees and hears will not be a
lisping bloodthirsty idiot!* And

(oh thank God finally a little luck)

just like that, they slid back out of sight. Even my fangs
didn't want to mess with me tonight, it seemed.

"Mess!" I nearly shouted down at her. "Look at this mess."

She managed to grin up at me. "I might." Stopped.
Breathed. "Not've. Thought this through."

Ya think? I managed—barely—to keep that behind my
teeth. She was going. Piling it on at this point would be not
only gross, but pointless.

But . . . she didn't have to be going. She could be fine. I
could see to it. Her wounds were horrific and terrified me but
I could whisk her down to Hell and cure her, probably. I
could—there were lots of things I could do. Grab Marc and
Laura and teleport them straight to the ER of Marc's choice,
using Hell as the transfer station. Promise Marc anything in
the world if he would just help my sister. I could—

"Don't," she said. "Don't help me. Don't save me. I want . . .
to go."

"I—"

"Promise."

"Okay," I whispered.

"Don't turn me," she whispered, enormous blue eyes filling
with tears. Pain? Regret? Or just the smoke making her eyes

water? It was awful that I didn't know. She was my sister, and I truly didn't know what she was thinking, even now. "Not into a vampire, or a zombie. Please don't."

"I don't know how to make zombies," I said tearfully. "I never have. Ancient Me turned Marc."[42]

"You do know. You just never tried because you don't *want* to know. That's you, Betsy, you all over: you hide from things."

"That's not—"

She coughed, a harsh bark that cut me off. After a few seconds, she finished. "And don't let your other friends make me a werewolf."

"That's not how it—" Was I really going to argue with her? She was dying. She'd lost. She could have the last word. She could take the credit for leaving this one last time. "I won't, I promise. I'll let you bleed out like a good sister would."

I got the barest curl of a smirk for that.

"You're not lisping. You've got blood all over—mostly other people's—"

"It's almost never my blood," I said, miserable. "These days, anyway. Other people—" *Have to pay the price.*

"Still. You're not lisping."

"I think I got a handle on that, finally." It was like a switch had flipped in my head. Every time my fangs wanted to peek out, I just willed them back. And all it took was being outed to the world, bitched at by werewolves, sneered at by a mermaid, attacked by my sister, intimidated by a child, and then watching my sister die. Piece of cake.

"I handled this. Badly."

Understatement! I groped for something else to say. Some-

---

[42] *Undead and Unfinished.*

thing nice. Something not stupid. "No harm done," is what came out of my eternally moronic mouth.

"How can you lie . . . to someone on their deathbed?" She blinked, glanced around at the mess. "Deathpile. Ugh, you're right. The basement is awful."

"Because I can't think about what to say to make you feel better about . . . about—" Dying in blood and pain. Knowing you failed. Getting innocents killed. Letting your petty emotions rule over your kindness—because she *was* kind; Laura had the capacity for great goodness. She just let herself get distracted by her darker emotions. We all do it. But when ordinary people indulged, there wasn't usually millions in property damage and a death count.

"You were right about Ronald." I imagined I looked like the center of a rapidly narrowing tunnel to her, with my dirty hair and face and the ruin of my outfit, and somewhere I'd lost a shoe. The last thing she'd see in life would be me looking my worst, wearing only one Rupert Sanderson Isolde Point-Toe flat. That shouldn't bother me almost as much as her treachery and impending death, but it did, because I'm awful. "You tried to warn me. I. Wouldn't listen."

"I won't make a habit of it," I babbled. "Being right. I swear! You know what they say about stopped clocks."

She sighed sarcastically, which I hadn't known was possible. "You always know. What to say. To make me feel better."

I started to shake my head. Then it hit me. "That's—yeah. You're right. I do know what to say." This once, I knew exactly what to say. I squeezed her hand but she didn't squeeze back. Sulking, or dying. Or both. Yeah. Both.

I paused for a second, made myself concentrate. *Think! Remember! Do this one thing for her, since you didn't do much else. You made her feel like this—this!—was a viable option. She's responsible, but you fed the flames.*

A shadow above me—I don't even know how I saw it, we were in so much darkness—and then the shadow moved and Sinclair landed like a cat in the rubble beside me. "Beloved, I can help you move—" he began, bending toward Laura with obvious intent.

"No! Don't touch her!" I grabbed his reaching hands and shoved. He stumbled but didn't overbalance. "She doesn't— don't. Look. See? She's afraid of you. Don't touch her."

"I will not," he said quietly, holding his hands up, palms out. He crouched beside me. He wouldn't mourn her, I knew, but he'd regret the waste and loss of life. "You've nothing to fear from me, Laura."

She was trying to move, was thrashing weakly on the things sticking through her body to keep away from him and it was awful, it was pathetic and horrifying and sad and gross all at once. "Don't move, Laura, don't! And listen. Look at my face. Look. Listen to me. I banish you from—from this earthly plane. Your body will remain, but you—you shall not. You are forever banished." I gulped. "From here."

She closed her eyes. Breathed. Listened.

"And—and I forbid you the solace and succor of my lands, those mine by—by right of conquest. You shall find no— no—" Fuck! What was the rest of it? I could picture the *Book of Shadows* on my nightstand, but I couldn't remember the next line of the spell.

Sinclair's prompt popped into my mind. *You shall find no shelter there . . .*

"You shall find no shelter there, neither now nor aeons from now," I gabbled, desperate to get it all out while she could hear me. While she was still with me. "I deny you forever."

"Thank you," she managed, a bare breath of sound. "But."

"You really shouldn't talk," I fretted. "Just—take it easy, okay?" *Take it easy. Good God. Useless. I am useless.*

"I'm afraid." I could actually hear her lungs laboring to work, heard a faint crackling that Marc had once told me meant bad news.[43] "Isn't that pathetic? After what I've done?"

"No," I choked. "I—I was afraid, too. The times I died."

"As was I," Sinclair added quietly.

"It's silly."

"Yes! Completely, totally silly! Listen, there's nothing to sweat. You won't be trapped here; I banished you. And you can't go to Hell—I pitched the welcome mat. There's only one place for you; you don't have the spiritual equivalent of a transfer pass."

She rolled her eyes but still looked worried.

"It's silly to worry because you know where you're going and you know He'll forgive you so don't even worry about it," I gabbled. "Straight to Heaven, no waiting."

"He never forgave my mother." Her pale hand fluttered, came up, wiped the foam of blood off her mouth, and then her arm flopped back down, boneless. The other was stuck, impaled above the elbow and below her shoulder. The smell of blood was maddening, maddening.

"Your mother never asked for it!" I insisted. "Apples and oranges! You *know* that's all God asks, and you're sorry, now, aren't you?"

A thread of sound. ". . . yes . . ."

"Satan wouldn't have asked God for shit, but you're not her. Don't you understand? You've never been her." *I've* been her, but now wasn't the time. "This is a totally different scenario. And if you can't—if He won't let you in—you come find me somehow. Any way you can. Haunt me or whatever. Figure out a way. You find me and—and if I have to, I'll go up to

---

[43] Bilateral rales. Very not good.

Heaven and kick God's ass and take *that* over and you can be there forever although how I'll shoehorn running Heaven *and* Hell *and* queening *and* Jessica's weird babies *and* house training Fur and Burr *and* giving mermaids and werewolves the boot but doing it nicely is a goddamned mystery. But that's not your problem! See? Either way, you're covered."

"Utter blasphemy," she said, and giggled. She took a breath, let it out, and her chest didn't rise again. She died laughing at me. Under the circumstances, it seemed appropriate.

CHAPTER THIRTY-EIGHT

Sinclair helped me climb out of the rubble and we both emerged from the wreck of our home into the yard. I was relieved to find the world was still there; wasn't that dumb?

It was a much busier place than it had been five minutes earlier: fire trucks, police cars, an ambulance, looky-loos, neighbors in robes and slippers along the sidewalk, werewolves keeping back, vampires doing the same. Somebody—a medium-sized blond woman who had her back to me—was off to the side . . . organizing, I think? It looked like neighbors wanted to drop some things off and she was directing them where to go and what to leave, and keeping them away from Sinclair and me.

What are all the vamps still doing here? Jeez, they should be long gone; I bet some of them don't even have righteous ID.

I gave them leave to depart; they respectfully refused until you—Ah, see? They see you.

Tina rushed over with the assembly, which was equal parts reassuring and scary. That was a *lot* of vampires to have

running at you. "Majesties, you're well? Oh, thank goodness.
I heard you went back in for Laura, but you didn't—" She cut
herself off as she realized what that meant. "Oh," she added
flatly. "Well. The important thing is—"

"Don't," I warned. Laura had screwed up and paid for it in
blood—and not just other people's. People were maybe right
to think, *Good riddance*, but I wasn't ready to hear it yet.

"Dread queen, I overstepped." Tina's gaze dropped to the
ground and I realized she looked like hell, too. She'd been
worried and could have been hurt or killed. Could have left
or shepherded the assembly far, far away. But because she was
everything my sister wasn't, she'd done none of those things.
"I must beg your—"

"No, *I'm* sorry. I'm glad you're okay." I looked around at
the other vampires. "I'm glad you're all okay. I mean that,
thank God." At their flinches, I added—

Don't apologize, my own.

Ah. Sinclair wanted the other vampires to see we could bear
light, and the Lord, could sing hymns and take the Lord's
name in vain and it wouldn't hurt a bit.

"It's been a long night?" I managed.

"We were glad to see you emerge," one of them said, a
curvy redhead with a splash of big freckles all over her face.
Needless to say, pale was a good look for her. The black clothing was a bit of an overdo, but now wasn't the time to chat
about fashion.

"We can start investigating after the police leave," another
one volunteered—Jack, I wanted to say? I'd met them all an
hour ago, but the names were a blur in my brain. "We'll find
out who did this and ensure they pay. They cannot attack our
queen with impunity. Especially now, with the world
watching."

"Uh, whoa. I already know who did it. Also, don't make

anybody pay for even a candy bar without checking with me first." Still, it was nice of them to linger. I wouldn't have expected that. "Clear?"

"Yes," they chorused.

"We're a nation now," the redhead elaborated. My face must have been pretty easy to read, because she answered the question I didn't ask. "You made that happen. We're not just a bunch of individuals in hiding anymore. We're all one, so we have to help each other."

"Yep." Totally, definitely my plan all along.

Wait, they're into it? That's why they came to town?

As you'd know, if you had paid attention during the meeting. They did have grievances, but those were more about nailing down specifics than advocating a return to last month's status quo. They came to say that they're with us, that after some thought they decided leading vampires into the light of society wasn't the worst plan ever conceived.

Duh! What I've been saying all along!

And after they heard out Dr. Bimm, the werewolves and vampires agreed with her plan.

. . .

You don't know what I'm talking about, do you, my own?

. . .

Luckily, the organizer had by then moved over to us. "Excuse me. Quite a few of your neighbors came over to donate blankets and clothes, and at least three different houses have offered to let you spend the night. I've got them all lined up over—"

"Holy crap, Jennifer Palmer! What are you doing here?"

She blinked at me, like it was a strange question. Like, where *else* would she be? "I saw you on TV in the hospital. Well, not you. Your picture. And your house was on fire. St. Paul's only twenty minutes from Burnsville, so I came right over to see what I could do."

I stared at her. She was dressed exactly the way she had been when I'd pulled her out of Hell about eight hours earlier. "Wait, Burnsville? I left you in Cannon Falls. And what hospital? What have you—"

"Betsy!"

Dammit, what now? I turned and beheld a sight that did not work for me: ambulance attendants loading Will's body for transport. Nope. Nope.

I grabbed Sinclair by the elbow hard enough to wring a wince out of him and started to haul him over to the ambulance. "I need that body," I hissed. "I have to take it to Hell, and the sooner the better. I do *not* want to break into a morgue tonight. But there's reporters and cops and—"

"My Maybelline mascara!" Jennifer Palmer screamed, and I almost turned around and slapped her, I was so startled. That shriek came out of nowhere and gave the sirens serious competition. "And my eye shadow! And apps! And my Kardashians! Those are all very important to me—I can't let them burn!" And she ran—sprinted—right for the flames.

And of course everybody went after her: cops, firemen, reporters.

CHAPTER
THIRTY-NINE

No time to be fancy. I just grabbed Marc, seized one of the rails of the ambulance stretcher, shut my eyes, and thought really, *really* hard, and when I opened them we were in Hell.

"Hey, Will." I shook the stretcher a little. "Open your eyes." *Too easy. This'll never work.*

It worked. He blinked up at me and started to sit up, glanced down and saw he'd been strapped in. I helped him undo the straps and he sat up like Frankenstein's monster, if the monster had been a slender blogger who reeked of blood. He reached behind himself, felt, then brought his hand out. A bullet rested in his bloody palm. "Um. Okay. I'm confused."

"Well," I began, because it was an exciting story, and hello, now I could raise zombies! That made me the good guy, right? Then I realized he hadn't been talking to me.

"Someone set the mansion on fire and when we made it outside, you were dead on the sidewalk." Marc ran shaking hands through his already mussed hair. "I tried to bring you back, but . . . You were gone."

"And I *did* bring you back," I said, in case he forgot the best part of the story.

"C'mere," he said, and Marc sort of staggered closer and Will wrapped him up in a firm hug. "It's okay," he said while Marc's arms went around him in a strangler's grip. He looked over Marc's shoulder and saw me. "Ronald Tinsman left a bomb in your house two days ago. When I found out, he shot me." He paused, thought about it. "Killed me, I'm pretty sure. This isn't Heaven. And why am I on a gurney?"

That surprised a snort out of me. "They were about to transport you, probably to keep trying to resuscitate until a doc pronounced you dead. And no. This is not Heaven." We were at my usual point of entry: the food court.

"So I'm in Hell now?"

"Yeah, but not to live." I'd given up on telling my story, or expecting praise. Hopefully when the shock wore off, I'd get a thank-you. "Look at this." I produced a knife from nowhere, took Will's hand, slashed the blade across his palm.

"Ow!"

"Oh, stop it, you big baby."

For a long moment, nothing happened. Then reddish black blood sluggishly welled, but before it could even drip down his wrist, the cut begrudgingly healed over. (Even zombie *injuries* had attitude.) "You're not stuck here. I'm taking you back to the real world. The thing is, though, now you're—"

"A zombie," Marc breathed. He looked at me. "How'd you do it?"

"Laura told me how." She'd said, *You just never tried because you don't want to know.* She'd said, *You hide from things.* Well, she was half right. "Will, if you don't want to be a zombie, I can try to—"

"No! No, it'll work. I feel . . ." He patted himself. "I feel exactly the same." To Marc: "Do I feel the same?"

"Yes: skinny and too many elbows."

Marc got a glare for that one, but I handled it with deft maturity by pointing and saying, "Ha! You're bony."

He was still feeling himself all over. "I don't feel any different; isn't that odd?" To me: "Is that normal?"

"What, like *I* know?"

"Wait, I'm breathing. Why am I doing that?" Slightly panicked. "Should I keep doing that?"

"You can," Marc assured him. "You don't need to, though. I like to run experiments on myself by timing how long I can hold my breath, but I got bored after three and a half hours. I'm so sorry I was too chickenshit to go out with you."

Will blinked faster at the rapid subject change. "That's—I mean, I understand why you were scared. We can—I mean, are you still scared?"

"Oh, sure. We're the only zombies in the world. Lots of pressure to live happily ever after. What if we're sick of each other in a hundred years?"

"I'll take that bet," Will said shyly, and they hugged again.

I snapped my fingers. "Yes! That reminds me. I want Cathie and the Ant." And a thank-you would be nice. Will? Helloooo? Anytime, pal.

And there they were. I could get used to this. Y'know, eventually.

"Good God, what's going on?" my stepmother asked with unbecoming avid interest. She took it all in: the gurney, Will, me, Sinclair, Marc. (Hey! Sinclair tagged along! Awwww. Must've grabbed the gurney before we went. Good reflexes.) "Who are you?" To me: "Who's this?"

"A new zombie; his name's Will Mason."

"Oh ho." Cathie's eyes narrowed as she observed the zombies canoodling. Flock of geese, assembly of vampires, canoodle of zombies? "That doesn't look like a man who's afraid of getting close to someone."

"You lost the bet," I informed the Ant with a credible lack of smug triumph. (I don't get nearly enough credit for my self-control.) "Marc *was* avoiding him out of fear, not duty, but as you can see, they're working on it."

"Oh," was the weak reply.

"Ha!" From Cathie, who turned to the Ant. "Go on. Do it. You lost. Do it."

The Ant looked at me for a long moment, then came out with, "Your hair doesn't look horrible today."

Cathie made a rude noise, like the sound you hear when a game show contestant gets the answer wrong. "First off, that's a lie—she looks like shit." This was true; I was all sooty and smudged and bloody. And still wearing only one shoe. "Second, that wasn't really a compliment. You have to say something nice. Stop me if you've heard this: you lost!"

The Ant closed her eyes, thought for a few seconds. Opened them. Came up with, "You aren't completely terrible at running Hell all the time."

"Wow."

"I know."

"Three times," Cathie insisted, because she was relentless in victory. "Better come up with another one right now; get in practice."

"And—you—" I was a little worried the Ant was going to have an aneurism right in front of me. "You—aren't—the— worst. Person. I've—ever. Met." She raised a shaking hand to her forehead. "That felt *so* strange."

For the first time in our lives, I was a little worried about her. "Are you all right?"

"No. May I go lie down?"

"Sure, sure." I dismissed her. And then, because I was a bitch, I called out, "Just one more nice thing to think of before I leave!"

She shivered and walked faster.

Cathie yelled, "Yeah!" in immature solidarity.

"So, no plans to be gracious in victory, huh?" Marc asked with a wry look.

"Never!" Then Cathie surprised the hell out of me by pulling me into an embrace. "I kind of love you right now," she said into my hair. Then: "Jesus, you stink."

"It's been a busy night." She let me go and I turned to look at Sinclair and almost screamed. Fred and the redheaded vampire and the vampire maybe named Jack and Derik the Werewolf were all there with him. And had been the whole time. Prob'ly should have picked up on that sooner. Wow, I needed a nap. "Where'd you guys come from?"

You're only now noticing, beloved? And why am I asking a question to which I know the answer?

Hey, a little focused on raising the dead, okay?

A fair point. You were glorious, by the way.

I wriggled a little at the praise. *And Cathie really caught me off guard. Hugs, now? Nobody ran that one by me. I'm not sure I want our friendship progressing to hug level.*

"We held on to the gurney," Fred said, like it was completely normal to run after a vampire queen and grab onto a gurney along with random vampires and a werewolf while Jennifer Palmer shrieked and drew away the cops and the reporters, only to end up in Hell and see me raise a zombie. "So here we are." She paused, glanced around. "Hell is a mall?"

"Long story."

"Holy *shit*." Derik couldn't stop staring at me.

"Yeah, you should take a minute. Most people get weirded out during their first visit."

"*First* visit?" He shook his head. "First and last for this guy. I hope. My God. It's all true. All the stuff they say about you. You really can do all that stuff. *Jesus*."

"So?" The curse of my life: now that Derik was prepared to take me seriously, it made me uncomfortable, and even a little sorry for him. "We get along; I've been your guest just like you're mine. And I freakin' love the next Pack leader, so." I figured it bore repeating. "We get along."

"Well, if we didn't before, we sure as shit would now!"

"I've got no problem with the Wyndhams."

"Nor do I," Sinclair added, but gave me a look like, *He's clearly not worried about* me.

"Thank God!" he nearly shouted. "Very happy to hear that! I will pass that on to my leader! But to do that I need to leave!"

"Are you all—?"

"I would like to go back to the real world now! Please!" He sucked in a big noisy breath and finished in a rush, "Everything is very strange here and it looks like a mall but it's not and there are dead people everywhere and I watched you raise the dead like it was nothing and there are a thousand smells I can't catalog and I would like to go home now, Betsy!"

Ever seen a hysterical werewolf? It's . . . disconcerting.

So we went home.

CHAPTER
FORTY

But not right away. We couldn't stay at the mansion for weeks, naturally. Tina made arrangements for us to crash at the Saint Paul Hotel just a few rooms away from the Wyndhams. It was temporary, and even unnecessary. The local vamps made it clear we could stay with them, and Michael invited us to come back with them to Cape Cod, to stay with them however long it took for the mansion to be livable again. Tina also started a search for nice houses that we could rent while repairs went on. And of course we were all welcome at Jessica's new house.

Fred didn't invite us for shit, which I appreciated. She thought I was interesting, like a bug nobody knew existed, but had no interest in being bosom buddies. This, I also appreciated.

The next day, she came to see us on her way to the airport. She took a cab, thankfully, not the Mississippi River, so she was as dry as a bone when I let her in. Good thing, too. Muddy Fred is Grumpier-than-usual Fred.

Sinclair and I had the Park Suite, so we made ourselves comfy at the glossy dining room table in the parlor. It was gloomy; Tina was in there, too, and was vulnerable to sunlight, so all the shades were drawn. She had a new laptop (she backed up her files obsessively, multiple times a day, so she wasn't missing a beat with her work . . . she was only missing her vodka) and was tapping away at the end of the table. Sinclair had gone to the swanky doggie spa where Fur and Burr were currently incarcerated, to check on them and terrorize anyone trying to feed them commercial dog food.

Fred opened the conversation by slurping something green in a Starbucks cup. "I hear you'll be able to make complete repairs."

"Seems like." Ronald Tinsman's parting gift was more an incendiary device than a blow-'em-up banger. Instead of the entire mansion going ka-blammo, the monitor room went ka-blammo and the resulting (thankfully smallish) explosion worked as a fire spreader. We'd heard the bang, but unless you'd been in the monitor room, you were safe from immediate immolation and/or being blown to bits. Unfortunately, you then faced slower immolation as all the lovely old wood that made up the mansion caught fire and helped the fire spread.

"I'm glad for you," was all she said, which was about as warm and sweet as Fred got.

"I'm glad for me, too. And I'm also glad you weren't hurt."

"No, just a little dehydrated." She smirked and slurped. "This is my fourth one of these in the last two hours."

"Yikes. Bathroom's over there on the left." Fun fact: mermaids *and* vampires didn't do well in fires. Michael and Jeannie Wyndham had helped Fred through the smoke and flames on their end of the basement, and Michael had carried her through the tunnel all the way to the dock. Then at her order

(I can only imagine the commands she barked at him), he unceremoniously plunked her into the river.

Five minutes later, she was much improved. The vampires and werewolves who'd come through the tunnel had found this as interesting as anything else that went on that night. Fred was the new paranormal Miss Congeniality, which was weird in about eight different ways.

"They—Michael and Jeannie—asked me to come visit, and I'm taking them up on it," Fred the suddenly social added. "One of the world's best marine biological labs is right up the road from them in Woods Hole."

"Which is good, I take it?"

"I plan to take full advantage," she said with relish. "I hope the Wyndhams won't do anything tiresome like expect me to make dinner conversation every night. Or have dinner with them."

"Oh good, there you are. I was wondering what happened to the real Fred."

"Shut your fang hole, you dolt." And she said it with such a lack of heat that the giggle just bubbled up out of me. "The reason I wanted to see you before I left—"

"I'm in love with you, too, Fred. What will society think?"

"That is not remotely amusing. But I had some thoughts about the triad."

Ah. The triad. Fred's bright, brilliant plan that, thanks to a timely house fire, everyone was on board with. I'd missed most of it, because I'd been in the corner coaching Marc on improving his love life while Will Mason bled to death on our sidewalk.

So here was the gist of it, as reconstructed for me later by Tina, Sinclair, and Fred herself.

FORTY-ONE

"Betsy's got the right idea," Fred began. It was unsettling to have the undivided attention of several vampires and werewolves, but she'd tolerated worse. Once you fought your father to the death, things like unblinking regard weren't nearly so unsettling. "And there won't be a better time for our three species to band together. Especially since we've always known about werewolves."

"Beg pardon?" This from Michael Wyndham. "I have to respectfully disagree, Dr. Bimm. Some individuals may know we exist, but in general, most people don't."

"Most *humans* don't," she corrected in a tone that was probably annoying or condescending or both. Mindful of her audience, she dialed down her near-constant impatience with people. "The Undersea Folk do. What, did you think in the history of both our species, no werewolf ever crossed paths with a mermaid?"[44]

---

[44] Because they did. And what a story it is!

From their expressions, Fred guessed it hadn't occurred to any of them, and continued. "Their—our—habits are different." She decided to use *they* instead of *we* so as to foster the impression of objectivity.

"The Folk can't hide from the fantastic and frightening; it's not in their nature. And there are so many astonishing and fantastic things in oceans and lakes and rivers, it's almost a matter of course for them to embrace the unusual. Things no human has ever seen, even now, when we've explored virtually every corner of our planet.

"Once enough of us knew about werewolves, that was that: they all knew. Because it's not in their nature to talk themselves into thinking it *wasn't* true. It's not in their nature to ignore the unusual. And, with respect to your current situation, avoiding it or trying to change things back is going about it all wrong. I know it's only been a few years, but the planet hasn't shaken itself apart because more people now know mermaids are real. How have any of your lives changed as a result of the Folk coming forward?"

Silence was her answer, eventually broken by the man in charge, who let her have the floor out of courtesy, and let her keep it out of interest.

"Perhaps because it may be a matter of territory," Sinclair began, and Fred nodded at once. Here was a concept she understood, that any of her folk would grasp.

"Of course. Yes. The Undersea Folk control the oceans. Anyone who has ever seen a globe understands that's three-quarters of the planet. That gives them tremendous leverage. And they're fantastically wealthy: by maritime law they own all the sunken treasure; any precious jewel or coin or natural resource in the water is ours. Use that; use *us*."

"I'm sorry," Jeannie said bluntly. "I don't get it."

That was fine. She was ready for that, and again willed her

impatience back. Giving in to her urge to snap, *I'm one of the smartest people in the room, I do my homework, I'm right, so just agree so we can put an end to the tedious explanations and get to work*, would have a deleterious effect.

"I'm saying the USF have the numbers and the money and the territory, so the nations of the world *have* to play nice with us. And to their credit, they realized that pretty quickly, which is why this has gone as well (so far) as it has. It may sound cynical, but that meant they couldn't marginalize us. And they couldn't pretend we were a hoax—too many people knew the truth. So they had to work with us, and they had to be decent about it. Nobody wants to look like the assholes bullying mermaids."

"But what would be in it for you, Dr. Bimm?" This from the small brunette, Tina, who had heard every word while never leaving Sinclair's side.

She thought about her father and his bad choices and how she'd had to kill him to save not only herself, but countless others. "Allies are always good," she replied simply. "I don't think there's a person in this room who would deny it." Not even Betsy, who was over in the corner giving Marc a piece of her mind—not that she could spare it. *Now, now. In her own way, she cares for her people easily as much as I care for mine. If she wants to yell at a doctor about shoes, where's the harm?*

"So rather than be your own separate small nations at the whim of the world, ally with us. I know about werewolves, and since I met Betsy I've known vampires were real, but I would never presume to guess how many there are. Less than a million in each case, I would estimate." She was being generous. She figured the number was quite a bit lower. "That's the population of Rhode Island."

"Yes, we are few, comparably speaking," Sinclair said. "And . . . ?"

"And now the world knows about vampires. My suggestion is, the three of us become the faces of all three newly acknowledged species. A triad."

"Us versus them?" Wyndham, always a predator, asked.

"Us combined with them." She turned to Sinclair. "This is your wife's purpose. It's mine, too, I think—why I was born. And"—with a nod at an expressionless Michael Wyndham—"my understanding is that Michael fought for his spot at the head of the Pack—to the death, I would guess." No one said anything, but Jeannie's gaze shifted to Lara, who blushed and looked down, fingering the hem of her New England Aquarium shirt.

"So here we three sit, so to speak," Fred continued, "controlling thrones (so to speak) by right of conquest. And maybe destiny is a lie; maybe there's no such thing and it's just an astonishing string of coincidences. Either way, we'd be fools to turn our backs on what is an unprecedented opportunity."

"I think Dr. Bimm makes some excellent points. We can—" Sinclair cut himself off and cocked his head. "I hear gunshots."

FORTY-TWO

"The timing just seemed to come together," Fred finished.
"And the consequences are fascinating, to say the least."

"You said consequences," I commented, "but this was a
good thing." A very good thing. Or a very bad thing: the day
was young. Either way, me, Michael, and Fred versus humanity was going to be interesting.

"*Consequence* doesn't denote bad," she explained. "It's simply
something that happens because of something else."

"Like a spring shoe sale in the spring?"

She snorted. "If that helps you."

My shoes. Ah, best not to think of them now. Hopefully I
could salvage most of them. The third floor had been the least
damaged, and our room the farthest from the device and resulting smoke. Better to focus on the positives: the triad, vampires accepting being out in the open, and we'd only lost Will.
And then only for twenty minutes or so.

Fred was chucking her empty Starbucks cup and preparing
to leave, thank God. One thing we had in common: we could

tolerate each other only in small doses. By the wry smile on her face, I guessed she was thinking the same thing.

"I know you don't think much of all the 'Elizabeth the One' rhetoric—"

I made a face. "It sounds like a *Matrix* parody."

"—but have you considered that this is, for want of a less hokey term, your destiny? Your rule was foretold—that's what Tina tells me—"

"Keep me out of it," Tina replied, eyes on her screen.

She smiled and shrugged into her sooty hoodie, which clashed with her stretch pants and faded T-shirt, because she dressed like a young bag lady. "And here you are, bringing the vampire nation into the light. And here you are, allies with werewolves while in a cordial relationship with the face of the Undersea Folk . . . *You* did that long before I came to town and talked about the triad. And that would have been impossible a hundred years ago. Perhaps ten years ago."

Have I mentioned I like Fred? She had a nice way of taking all my blunders and putting them in the "I did that on purpose" pile.

There was a short silence, broken by Tina's, "Majesty, you're doing it again."

"What?"

"Saying things out loud, instead of just thinking them."

"It was a test," I decided on the spot, "and Fred passed."

"Sure it was," Fred said, and shocked the shit out of me by hugging me good-bye.

"One Betsy . . . to rule the world."

"Will you knock it off?" I leaned over to cuff Marc on the back of the head, only to be body blocked by Will Mason, who was getting cockier every day he was a zombie. "The triad doesn't need a motto, and if we did, it wouldn't be that. Oof! Jeez, Will, you almost knocked me into a bush."

"Don't touch him," Will mock scolded. "He's miiiiine!"

"Yeah, *all* yours. Take him and go far, far away." We'd piled out of various cars and were eyeing the ongoing construction at the mansion. The fire had been two weeks ago; we'd come to check on the progress. Since it was the middle of the afternoon, Tina had stayed behind. Fred, the Wyndhams, and the assembly o' vamps were, of course, long gone.

"We're staying put." This from Marc, who had his arms twined around Will and was nuzzling the space behind his ear. Zombie PDA: exactly as weird as you'd expect.

"You couldn't chase us away if you tried," Will added,

because he was saucy now. *Note to self: don't make any more zombies.* At least he'd gotten around to thanking me. It had been sweet and a little embarrassing. Lots of "I'll be forever in your debt!" and "You'll never regret doing this for me!" And "I don't know why you saved a nobody but I'll spend the rest of my days paying you back!" and "I feel like giving you something—can I give you something?"

Marc had been way more sophisticated about it, snuggling up beside me on the couch while we watched *Deadpool* again, never saying a thing because he knew *I* knew what he was really doing. That sometimes there weren't words when a friend stepped up.

"Nobody's chasing any of us away. Nobody's making us leave our home. Well, permanently, I mean. We've been temporarily relocated by choice. We'll rebuild." I gestured at the scaffolding, the workmen, the cheerful progress in the sunshine. "It's what we're supposed to do."

I started to walk around to the side, Jessica beside me holding a baby carrier. She'd brought Elizabeth, solo. Dick was doing something baby related with Eric that I didn't care about, and so didn't listen when she explained. *Thank God they don't outnumber us,* she'd confided at the end of her super-long baby story. *We divvy them up and go about our day.*

"I've been meaning to ask you," she said. "How do you know? I mean—obviously that's what we're seeing, but you were saying that the night of the fire, when we didn't know how extensive the damage was. You always made it clear that you'd be back. We'd all eventually be back. But you couldn't have known that."

"This will sound crazy, but—"

"My babies told you."

"Or it'll sound completely sane, but only if you're us. And

yeah, they did." Just not in so many words. Their ease with the mansion made me realize anew that in every timeline, the twins grew up here. So, obvious choice: rebuild.

And like she'd been conjured from thought, the door to the mudroom opened and a tall, slender teenager was standing in the doorway, waving us over.

We all looked down. Jessica's baby carrier was, of course, empty.

"So!" Elizabeth Berry said with a bright smile. "Your house is trashed, Onnie Betsy. And it's not even homecoming season. Be desperately ashamed."

"I will not," I snapped back. "And it's deeply, *deeply* unfair that you're gorgeous and fresh faced and have a flawless complexion at oh-God-thirty in the morning." It was true. Same foxy, pointed face as her brother, but with a feminine cast to her features. Her small rose gold earrings set off the gold undertones in her skin, and she was wearing stuff, I couldn't say what. That's how great she looked: her outfit was irrelevant. Which was a thought I had never entertained before. "You're not even wearing makeup; what a show-off."

"Oh-God-thirty? It's past lunchtime."

"Who cares?" But hanging on to my grumpy mood was tricky. The mansion was coming along nicely, though Elizabeth and I were standing on plastic in the kitchen, and the main fridge had been pulled like a tooth and toted away. Just as well Tina wasn't able to visit the vodka crime scene.

Elizabeth hopped up on the one stretch of counter that wasn't filthy or covered in plastic. "So any new plans to, oh, I don't know, step up the security setup? Cameras *and* motion detectors *and* bug detectors, and everywhere for a change?"

"Ya think?" Just like that, my bad mood was back. Should

have done it years ago. Like, the day we moved in. We'd been lucky something wretched hadn't happened before now.

Laura had planted the bomb in the one room that wasn't bristling with sensors and cameras: the monitor room. Because duh. We had no clue until the ceiling fell on us.

"No harm done." And she wasn't smiling anymore. And I jerked my head up, shocked, because she must *know* that Laura was dead; she seemed to know an awful lot, just like her brother. But she didn't falter. "I'm sorry if that hurts you," she continued gently, "but it's the plain truth, Onnie. No. Harm. Done. What can be fixed will be fixed. And what's gone should stay gone."

"Maybe, but that's not for you to say to me today. It's still a little raw. Or, as we fuddy-duddies like to say, 'too soon.' Change of subject. Now."

"Um . . . good job spinning it for the media?"

I was silent, because I wasn't proud of that. We'd returned from Hell and vamp-mojo'd the firemen, police, ambulance attendants, media, and a few of our neighbors, just to be on the safe side. It was the first time I was glad there was an assembly of vampires to lend a hand.

We didn't mess with them too much—we weren't trying to trick people into thinking the fire didn't happen. But the reporters reported that the fire was started quite accidentally by bad wiring. And the subsequent investigation

("Your investigation will match those findings."

"Yes, my investigation will match those findings.")

matched those findings. And Will Mason—whoever that was—had never been shot. And he certainly hadn't died. And the man who had tried to bring him back definitely wasn't a zombie.

It didn't hurt that the media broadcasted pictures of all of us being calm and cool and our neighbors helping and nobody eating anyone alive or drinking from jugulars. We'd just looked . . . normal. Which the world was fine with.

Besides, the fire had been two weeks ago. And everyone had learned vampires were real last month, and Undersea Folk were real last year. What's new *now*?

"Look, kiddo, I'm an American, just like you."

"Actually, I identify as an Earth-bound carbon-based life form. Brunette."

"Adorable. As I was saying, the media's not mine to manipulate and it would eventually backfire, anyway. One of the great things about our country, the media won't put up with that kind of overt manipulation. It's not like, I dunno, Communist Russia. Or China."

"Uh-huh, and in response to your adorable 'the American media isn't easily manipulated' nonsense, here is my rebuttal: *Bwah*-ha-ha!"

"I've also been thinking about recent events."

Elizabeth stopped in mid-bwah. "Natch. It'd be odd-odd-odd if you weren't."

"My sister's dead, and my dad's a dead stick." Gone, left town probably the day Lara Wyndham got her tiny deadly hands on him. No trace of him anywhere. Good. His money had bought Laura's campaign to expose me and mine, and all that came with it. Which meant he'd bought the bomb, too. I was no longer ambivalent about how to handle our next meeting. It'd be our last. My mom hadn't tried to talk me out of it like she had earlier this year. She either knew it'd be futile, or—after a look around the mansion the day after the fire—decided he deserved whatever I was going to do to him.

I kept going, because I wasn't sure if she was inclined to be as helpful as her brother, but there was no harm in trying to find out. "The mermaids and the werewolves are going to band together and work with us, so it's not just a few hundred thousand vampires exposed and vulnerable to anyone who wants to stake them; we'll be a formidable nation with allies who are not to be fucked with."

"All good, right, chieftess?"

"Extremely good. So in a way, this mansion, this *life*, will never be safer. It looks like—anything can happen, but it looks like Sinclair and I will be in charge and we'll all be working together and running things for a long, long time." Centuries. Maybe longer. Werewolves weren't especially long-lived, but the next Pack leader thought my husband and I were peachy keen. The next Pack leader had risked her neck (and her beloved New England Aquarium shirt) to save my son. We were going to get along fine.

And mermaids *were* long-lived. I could expect to work with Fred for decades, barring something unforeseen, or me punching her *so much* when she pissed me off, which I foresaw could be frequently. I mean, yes, to give credit where credit was et cetera, she'd come up with the triad and we were going to play nicely with others, but . . . come on. She was still Fred Bimm.

"Yep-yep-yep," Elizabeth said. "I can see that. Sure."

She could. She was living it. We were from different timelines, but in hers, Laura died and things got better. And stayed that way.

"My half brother, Jon Taylor, can't be harmed by anything paranormal," I told someone who already knew. "And I can't think that's a coincidence."

"Onnie Betsy, we all give you shit for being silly, but you've never been all-the-way stupid."

"Thanks?"

Her gaze was kind but relentless. "You don't think any of this is a coincidence."

"No." I drummed my fingers on the counter and watched my friend's daughter, a confident young woman who, along with her brother, had seen things that would send most people sprinting to a shrink. "I can't say I do. Not anymore."

She stretched, long bony arms over her head, and yawned. "Sorry. College graduation coming up—last night was the party to celebrate the party we'll throw on graduation day. I feel like I mainlined a liter of rum. And ate . . . cotton balls, it feels like?"

"Poor thing." So, twenty-one. Drinking age. Unless she was a genius and had skipped some grades. Which was certainly possible. Also, I sucked at estimating ages. She could be seventeen or twenty-four (and either way, couldn't legally rent a car, so I had her beat in one area at least).

"I need to rush. Mom's still roaming the upstairs with the others, right? Won't be a better time to slip away." Oh, was that what they called their mysterious comings and goings? They were like beautiful biracial Batmans. Batmen? "I only came because—"

"You can tell if we need you," I whispered, and I don't know why. Maybe I wasn't ready for anyone to hear the theory until I'd thought it over more. "That's when you come. You do what you can and then you go back. Every time. Even when you're tiny."

She smiled and took my hand. "It's not entirely altruistic, Elizabeth the One." She laughed when I made a face. "We get a sizable emo-boost from the trips. It's so *severely* wonderful to see you guys in your carefree days."

I snorted. *Carefree* was never a word that leaped to mind when pondering our lives.

"But yep: I must motorvate. I was hoping to see BabyJon."

"Sorry—my mom enrolled him in some kind of *Lord of the Flies* day care three mornings a week. Lots of emphasis on interacting with other toddlers. Apparently socializing is huge. But I dunno. Seems overrated." I'd gone with them. Once.

Soooo many sticky fingers, and they all wanted to touch me. I hadn't salvaged six-eighths of my shoe collection only to be severely smudged.

"You should take my brother's advice about the kiddo. Like he said, BabyJon's the last one you need to worry about."

"Yeah, I've been thinking about that."

"This entire time?" she teased.

"Shut up, it's my process." I took a breath and said the thing that had occurred to me when Lara Wyndham saved my boy. "He's my heir. Mine and Laura's. She's dead, so he'll inherit her abilities. And since he's a blood relative, like Laura and I were, I'll be able to teach him how to go back and forth from Hell."

She studied her (beautiful) nails and said nothing.

"I'm right, aren't I?" I pressed on. "Sinclair and I will rule for a long time and when we're done, and dead, Jon Taylor will be the new king." Of vampires . . . and perhaps Hell, too. Who knew?

Elizabeth rose to her feet, put a hand over her breast, and sounded like the world's biggest, dorkiest Girl Scout as she said with prim precision, "I can neither confirm nor deny that theory, Ms. The One, out of respect for the always fragile timeline, and also, I gotta pee and maybe get a sandwich, and I can't do that here, so farewell, chieftess, time to arrivederci." Only she pronounced it the way Brad Pitt did in *Inglourious Basterds*: uh-ree-vuh-DER-chee. Even *I* knew that was screwed up.

"Oh, go, then." Should have known she wouldn't confirm. Not that she had to. The smirk said it all, really.

She started to amble past me toward the mudroom door, then paused and rested a warm hand on my shoulder. "Gosh, if only BabyJon—he never ditches that nickname, by the way, poor bastard—if only he was raised by vampires and a zombie and was used to extreme weirdness and hung out with were-wolves and mermaids and saw all kinds of amazing shit all the time. And if only that same guy had two best friends who could travel back and forth between parallel universes and figure out how to get him whatever he needed whenever he took on the bad guy du jour. Wouldn't that be something?"

I *stared* at her. It was. It was all. It was literally all I could do. Because. I. Wow. Holy. Wow!

A giggle. "You should see your face!"

Then she left, the little jerk.

Jennifer put the cereal box back in the cupboard, put away the milk, wiped down the counter. Looked around the small, sunny kitchen with satisfaction, hung the dish towel neatly on a hook by the oven.

"Y'know, I have a cleaning lady. You don't have to do all those things for me plus clean."

She turned to look at Lars, who was much improved since his hospital stay. After breakfast, he would telecommute—amazing, genius concept—for a couple of hours, then nap. His job title was something she could never remember that hadn't existed thirty-one years ago. Computer stuff.

"Don't be silly. It's my pleasure. Okay if I head out?" She checked her watch. Watches were almost gone; everyone used their cell phones to tell time. She *liked* watches; she had no interest in giving them up. "Starts in forty-five minutes."

He flapped a big meaty hand at her. "Sure, sure. See you tonight. Your mom still joining us for dinner?" At her nod, he added, "Listen, don't worry. You'll love it."

"We'll see," she replied, and went for her jacket and car keys. "If it's going to cut too much into my time here, it doesn't matter how much I love it."

"Well, that's the spirit, I guess. And don't tell me about the so-called 'snacks' you've left me. Carrot sticks and granola aren't snacks; they're what you feed petting zoo animals."

"Tough nuts. And there's more where that came from. I know you haven't been eating the rice cakes, just crumbling them up and tossing them. You *will* devour your rice cakes, Lars. If you're good, you can put some Greek yogurt on them." Greek yogurt put Yoplait in the shade, she had discovered.

"Aw, jeez, just leave already." But he gave her a smile that made his small eyes seem to disappear in a fit of good humor, and she took that as her dismissal.

Today she was taking a tour of the U of M campus, which she anticipated would be different from the tour she'd taken thirty-one years ago. Her mother had never touched her college fund in all the years Jennifer had been in Hell, though due to inflation that money would pay for only about half of the tuition for the nursing program.

To her amazement, Lars had offered to pay the balance. He'd casually made the suggestion a few days after his discharge from Fairview. She had practically moved in at that point, was essentially his caretaker as he slowly regained his health and strength. She'd left only late at night to go back to her mom's house to grab six or seven hours of sleep. She'd be right back in his house before the sun was all the way up.

"You don't have to do all this for me." He'd been on the couch with the remote nearby, comfortably clad in flannel pajamas and propped up with pillows. The remains of his breakfast were still on the coffee table and she started to clear away the dishes. "Y'really don't."

"Of course I do. It's my fault—again—that you're in some

difficulty." While she waited for Betsy to come fetch her for another three decades of torture by boredom, Jennifer had followed her own adage. She had controlled the things she could and let the rest work itself out.

"Listen, you were a dumb kid back then. You paid for it, okay? We're square." She'd just hummed in response and wiped down the coffee table. "You like it, though, right? I mean, it's not all for my benefit. You still want to be a nurse? I remember you going on about it in school."

"I haven't thought about it," she'd replied, and it was the truth. "Sorry about the cliché, but I'm taking it one day at a time."

"You should go back to school," he'd suggested. "Get your GED and then take some college classes. I'd be glad to help pay."

Shocked, she'd just stared at him.

"What? I got the money. So who cares?"

"I can't let you do that." Preposterous. She should be giving *him* money. She would, if she had any.

"Ah, bullshit. You're not listening again. Enough with the punishing yourself. You explained what happened. Not just that. I mean, jeez, you came from Hell to try to make it up with me. 'Sfar as I'm concerned, that was more than enough. But you can't live out the next decade making me eat that awful fucking granola. I won't have it, Palmer, no way. Go to school already. If that money helps you, what the hell do I care?"

"*You* could go to college," she'd pointed out, and he just laughed at her.

"Too old."

"We're the same age," she reminded him.

"Too fat."

She said nothing, and her tact made him laugh harder.

* * *

Then: the incredible, most amazing thing. Betsy had popped up when Jennifer was on her way to restock Lars' pantry with stuff that *wouldn't* give him a heart attack. And there she was, sitting on the hood of her mom's space shuttle, like the new devil hanging in the Minnesota suburbs was "a thing" (lots of things were "a thing" these days).

"Keeping busy?"

Jennifer had almost dropped her purse (she had a purse now, and a wallet, and clothes—her mother had brought her to Target the day after the fire). "Yes, ma'am." She quit fumbling for her car keys and said, "Would you please let me say good-bye to my mom before you take me? And maybe give me a minute to explain to Lars?"

Betsy's answer was to frown. "Take you where? Do we have plans I forgot about? Oh damn, that's it, isn't it? I need to start keeping a calendar. One that doesn't burn up in a house fire."

Jennifer hadn't expected her to play dumb. Or worse—toy with her. "To Hell, obviously," she'd replied, almost snapped. "That's why you're here. I failed."

"Failed."

"*Yes.*" Oh cripes, was this how it was going to go? Did she have to confess all before Betsy took her away? "I gave Lars a heart attack. Then I left him alone to go to your house."

"The guy was a walking time bomb—having recently been around a time bomb I know what I'm talking about—and could have popped a valve at any time. You probably saved his life by getting the ambulance so quickly. Then when you'd done what you could and visiting hours were almost over anyway, you saw I was in trouble and came to help. And *then* you confronted your worst fear by running toward a burning house to distract people so I could get Will away." Betsy shook her head. "I mean, Jesus."

"That's . . ." *A generous interpretation of events*, she'd been about to say, because *completely wrong, you well-meaning dope* probably wouldn't have gone over well. "Not how I see it."

"And now you're here . . ." Gesturing to the house. "Fifteen hours a day, busting your ass to nurse this guy back to health. Of *course* I'm not going to take you back to Hell. You passed. You did great."

"I did?"

"Sure. I didn't expect you to fix everything, to make it all perfect. But you owned your shit. Repeatedly. That's plenty good enough."

"Oh. Huh." She wasn't Hell bound? She could stay? "Wow. Okay. That's . . . wow." She looked up into the other woman's kind eyes. "*Thank* you. I wasn't expecting that."

"You're not going to hug me, are you?"

"No."

"Great." A sigh of relief, and then she hopped off the car. "I just wanted to check on you, is all. And to thank you for your help."

"Okay." She had years, maybe. Decades, possibly. To fill however she could. Any way she wanted. It actually hurt to try to grasp that. A mortal lifetime yawned before her.

"I wish you the very, very best of luck." She held out a hand. Jennifer shook it, felt like she was falling, or getting too much oxygen. "And don't take this the wrong way, but I hope I never see you again. In Hell, I mean."

"Oh, me, too! In Hell."

She'd stepped back so Jennifer could get to the driver's side door. Stood there while Jennifer climbed in, buckled her seat belt (it was the law now), started the car. Rolled down the window so Betsy could finish.

"Tammy sees you," she said softly. And was gone.

Jennifer clutched the steering wheel and wept thirty-one years of tears.

'NOTHER EPILOGUE

"Okay, okay, that one now. Let me smell it."

"This is the most disgusting game in the history of games."

"Marc is correct, Elizabeth."

I took a big whiff, then straightened. "Ha! See?" I opened my mouth and pointed. "No fangs!"

"And now, no appetite." Marc swept the almost empty blood bag out of sight. We had no idea where he'd gotten it, and didn't ask. Something about biohazard garbage being a treasure trove of grossness, which is the exact moment I stopped listening.

It was the end of Moving Back Day, and the beginning of smoothie time. The only person missing was Tina, and I could hear her steps in the hall. She came into the kitchen, smiling a little at the old-fashioned swinging door. We'd restored what we could and changed as little as necessary.

"Two packages for you, Majesty." She had a sizable box in her arms and a Priority Mail envelope on top of it. I knew without asking that they'd been scanned, weighed, fluoro-scoped, et cetera, or she wouldn't have brought them anywhere near me. There were some security upgrades to adjust to.

I tore open the first envelope while Sinclair topped my glass with more Dreamsicle smoothie. He nearly dropped the blender when I yelped to see the book and the enclosed note.

Dear Betsy,

You might not remember me but we met the day of our KARE 11 interviews. I saw on the news that you had a fire and thought you might like a new copy of Smoothie Nation. Thanks again for being so nice to me when you knew I was scared of you.

Best, Carol

"Oh, *yay!*" I showed them the book. "Isn't that nice? Now I'm super glad I didn't bite her. Or any of the sound guys. Or Diana Pierce."

"No need to immediately make work for Detective Berry," my husband pointed out. Except he wasn't Detective Berry anymore; he was now the official Police Liaison to the Twin Cities Vampire Community Berry. His twins

(One way or the other, Dad's always fuzzy.)

had nailed that one, too.

I picked up the paring knife we'd used to clean the straw-berries for Smoothies: Round Two, and slit the top of the UPS box. "Where's Will? He's missing the most important event in this house."

"Unpacking. He's . . . a tiny bit anal about placing his belongings."

"Yeah, well, tell him to keep his anal attitude away from me." I was still a little touchy about some of *my* belongings, specifically the ones that I'd had to toss due to smoke damage and worse. "And don't forget, we're going back to Hell first thing in the morning to pull together some more parole board committees." Jennifer Palmer had set the bar high for future parolees, but thanks to her, there'd *be* future parolees. I wanted to get them back into the world as quickly as possible, which meant I needed a lot more bodies to help.

I'd offered Lawrence *and* Cindy parole, and they'd both turned me down. Cindy because she'd found her purpose—she was now in charge of all social media and gossip in Hell, reporting to the Ant (and, I was sure, suggesting compliments the Ant could use to satisfy the parameters of the bet), and Lawrence wouldn't leave her. Nor did she want to return to a world where her father was dead.

Ronald hadn't shown up in Hell, so unfortunately I couldn't tie off that loose end. Wherever he was, I hoped he had found some peace. I blamed Laura a lot more than I blamed him. And blame aside, even if I hated them, they had both paid for their grotesque mistakes.

I got the box flap open and stared at a familiar box.

No.

Couldn't be.

But there was no mistaking them; I'd know those beautiful shoe boxes anywhere, all glossy black and purple and pink, as much works of art as the shoes inside.

I grabbed the note with trembling fingers.

Dear Ms. Taylor,

My assistant has been following your story on the news and told me you lost some of your shoes to a fire. I thought you might

like some new ones so enclosed please find my summer collection.
Would love to talk to you about repping my brand!

Sincerely,
Beverly Feldman

"Eeeeeeeeeeeeeeeeeeeeeeeeeeeeeeeeeeeeeeeeeeeeeeeeeeeeeeeee—"
"My God."
"—eeeeeeeeeeeeeeeeeeeeeeeeeeeeeeeeeeeeeeeeeeeeeeeeeeeeeeee—"
"The neighbors are gonna think there's another fire."
"—eeeeeeeeeeeeeeeeeeeeeeeeeeeeeeee!" I fought, and conquered, the urge to burst into tears of transcendent joy. "Look! *Look!* So many shoes! Oh my God! Oh, look at these! And these! Heels *and* flats! Look!"

Home.